A WILD AND HUNGRY PLACE

By EE Ottoman

A WILD AND HUNGRY PLACE: EE Ottoman
Copyright © 2025 by EE Ottoman
Credits: Dust jacket images: *Interior of a Forest* by Alexandre Calames, courtesy of Kunstmuseum Basel. *Still Life With a Gilt Cup* by Willem Claesz Heda, courtesy of Rijksmuseum Amsterdam. Case cover image: embossed design from "Histoire naturelle des champignons comestibles et veneneux" by Guillaume Sicard. Courtesy of the LuEsther T Mertz Library, New York.
Cover design by: EE Ottoman Original
Interior illustration by: Hippolyte Girardin
Edited by: S.T. Gibson, May Peterson, and Jessica Cale
All rights reserved.
ISBN: ebook 9798999188304
ISBN: paperback 9798999188311
ISBN: hardcover 9798999188328

Also by EE Ottoman

The Companion
The Longest Night
The Craft of Love
The Doctor's Discretion
A Sweet Yuletide
Documenting Light
A Matter of Disagreement
Song of the Spring Moon Waning
Zi Yong and The Collector of Secrets
Heart of Water and Stone

CONTENT NOTES

A note on the gender identity of the characters: this book depicts a nonbinary person, Cricket, a transman, Gabriel, and a cis woman, Rosaleen. Due to the historical/fantasy setting, however, this is not the language these characters use for themselves.

Content warning: This work of fiction explores dark themes, which include mentions of the suicide of a close family member, mentions of suicidal ideation, mentions of drug use, mentions of controlling and abusive behavior by a domestic partner, and their family. Fear of incarceration in a mental hospital, murder, attempted murder, graphic descriptions of cannibalism, graphic violence, and the undead. Discussion of parasites, particularly parasitic worms and fungi. Gender dysphoria and discussion of gender dysphoria. Animal death: a stag and birds. Depictions of caves and drowning. Sexual content, including sexual fantasies and on-page masturbation.

A WILD AND HUNGRY PLACE
EE OTTOMAN

~~~~~~~~~~~
~~~~~~~~~~~

CHAPTER 1

If it hadn't been for the curse, Cricket never would have come here.

Berwick was a tiny speck of a rural New England community, more like a cluster of farms than a town at all. According to Cricket's limited research, there were some mining operations nearby as well. Still, it was the sort of place Cricket would have only sought out if her life depended on it, which unfortunately it did.

Outside the train window, the trees sped by, creating dark green and gray-blue smears across her vision.

Cricket wished she was heading north. If only she could flee back to the seclusion of the mountains, the deep forests and deeper lakes. Her family's home, a great stone house where she'd grown up, had sat perched high above one of those lakes.

You could sit on the back terrace and look down across the dark waters of the lake. All around the house had stretched forests and mountains barely interrupted by any human settlements, the nearest town being many miles off. The only thing that could be heard from that terrace most days was the sound of the wind through the trees, the lap of the water, and the cry of dark birds circling overhead.

Cricket loved it there more than anywhere else on earth.

Early on in their marriage, Cricket had tried to convince Walter to move into the big stone house and make it their own.

He'd scoffed. "Out in the middle of nowhere?" He'd said like it was the most absurd thing he'd ever heard. "Why would I want to do that? No, much better to stay here, close to Mama and civilization."

'Here' had been Walter's townhouse in Westchester, an easy train ride to both New York City and his own family's home in Connecticut. Cricket did not care for its fashionable interior or its well-manicured exterior. She particularly did not like that it existed in such close proximity to her mother-in-law or, quite frankly, that Walter also lived there.

Too many nights she'd lain awake in bed and dreamed of fleeing north.

Now sitting on the slowly rocking train, she supposed she was, just not as far north as she would have liked.

The train came to a lurching stop and Cricket stood, gathering her skirts up enough to not trip over them. She made to pull the carpetbag down off the rack above her head when one of the train porters called out to her. "I'll get that for you, Madam."

Cricket obediently stepped back out of his way and let him pull the carpetbag down for her and carry it out of the train and onto the platform. The air was pleasantly cool and crisp against her face when she exited the train.

"There you go, Madam." The porter smiled at her. A young man with impressive sideburns. "If you can just direct me to the carriage or parties waiting for you?"

"No one is waiting for me," Cricket told him, taking the bag from his hand herself. "But thank you for getting it down for me."

His brows furrowed as he took in her appearance, her fine dress and shoes in the deepest of mourning black. Cricket knew she looked like a lady, not the daughter of a farmer. She wasn't exactly going to blend in here but that couldn't be helped. She hadn't had time to find more appropriate clothes.

It was already getting late in the day, and no doubt he was wondering where she was planning on spending the night if there was no one waiting for her arrival. It was a good question, one Cricket had been trying not to think about during her long hours on the train.

She pressed a coin into his hand before he could share his opinion on her situation and headed down the road at a brisk pace.

Her carpet bag was too heavy. She had to carry it with two hands. It knocked painfully against her shins with every step, slowing her pace somewhat. On top of that, the road that led from the train station turned out to be beaten dirt, which her dainty button boots had not been made for.

She clenched her teeth and trudged on.

From time to time there would be a gate on either side of the road with a number or a name on it, but none of them was the house she was looking for. She had expected the houses to become more closely set in, indicating that she was drawing near whatever passed for Berwick town proper. Instead, the houses seemed too thin, with even longer stretches of fields and wooded areas on either side of the road and fewer gate posts as she went along.

Cricket's boots were beginning to rub the sides of her feet painfully, and she had to pick her way carefully down the road to keep from turning her heel on a stone or pothole. The trees on either side of the road became thicker, a veritable wall of green foliage, their branches spreading out overhead until it felt at times as if she was walking through a deep green tunnel. She took several deep breaths, breathing in the scent of pine trees and green leaves mingling with the scent of dirt.

Even though her emotions were a tangle of anxiety and foreboding, she felt herself relax just that little bit.

It had been too long since she'd been in the company of trees.

She almost walked by the stone pillars set on either side of an iron gate among all that green. *50 Church Lane* was carved into one of the pillars. Cricket stopped in front of the gate, letting her carpet bag fall to the ground, and stared through the gate at the house.

It was not terribly big, a modest-sized brick two-story building. The house she'd grown up in had been three times as large, and even Walter's fashionable townhouse had been bigger. Ivy snaked its way up the front of the house, and the yard in front was an overgrown mess of brambles and bushes that had been allowed to grow as they pleased for a very long time.

Cricket felt some of the tension leave her shoulders. She still felt on edge, her stomach roiling and her heart beating just a little bit too fast, but there was something about the house in all its wild rundown glory that pulled at her. It reminded her of the dust-filled forgotten places and deep forests of her youth. Different enough from the pristine parlors of her in-laws' house to make her think that maybe she'd made the right decision coming here.

She pushed the gate, which opened surprisingly easily, and made her way up the path toward the house.

Once in the yard, she could see that the space was not completely uncared for. Someone had cut back the grasses and foliage from the path but simply had not bothered with the rest of it. Likewise, the stone steps leading up to the house had been cleared.

Standing at the front door, she could see that the house was in good repair underneath the ivy, not nearly as neglected as the yard. She reached out and pulled the chain beside the door. Deep in the house, she heard the heavy ring of a bell, followed by a very long silence.

She was just about to reach for it again when the front door was pulled open.

A man stood on the other side of the door, partly in shadow.

He was taller than she was, with a large stomach and wide-set shoulders. His hair was dark, and he was wearing the somberest suit she'd ever seen outside of a funeral. Like a mirror image of herself, he was dressed in pure black right down to his shirtsleeves. He frowned at her. "Can I help you?"

She squared her shoulders. "Mr. Throckmorton, my name is Gertrude Mallory." She began the speech she'd spent the last week composing and the better part of the day practicing in her head. "No doubt you don't know who I am, but I am the widow of Walter Mallory, your late cousin twice removed—"

"I am sorry for your loss, Mrs. Mallory, but I don't take callers and I've not been in communication with my family for quite some time." He started to swing the door shut.

"Wait!" Cricket stuck out her foot, wedging her already abused boot in the doorway. "I know I'm a stranger and I respect that you don't want callers, but I don't have anywhere else to go. My mother-in-law has cursed me, and I need your help."

He paused and considered her for a long moment, but then he shook his head. "I am sorry, Mrs. Mallory, but I can't get involved in family affairs." He nudged her boot out of the way with the toe of his own shoe and shut the door.

Cricket stared at it as the lock was thrown for good measure.

She stood there, listening to herself breathe, wondering if there was any possibility that he might open the door again.

Minutes passed. The door did not open.

She sank down onto the stone steps. Her feet hurt with a dull throbbing pain, except for the side of her heel, which burned from being chafed raw. Her stomach felt leaden, but she was grimily sure that sooner rather than later she would start feeling the pangs of hunger instead.

She rubbed one hand across her forehead.

There might be a tavern somewhere in Berwick, but she didn't much feel like traipsing through the growing dark on her own trying to find it. Besides, even if she could find her way into Berwick, she had no money with her. She'd spent it all to buy the train ticket to get out here in the first place. She'd been desperate and hadn't let herself think of what she'd do if Mr. Throckmorton turned her away.

Dusk was gathering fast around her. Cricket pulled her knees up close to her chest and wrapped her arms around them. Surely he'd come back out if she waited long enough. He wouldn't leave her to sleep on his front stoop; he couldn't be that heartless.

Still, he was related to Walter, Lydia, and Mrs. Mallory, so maybe he was.

At least it was too early in the year for her to worry about the temperature dropping below freezing that night.

Cricket stood on sore feet and picked up her carpet bag, heading farther up the road until she came to a tiny weather-worn church at the corner. She climbed the wooden steps up to the whitewashed double doors and pulled on the handle, but the doors were locked tight. There would be no chance of her sheltering in the sanctuary like a hunted noble of old tonight.

She trudged back to Mr. Throckmorton's house, her other options depleted.

Lights were on in the house now, bathing the windows with a warm glow.

Cricket tugged the doorbell chain again, but this time no one came. She sat down on the stoop, debating if she should actually spend the night there. On the stoop, she'd be in full view of the road. While there was the gate between her and any passersby, it wasn't locked and that made her feel vulnerable and exposed. She stood again, picked up her carpet bag, and stepped off the path and into the overgrown wilderness of the yard.

She pushed her way through the long grass, the ends of the prickly blades sticking and pulling against her long skirts, the ground sinking slightly under the heels of her poor boots. She put her hands up, using her forearms to push through the overgrown shrubbery heading toward the back of the house.

Her way was barred before she got there. Around the side of the house, she came to an ancient wood fence separating the front yard from the back. The fence was covered in ivy and other creeping plants.

Still, it really wasn't that high.

Cricket dropped her bag into the weeds on the other side, hitched her skirts up as high as possible, and curled her hands around the top of the fence. It took her a few tries to get herself up and over it. Luckily, true to her name, Cricket was small and light and deceptively strong.

When she dropped into the weeds and scrub on the other side of the fence, she had scrapes across both knees and her dress was definitely torn in at least one place. Her hair was no doubt a mess, and there were flakes of deadwood and dirt under her fingernails and sharp little burs stuck all through her clothing. A certain wild exhilaration filled her chest. It had been so long since she'd been allowed to be dirty and unkempt.

The backyard was just as overgrown as the front. Cricket couldn't tell if there had been a garden there at one point or if there was a stone walk or terrace under all of the tall grasses, weeds, creeping ivy, and overgrown bushes. It was just a tangled mass of terrible, glorious, untamed greenness.

Cricket bared her teeth at it, half in triumph, half in warning. She picked up her bag and waded in.

She found a stone bench among the tall grasses when she almost fell over it. It was covered in a thick layer of leaves and other dead and dried plant matter. She cleared it off and sat on it, swinging her legs around to put her feet up too.

Behind the bench and to either side, what once must have been decorative bushes had gone wild, spreading out and pushing up so that her position on the bench felt like sitting in a green cave.

A safe haven for birds, insects, small creatures, and now, Cricket.

Cricket pressed her hands against her face and wondered what she was going to do. Staying on the bench for one night was one thing, but then what?

Would Throckmorton call Mrs. Mallory when he found her here? Would she need to go back?

I'd rather die, she thought fiercely, but the terrible truth of it was that she wasn't sure she would.

For a moment she imagined selling what few possessions she still had and using that money to buy a train ticket to take her farther north, back to her parents' house. She could lie on the shores of that still dark lake and let the curse take her.

Yet there was a fire that burned inside her still, a tiny wild thing with teeth and claws that said *stay* and *fight*.

She clenched her hands into fists until her dirty nails bit painfully into her palms.

Mrs. Mallory would not win.

Walter would not have the last laugh from beyond the grave.

Above, the sky had darkened. The birds had gone quiet, and she could hear the whisper of a soft breeze through the leaves of the plants around her, the sounds of small night animals beginning to stir, and the hum of insects. Beyond her little green alcove, the air filled with the winking light of fireflies drifting through the air.

Cricket's stomach grumbled but she ignored it, stretching out farther so she could lie as comfortably as possible. She let her eyes drift shut. Bone-deep exhaustion from the stress and exertions of the day settled over her despite how hard and cold the bench was underneath her.

Sleep took her but only fitfully, surrounded as she was by unfamiliar noises in an unfamiliar place. She dreamed of being watched from beyond the green cave around the bench. A large, hulking animal with gold eyes and a hungry, waiting mouth.

Every time she woke, ears and eyes straining through the darkness, there was nothing there.

CHAPTER 2

When Cricket woke, blinking against the gray light of early morning, the first thing she saw was a pair of trouser-clad legs.

That jolted her wide awake. She made to spring up on limbs gone numb and heavy from too long sleeping in the cold on a slab of stone. Instead, her body jerked ungracefully like a newly landed fish, and she fell off the bench into a crumpled heap on the ground.

"You know this is grounds to have you arrested for trespassing," Throckmorton said, his deep voice conversational. "And maybe also vagrancy."

Cricket sat up and bared her teeth at him, no longer caring what he thought of her. Yesterday she'd been ready to tell him whatever he wanted to hear, to play the damsel in distress, stroke his ego, and to call upon his gentlemanly sense of mercy.

That was before he'd literally turned her out onto the street for the night, knowing full well she had nowhere to go.

Now she was cold, hungry, dirty, and not interested in being nice to him.

"Luckily for you, the closest constable is several towns over and I'm not on very good terms with him," Throckmorton said. "Why on Earth didn't you get a train ticket last night and go home?"

"I told you I can't," Cricket snapped, standing and shaking her skirt out as best she could. "I don't have the money for a ticket, and even if I did, I am not going back to my late husband's mother."

"I will give you money for a ticket," Throckmorton said. "And a little extra too, if it will get you out of my garden. You can go wherever you please."

"Trust me, I would love nothing better." Cricket clenched her hands. "But like I told you yesterday, I am cursed; not as a figure of speech, but an actual, honest blood curse. I must reside with a member of my late husband's family or I will die."

Throckmorton stared at her for a long moment. "I suppose you should come inside, then."

He turned back toward the house. Cricket picked up her bag and followed him.

They crossed the overgrown garden, creating a path of trodden-down grass all the way back to the house, where Throckmorton pushed open a door and ushered her through a stone-floored entryway and into the kitchen.

Everything seemed slightly old and used, but the kitchen table, the huge cast-iron range, and the floor was surprisingly scrubbed and clean. Enough so that she felt a pang of guilt for tracking her dirt-caked boots across it.

"Sit." Throckmorton pointed at one of the battered wooden chairs at the kitchen table.

Cricket sat while he pulled a mug off a shelf and poured tea into it from a gently steaming teapot.

Throckmorton put the cup of tea in front of her, then pulled a loaf of bread from the bread box, sliced off a large wedge, and gave it to her along with a butter dish, a knife, and a pot of some sort of dark-colored preserves.

Cricket immediately reached for the knife and began buttering the bread as Throckmorton kicked out the chair on the other side of the table and dropped into it without ceremony. The chair groaned a little under his bulk as he slouched comfortably into it and crossed his arms over his chest.

"All right, Mrs. Mallory, please explain what is going on."

"I married Walter Mallory five years ago," she said. "I knew of course at the time that Walter and, for that matter, the Mallory family's primary interest in me was my money. My family, you understand, is quite wealthy. But I don't know, I suppose I thought when we were married, we'd be able to get along."

She paused, taking a sip of tea and warming her hands around the mug. It was a commemorative mug with an illustration in blue on one side depicting some sort of exciting sea battle, half worn away now.

Her mother had fallen into such a dark place after Cricket's father had died, and the morphine, that had always been her weakness, had consumed her life. She had worried so much about Cricket's future. Cricket had thought at the time that finding some genial, if rather pedestrian, young man to marry would soothe her mother somewhat and secure her own future besides. She'd thought at the time that Walter seemed like that sort of inoffensive young man. Their engagement had made her mother happy, even if she hadn't lived to see them actually married.

Cricket shook her head, trying to draw herself back to the current conversation. "We didn't get along. I was not the biddable wife he wanted me to be, and he turned out to be a spoiled child and not a very nice person."

"That has been my experience of the entire Mallory family." Throckmorton's voice was dry, but his expression remained grave and somewhat unreadable.

"Yes." Cricket pressed her hands harder around the mug. "After our first real fight, I told him I would leave, and he told me I couldn't. That they'd arranged a blood curse when we'd been married so that if I tried to leave him, I would die. I thought he was bluffing at first. Walter was such a sniveling little snail—what would he know about curses? And Mrs. Mallory seemed far too holier-than-thou for something like that. So, I called their bluff and left."

To this day Cricket couldn't imagine Mrs. Mallory, who wielded her refinement and station as a weapon, crawling through the dark and the dirt. Digging and scratching into the rotting muck-filled places, giving of her self, hair, skin, blood, and spit before she pulled the curse, a gnarled and twisted root, from the ground itself.

How many of Cricket's things must she have poisoned with it? Feeding it to her one scrap, one morsel at a time in her food, in her coffee, rendered down into the soap Cricket bathed with. It must have started from the moment Cricket and Walter had become engaged, if not before.

That first meeting, when they had all sat stiff in Cricket's parents' parlor sipping tea, had Mrs. Mallory managed to slip it to her even then?

Her stomach growled. She reached for her bread and began to eat to soothe it, even though these particular memories didn't leave her with much of an appetite. "The first day I was fine, but the day after that, I began feeling distinctly unwell. The day after that I could barely rise from bed."

She pressed her lips together, remembering her body shaking with fever, the blood that had come bubbling out of her throat, and the cold fear that had locked its claws around her.

"So I went back," she said, "and as soon as I did, my health began to improve. Walter told me all about it eventually. They— meaning mostly his mother, I think—had been afraid from the beginning that I was too wild, that I would leave him. They could have lost my money. So they bound me to the family for the rest of my life."

Cricket had wondered in the beginning if the curse might lift if Walter were to die, but that had not been the case.

"So you came to me because I am a relation," Throckmorton said. "But I am interested to know how you found out about me at all. I've been estranged from my family for quite some time."

"As soon as I discovered the true nature of the curse, I began looking for a relation of Walter's who was not under the family's control," Cricket said. "Someone who wouldn't be swayed by the family's interests." It had taken her years of careful searching, research, and planning—the quietest years of their marriage, as far as Walter and Mrs. Mallory were concerned. She hadn't gone out of her way to be a good or proper wife, but she hadn't tried to run away, launch legal proceedings, or murder anyone.

Instead, she had waited and planned her escape.

"Walter died six weeks ago, " Cricket said, setting aside her now empty teacup. "And I knew I had to get away."

After the funeral, Mrs. Mallory and Walter's sisters had descended on the house with the intention of repossessing Walter's belongings and assets, including Cricket. Cricket didn't know what would have happened to her if she'd been moved into Mrs. Mallory's care, but she couldn't imagine it would have been pleasant. Walter had been the petty sort of bully that many privileged young men became. Living with him had not been pleasant or easy, but Mrs. Mallory's cruelty was a wickedly sharpened knife.

Cricket had stolen enough money to buy the train ticket to Berwick and left the first chance she'd had.

"I won't go back to Walter's mother," she said flatly. "I will die first."

Throckmorton reached up to pinch the bridge of his nose and shut his eyes briefly. When he opened them again, they were as cold as stone. He leaned forward, resting his forearms against the table, all but looming across it.

It reminded her, not pleasantly, how very large he was. Not tall, perhaps, but far, far heavier than she was. His arms were thick under the dark wool of his coat, and his hands could have swallowed her tiny ones up.

She frowned at him, hating to feel small, although she knew full well that compared to pretty much everyone else, she was.

"I don't want to be dragged back into my family's schemes," he said bluntly. "I don't know you, and I don't want you here. As far as I'm concerned, you are a stranger. There is no one I know that I would be happy to share a house with, much less someone I've barely met." He stared at her hard for a long moment. "But of all the branches of my extended relations, I like and trust the Mallorys the least. You can stay here"—he raised one hand when she opened her mouth—"*temporarily* until I figure out how to lift the curse."

She took a long, deep breath in through her nose as relief slowly washed through her body, replacing the fear that had lived there for far too long.

"It sounds reasonable," she said. "And thank you."

He made an impatient gesture with one hand. "I barely have a choice in the matter. I don't have a guest room, but you are welcome to the sunroom. There is a sofa in there which should be big enough for you to sleep on."

He stood, gesturing for her to follow him, so she picked up her carpet bag and trailed along behind him.

The doorway to the sunroom turned out to be right next to the kitchen, down a short hall and through a door that Throckmorton unlocked. It was a small room, the two outer walls made mostly of tall windows looking out onto the bedraggled and overgrown back garden. There were bookcases containing some very dusty old books against one of the other walls, and a few storage boxes and crates stacked against another. An ancient, extremely dead plant in a large ceramic planter sat on a small table next to the sofa Throckmorton had promised, which was covered by a drop cloth.

"Make yourself at home," Throckmorton said a touch sardonically.

"Well, it's far better accommodation than where I slept last night." Cricket dropped her bag onto the floor by the sofa. "Do you have somewhere for me to wash?"

Throckmorton nodded and led the way back out of the sunroom, down the hall, and toward the rest of the house. They passed an open doorway that looked into a sitting room filled with bookcases, a few comfortable looking chairs, another sofa, and some actually living potted plants. There was another book-lined room, probably a study, to the left and a staircase leading to the second floor.

The stairs took them to a long hallway with several closed doors on either side. Throckmorton pushed open the first door on the left, which revealed a narrow bathroom with a sink and tub.

"Feel free to do what you need to do," he said. "I'll be leaving soon to run some errands. Meanwhile, make yourself comfortable, I suppose. But if all of this is some kind of elaborate ruse to rob me, I wouldn't recommend it."

Cricket couldn't imagine Throckmorton owned much worth stealing. From what she'd seen so far, this was not the sort of house in which grand heists occurred. She did not tell him this, though.

"Here." He pulled out a metal ring of keys and extracted one, pressing it into her hand. "A house key. In case you want to go out." Then he was already turning away from her, heading down the stairs and toward the front door, where his hat and coat hung on a coat rack in the corner.

Cricket drifted toward the stairs but did not descend, listening to him move around the front hall. The front door opened and shut. Cricket held her breath and counted to ten before slowly letting it out.

She was alone.

Slowly she descended the stairs, listening to how each of the steps creaked or settled under her slight weight. She went back to her abused carpet bag and opened it, fishing out some of the very few items of clothing she'd packed. Fresh underclothes, a plain blouse, and a utilitarian tweed skirt. Sitting on the still-covered sofa, she finally eased off her almost completely ruined boots and the socks underneath and wiggled her freed toes against the floorboard. She inspected the blister on the side of her foot and determined that once she cleaned it, it would be fine.

Picking up her fresh clothes, she limped back through the house and up the stairs to the bathroom.

The door did have a lock, to her relief, which she threw before turning on the taps and watching the deep bathtub fill. The room slowly began to fill with steam, and Cricket began pulling hairpins out of her hair and dropping them into the sink. Once her hair was loose, she stripped off the rest of her clothes as well and climbed into the bathtub.

She dunked her head briefly under the water, scrubbed herself briskly with the brush she found on the corner of the tub, and made sure the sores and rub marks on her feet were washed out.

Generally, she would get out of the water once the bare minimum of cleaning had occurred. She hadn't felt safe taking longer when bathing in quite some time. She didn't feel wholly safe now, in this strange house that belonged to a man she'd only just met.

Still, she didn't rise out of the warm water quite yet. Her body ached and the water soothed it as her mind worked.

There was a bone-deep relief making her feel lighter than she had in years. For the first time since she'd first laid eyes on Walter in her parent's parlor she was truly free of him, of his mother and the clutches of the Mallory family.

Throckmorton had not turned her out and had said he'd try to help her lift the curse. Not that she fully trusted him to do that. There was always the possibility that he was out contacting Mrs. Mallory even now. But unless he did indeed mean to betray her, she had at least a little bit of time to work on lifting the curse herself.

The water had started to cool, so she rose and climbed out of the tub.

The sink was across from the tub, and there was no way of avoiding her reflection in it showing her small narrow face, now half obscured by a heavy tangled mess of dark wet hair. Cricket was bird-small and always had been, shorter than most and willow thin without any defining curves to her figure.

She was not a pretty young woman. Walter, along with his mother and sisters, had told her often enough how not pretty she was over the last five years.

She'd never aspired to be—pretty or a woman. So, the fact that she was neither had never truly bothered her. Cricket was a changeling child, a thing that, while she might have some womanly features, was distinctly not a woman. In her truest form, Cricket liked to think she was a sort of goblin living in the woods somewhere with dirt under her fingernails and blood on her teeth.

She heaved the hair out of her eyes. It curled by nature and would dry a mess, but she desperately hated combing it and only had for the last five years because Walter insisted.

"My wife needs to look like a lady," he'd told her once, his grip on her arm hard enough to leave finger-shaped bruises. "Not an urchin child."

She left it wild now and began putting on the clean clothes she'd brought with her instead.

Once she'd done the bare minimum, she bundled up her dirty black dress and clattered down the stairs to the ground floor. She deposited the dress on the sofa in the sunroom and left to begin exploring the house.

The kitchen she'd already seen, but she walked through it anyway, opening cupboards and rifling through shelves and inspecting the pantry off of it.

She wandered out of the kitchen and down the hall to the sitting room, which turned out to be attached to a very disused-looking dining room, its sideboard cluttered with books, little knick-knacks, opened pieces of mail, and an abandoned cup of tea that had been there long enough to have a fine film of dust floating on the surface.

The furniture in the sitting room was old and ordinary enough to look at, not cheap but not expensive either, the chairs showing several worn patches on the upholstery. The sofa had been torn across the back at some point, and it had been carefully stitched shut.

The entire house felt shabbily middle class compared to the ostentatiousness of the house she'd lived in with Walter. There had been a sort of careless wealth about the house she'd grown up in as well. Every room in the looming stone mansion was filled with priceless art, heirlooms, and artifacts her father had collected around him.

Cricket turned away from the repaired sofa and began to inspect the bookcases. There was an interesting mix of books. Throckmorton seemed to have a little of everything—novels, history books, science books, books on politics, horticulture, poetry, mythology, and folklore.

She ran her fingers across the spines and wondered how hard it would be to access her father's money, and if she could, whether she might be able to buy Throckmorton's cooperation over the long term. On the other hand, Mrs. Mallory was no doubt in contact with her father's banker, and there was always the chance that she'd manage to squeeze Cricket's whereabouts out of the man. Maybe best not to risk it right now, although it was something to keep in mind.

The bathroom she'd already seen, and the next door down the hall opened onto an ordinary bedroom with just enough of a lived-in look to make her think it was Throckmorton's. She considered searching the room—it might give up important clues about the nature of the man she was going to be living with for the foreseeable future—but she hesitated at the door. Actually going inside seemed too much of a violation, and she turned away without entering and pulled the door shut.

There was another door on the right side of the hall, but it was locked when she tried it.

Back downstairs, she discovered the door to the cellar between the kitchen door and her sunroom.

The smell of wet earth hit her as soon as she unlatched it and pulled it open. There was no light that she could see, and a rickety flight of wooden stairs descended into darkness. Cricket took two steps down, peering below her, but even with the light from the open door, everything was bathed in murky shadow. She did not go any farther down but turned back toward the house and light instead.

That brought her back to the sunroom, her bag and dirty clothes waiting for her in the dusty sunlight filtering through the windows.

Her hair was drying tangled, still tumbling into her face. She needed to comb it and pin it up out of the way again, but just thinking about it made her tired and angry. She pushed the heavy mess away with a frustrated sweep of her hands but didn't try to fix it nicely in any way.

Instead, she looked around the little sun-dappled room. The sunroom would be perfect for a greenhouse, Cricket thought, once more reminded of her father's big house and the greenhouse she'd had there, the plants and flowers she'd grown.

Neither of her parents had been plant lovers, but for as long as Cricket could remember, she'd loved nothing more than to get her hands into the dirt. She was forever coming back from the forest or lakeside with a cutting to try to propagate within the safety of her little glass sanctum.

Her laboratory, her father had called it. When she'd visit his sickroom in the afternoon, he'd ask, "What are you working on in the laboratory today, my little Cricket?"

Her mother hadn't been as supportive. "It's a strange pastime for a child," she'd once said, her lovely face pinched up in a frown as she elegantly draped herself across a wicker chaise lounge on the veranda overlooking the lake.

Still, she'd allowed it as she allowed Cricket to do most things whether or not she approved.

Cricket had always suspected that her mother was more relieved to have her out of the house than anything else. It wasn't that her mother didn't love her, more that she found most things to be exhausting and anxiety inducing, raising a child very much included. That Cricket spent most of her time out of sight and out of mind, running wild in the forest or holed up in the library or the greenhouse suited her mother just fine.

Whenever they had guests, which was rare, Cricket would make a point to wash, do up her hair, and put on a nice dress. She'd found that was all the placating her mother really needed.

She walked over to the potted plant in the sunroom, reaching out to touch one of its brown and dust-covered leaves. It dropped off as soon as her fingertips brushed against it and fluttered down to the cracked earth at the bottom of the pot. She contemplated it, wondering if she'd be able to bring it back to life if she cut it down and watered it diligently. Probably not, but she dug out a pair of gardening shears from her carpet bag and cut off the dead growth anyway before going to fetch water from the kitchen. The soil in the pot was so dry that it took her several minutes to get it to absorb any of the water at all. Once the water began to penetrate down into the pot, it took as much as she could pour on it. She only did the one cup from the kitchen, not wanting to swamp it.

Cricket straightened up from the sad little potted plant and pulled the drop cloth off the sofa, revealing very faded, old-fashioned rose upholstery. When she sat on it, the springs groaned and a small cloud of dust was flung up into the pool of sunlight around her. It was not particularly comfortable, but it was a good deal softer than the stone bench. She let her head fall back and her eyes drifted shut. For several long moments she sat, body relaxed, thoughts settling like fallen leaves coming to rest.

When her eyes blinked open at last, a movement out of the window caught her eye. It was a quick, dark flash at her peripheral vision that nonetheless made her jerk around, her gaze sweeping across the garden.

There was a woman in the yard.

CHAPTER 3

Cricket froze, like a small animal catching sight of a predator.

The woman was not close to the house, standing knee-deep among the weeds and tall grass. She was dressed in stark white as far as Cricket could see, a mass of blonde hair pinned artfully on top of her head. Her face was mostly turned away from Cricket, so she could not clearly make out the woman's features.

For a moment there was something about the woman that reminded Cricket so much of her mother that her entire body ached with it.

As Cricket watched, the woman's head lifted as if she had heard something. Cricket took several quick steps forward in order to get a better look. She had forgotten about her carpet bag on the floor and stumbled when her foot caught on it. Spitting out a curse, she straightened up as quickly as she could, but when she looked back out the window, the woman was gone.

It could have been a neighbor, Cricket told herself, her gaze sweeping back and forth over the yard. It could have been a vagrant like Throckmorton had accused her of being that morning. Certainly, she'd found that it wasn't exactly difficult to break into the backyard. Yet the space had seemed deeply disused, without any sign that there had been other people traipsing around back there besides herself.

She pressed her lips together, picked up the water glass she'd used for the plant, and went back into the kitchen to deposit it into the sink.

Around her the silence of the empty house bore down on her, making her too aware of every little creak and groan. She flinched away from nothing, drawing her arms up around herself. The last thing she wanted to do was stay here alone in this house.

She walked as quickly as she could back to the sunroom, trying not to look at any of the windows as she pulled on her battered socks and boots and found the house key Throckmorton had given to her.

Her hair was still a mess. She finally ran a comb through it perfunctorily and decided it was good enough.

Cricket headed out of the house, picking her way down the overgrown walk to the gate. Once on the road again, she steadied herself, taking in the forest around her. The back of her neck still prickled with tension and the sense of being watched. She tried to shake that off, starting down the road at a brisk pace.

For a number of minutes, she passed forest stretching on both sides without a sign of another house or farmstead on either side. Then off to the left, she spotted a path through the trees. It was weed-choked and overgrown, but she turned down it anyway, picking her way along it.

When the trees closed in overhead, there was less undergrowth. Just soft ground bedded in pine needles broken by long ribbons and tufted swells of moss and twisting tree roots poking up through the soil. The path wove through the trees. Cricket let herself relax just a little, listening to the call of birds and the hum of insects.

Someways into the forest, far enough that Cricket could not see the road and had not been able to for some time, the forest opened up into a clearing to reveal the ruins of a house.

A low stone wall marked where the house plot had stood, and some of the walls still remained although weather and the forest itself were doing their best to disassemble them stone by stone.

Cricket picked her way among the ruins, inspecting the weathered moss-covered stones.

She had seen decaying house plots like this before, failed towns, and abandoned farms. Silent markers where some young family had tried to own and work the land only for it to resist them too strenuously. There were places too where sickness had set in and its gray shadow had not left until most of the settlement had died off, leaving only ghost houses in its wake.

Cricket wondered which this house represented. Had this lonely house plot been ruined by an illness or just bad luck? Had there been a yard with chickens here once, with a kitchen garden out back? It was impossible to tell now.

Among the crumbling walls she found what she thought might have been a hearthstone and knelt by it, running her hands over its cool, lichen-covered surface.

The faintest breeze, like a breath, ghosted across her cheek and lifted tiny strands of hair around her face.

All around her, the forest was still. Cricket breathed in and then out, so aware of the rise and fall of her own chest in the stillness, the warmth of her hand against the stone.

She rose, quiet and careful, as reverent as she would be at a grave now, and turned back, making her way through the trees and back to the road.

Cricket walked slowly back the way she had come with no plans of where to go next asides from the fact that she was not ready to face Throckmorton's empty house quiet yet. She came to a small cow path leading into the woods on the opposite side of the road and turned down it.

Her boots crunched against dead leaves and new smaller tufts of green plants pushing up between them. Moss crossed the roots of the trees on either side of the path, and Cricket once more inhaled air fragrant with fallen pine needles.

It was a beautiful country here, she decided, no matter what she might think of Throckmorton.

She would simply need to spend more time out of the house. Maybe next time she would bring her penknife out into the woods and find plant samples to take back with her, cuttings she could propagate, plants she could experiment with or dry for teas or turn into tinctures. Next time she'd bring a basket and really go foraging.

There were some experiments with fungus she'd had to put on hold when she'd married. Although her marriage to Walter had presented her with a grim sort of case study for the use of certain plants and their effects on several occasions.

Her working notebooks were piled at the bottom of her carpet bag, and she would have to get them out and read up on the more enjoyable sort of work she'd done before she'd been wed.

The woods thinned out, and Cricket followed the path into a large sun-dappled field instead. The tall grass was threaded through with wildflowers, and the entire field whispered as a light breeze rustled through it. Cricket paused in the shadow of the trees to admire the sight before stepping out into the field, the grass brushing and clinging to the wool of her skirt before ultimately bending under her tread.

She closed her eyes again, enjoying the sounds all around her, savoring her solitude.

The breeze carried a scent to her, the sickly sweetness of death and decay with something else underneath it, something that prickled along Cricket's senses like the slow sweet drag of fingernails against her scalp. So familiar and yet she couldn't place it.

Her gaze swept the field, but she didn't see anything out of place. Still, some of her peace had left her as she continued her way across it, the breeze still moving the grasses and flowers that stretched out around her. It was cool against her face although the sun beat down quite warmly now that she was no longer protected by trees.

The scent of decay was stronger now. Cold fingers of unease stroked up her spine.

Cricket told herself that it must have been some unfortunate animal dead somewhere in the field, its carcass turning bloated and black under the sun. Although in such a place as this, carcasses rarely stayed intact long enough to stink.

She dropped down to squat in the dirt, the grass pushing up around her. She quieted her breathing, trying to calm her racing heart as best she could. Now that she was down lower, she could see that there was a space in the long grass.

Ahead of her was a gap in the grass due to the large hole someone had dug in the field.

It was about four feet wide, if Cricket had to guess, and crudely irregular. She crept forward. When she was close enough she leaned forward so she could see down into it. It was quite a deep hole, but not so deep that she couldn't see the bottom.

There was a dark shape at the bottom of the hole. She could hear the faint but persistent buzz of flies and other insects too, and that scent of rotting meat with something else underneath it filled up her sinuses and clung to her tongue.

A deep sense of wrongness gripped her, churning up her stomach and making her chest tighten.

She sank down to the ground on instinct alone, as if to make herself smaller, and crawled just a little bit farther until she could look down into the hole.

There was a horrible, terrible fear radiating from her gut that whatever was rotting at the bottom of that hole had once been a person. On her knees, though, looking down at it, she could see the dark fur pelt. The heat of the sun on the back of her neck, she could smell the rot and hear the sound of the flies on the carcass below her mixing with her own ragged breath, but besides that, everything around her was calm and quiet.

Cricket felt a bit foolish.

She leaned away from the edge and sat back on her heels. When she was no longer leaning directly over the hole, the smell wasn't nearly as bad, almost completely covered by the fresh scent of the breeze and wildflowers.

A hole in the middle of the field was a bit strange, but it could have been the beginnings of an abandoned well or lots of other things. That fact that some animal had fallen in and died was sad but no cause for alarm.

She rubbed the dirt off her hands onto her skirt and made to stand up.

Again, the scent drifted to her on the breeze that ruffled her hair, not just the scent of the animal in the hole, but a different scent this time, like brackish water or the scent of mold growing in old damp closets. She froze where she was, still kneeling on the ground as it filled her head up, putting her teeth on edge and tugging at her stomach. Her heart began to hammer and a cold sweat broke out across the back of her neck and between her breasts. Why, she wasn't sure. She was reminded of pressing her fingers against a healing bruise gone all purple and green around the edges, that sweet aching pain.

She put both hands flat against the cool solid ground and leaned forward again.

The matted stinking pelt in the hole jerked, its sides heaving in a deep moaning breath.

Cricket jerked back so fast she almost fell flat on her back. Her heart drummed wildly, battering against her ribs like a bird trapped in a room, so hard she could barely breathe.

She scrambled to her feet and put as much distance as she could between herself and the hole.

Once she was moving, she didn't let herself stop, her hands shaking and entire body cold as she ran through the field of wildflowers, back toward the forest and the way she'd come.

CHAPTER 4

Back under the shade of the trees, Cricket felt safer but still didn't let herself stop. She told herself that there were scientific explanations for what she'd seen. Carcasses bloated and off gassed at unpredictable rates sometimes. Or as grim as it was, maybe the unfortunate creature was still clinging to life somehow and she had been there to witness its death throws.

That thought made her half want to turn back, if to do nothing else but to put the poor thing out of its misery.

She didn't slow her pace or look behind her, not as she hurried down the path through the woods, and not once she stepped back out onto the road. There would be no way for her to get safely in and out of a hole that deep, and the thought of going back there made a strange sort of nausea rise up her throat. There had been something very wrong with the carcass in the pit, and the animal part of her brain was screaming at her to keep her distance.

Striding to Throckmorton's front gate, she pushed it open, hurried up the path, and jammed the key into the door lock as quickly as she could. The door gave and she all but staggered back into the house. She was out of breath, and her face was hot against the cooler air of the front hall.

There was a soft noise to her left, and she whirled, her hands coming up before she saw Throckmorton's large bulk framed in the doorway into the sitting room.

He was frowning at her.

It was a testament to the fear still coursing through her body that she was actually glad to see him. Pathetically relieved not to be alone in the house again.

"Mrs. Mallory," he said. "Did you run here? Did something happen?"

"There's a hole," she got out, still trying to steady her breathing and bring her pulse down.

His frown deepened and he stared at her like she was speaking in another language. "A what?"

"A hole. Out in a field not far from here. A very bad hole, something"—she swallowed hard—"an animal had fallen into it and died."

He stared at her for a moment longer, then grunted and shook his head as if dismissing it. "Shall we see what we can do about this curse? I was doing some reading this morning, and I have a few ideas we can try before dinner. I'm sure we both want this business cleared up as soon as possible."

Cricket did want it cleared up. Honestly, she did not want to stay here any longer than she absolutely had to. The sooner she could leave this house with strangers in the garden and mysterious holes in the neighborhood, the better.

She nodded and followed Throckmorton back into the sitting room.

There were multiple books, both large and small, all open and spread out.

Cricket eyed them with a certain kind of cautious interest. She knew of learned magicians who practiced ritual magic. She had heard of words of power, chanting, incense, old tomes, and secret histories. Never had she experienced it, though.

For Cricket, power was to be found in the dark spaces between the roots of trees, the secret holes and crevices within the silty floor of lakes, and inscribed into the chemical makeup of leaves, plants' oils, pollen, sap, and toxins.

She watched Throckmorton, wondering what kind of show he was going to put on for her. Would there be candles? Would he speak in Latin?

Instead, he turned to her and said, "I will have to get quite close to you, I'm afraid."

She squared her shoulders but stood her ground. "How close would 'quite close' be?"

"May I put my hand on your shoulder?"

She nodded.

His big hand settled on her shoulder, a warm heavy weight.

Cricket held herself very still, trying not to flinch, particularly when he leaned forward. She could feel a puff of warm air as he drew in a long slow breath right below her ear.

"I can smell the curse on you," Throckmorton said, voice very deep and low, lips far too close to the curve of her throat.

She swallowed hard and willed herself still while her left hand balled into a fist into her skirt, ready to hit him if he made any sudden movements. "What does it smell like?"

"You smell like bitter herbs and soil," Throckmorton said, his voice still too low and too intense, each word like claws scraping the back of her neck. "But there is another scent on you, like iron and rot."

His hand fell from her shoulder, and he took a step back. She swayed a little, feeling a wash of relief at no longer having to bear the heaviness of his touch or the intensity of his gaze.

Her relief was short-lived. He reached for her hand, taking it into his larger one.

"May I bite you?" he asked, his voice sweet like honey pooling across the palm of her hand.

She felt the shudder of the words go right through her, caused by his voice and tone as much as his actual request.

"W—what?" She hated that her voice was a little too breathy with a tremble just under the words. She locked her knees and straightened her spine just in case that tremor was able to pass from her vocal cords to the rest of her.

"According to my—albeit limited—research, blood curses are like venom from a snake or an insect," Throckmorton said. "In fact, I believe that is how yours was transmitted to you, through the bite of a wasp or some other stinging insect. But I may be able to draw it out as one would with venom."

Cricket's eyes narrowed. "It can't be that simple."

Throckmorton made a noise in his throat, deep and impatient. "Of course not."

"Do you have a book that tells you these things?"

He turned to the half dozen open books piled around them and picked up a smaller one with an unpresuming dark green cloth binding and handed it to her.

It was open to a treatise on blood curses. Cricket read through it carefully, swallowing hard when she came to the detailed descriptions of several attempted treatments that the cursed individuals had not survived. She forced herself to read through it all the way to the end.

Throckmorton waited for her to finish, arms crossed over his chest.

She looked up at him. "Is there more?"

He wordlessly waved at all the other volumes, then walked to one of the armchairs and settled himself as she picked up the next book.

Blood curses were not something most people survived, Cricket concluded after finishing her third treatise on the subject. She'd known that, of course; there wouldn't have been much point otherwise. She had always assumed, though, that if she could just get away, outside of the Mallory family's clutches, she would be able to find some way to lift the curse herself or someone powerful enough to do it. But now, reading through these accounts of case studies and failed treatments, she saw the true complexity and deviousness of curses like the one currently inside of her.

She wished she had poisoned Mrs. Mallory for doing this to her, and Walter too, for good measure. Her fingers curled around the edge of the large leather-bound tome she was holding.

She wished she'd poisoned them and made it slow.

Closing the book with a snap, she finally looked back up at Throckmorton, where he waited for her to make a decision. "All right. Let's try it."

He stood, graceful despite the bulk of him, and moved across the room to stand before her again.

"Probably best for it to be a fleshy part of you." His gaze raked critically across her skinny, stick-like form. "Your arm, maybe."

Cricket knew perfectly well that her arm was quite bony and not what anyone would call "fleshy," but she was not willing to bare more of herself for him. She rolled up her left sleeve to the elbow, then pushed it up a bit higher.

He reached for her again, fingers wrapping around her wrist, this time encircling it with ease. For a moment he just held her, and she was terribly aware of how fast her pulse must be beating under his fingers.

She held her breath, then became annoyed at herself for doing it and let it out in a soft huff.

He raised her arm up and bent his head. For a fleeting moment, she felt his lips against her skin, soft and warm, like a caress.

Then he bit her.

She could feel every single tooth as it sunk into her flesh, sharper than she could have ever imagined. The sensation was less pain and more a white-hot agony she felt from the top of her scalp straight down to the soles of her feet.

Dimly, she thought she might have screamed. She tried to wrench her arm back on instinct, but his grip on her had turned to iron, completely inescapable. Throckmorton's mouth bit and suckled, and she felt her body go limp against the pain of it. His other arm wrapped around her to keep her from crashing to the floor.

When his teeth left her flesh, there was another bright blossom of agony. She made another animal sound she wasn't proud of but had no control over.

Above her, he was frowning, his mouth dark and red with blood. "It's no good. The curse has spread too far, embedded itself into the heart of you."

He supported her to one of the armchairs and picked up a cloth pad from where it sat on the side table along with a roll of gauze and a dark glass bottle. He knelt, pressing the pad against the large bleeding wound in her arm.

Cricket took in long, shaking breaths, feeling cold all over. The bite on her arm ached and burned, but the haze of pain was beginning to clear.

Throckmorton swabbed the wound with stinging disinfectant and bound it with practiced ease before sitting back on his heels.

Absently, he licked the blood from his teeth.

Cricket felt herself shudder and had to look away. Her guts felt all jumbled up, and there was a mounting certainty that a line had just been crossed.

Moisture gathered at the corners of her eyes and she blinked it back, trying to focus on the issue at hand. "It didn't work?"

"Unfortunately, no," Throckmorton said. "The curse is too deeply rooted."

Cricket stared over his shoulder at the late afternoon sunlight spilling through the parlor window and dappling the floor. "There has to be a way,"

Throckmorton sighed and stood, rubbing the back of his hand across his mouth where blood was still smeared, drying to a brownish rust blot on his lips. "I'll think about what we can do.

Conduct more research." He was silent for a moment, face turned away from her as he scanned the bookshelves that lined the parlor.

She rolled down her sleeve again, wincing as it pressed against the wound, sending a bone-deep pain straight up her arm.

"Strange," Throckmorton said, more to himself than to her. "One would think poisons of the blood should be no mystery to me, but this one is persistent." He licked his teeth again.

Cricket pressed her own lips together, frowning hard. She eased herself up off the chair. "I need some air." She left the room without waiting for him to reply.

Since she'd had quite enough of the countryside for one day and could not stay inside for a moment longer, she headed out into the wilds of the garden. She picked her way through the long grasses and sat on the bench where she'd spent the night before.

For several long moments, she just breathed, drawing long pulls of cool, crisp air into her lungs. The garden smelled of verdant growing things with the faintest dark scent of rot underneath it. Dead plant matter littering the ground deep under all that growing green, breaking down and enriching the soil below.

She drew in one long breath after another, hands balled in her lap against the cloth of her skirt.

What if they couldn't lift the curse?

All these years and she'd never allowed herself to really think about it. She'd always believed there was a way. Somehow, through trickery, cunning, or just plain stubbornness she'd find a way out of the trap she'd found herself ensnared in.

She would not give in to the Mallorys' control or the endless embrace of death, but carve out a third path instead.

But for now, she was tired, and the bite on her arm throbbed with every breath she took.

What would Throckmorton do when it became obvious that they would not be able to lift the curse? He would not let her live here forever, of that she was certain. Even if he did, would she want to?

She thought of the hole in the field, of the claustrophobic smallness of the house, of Throckmorton licking her blood from his teeth.

Her hands were shaking when she brought them up to muffle her mouth as she cried in great gasping, sobbing wails.

Every bone in her body longed for that beautiful gray expanse of lake in whose dark depths her father had chosen to end his days rather than the slow withering death of the sickroom.

She knew better now than she ever had what he had been thinking when he'd made that choice.

Even now she could feel the pull of its icy waters against her body, the only lover she had ever truly wanted.

She fell forward, body shaking, each heaving sob tearing its way out of her, yearning with every fiber of her body to just go home.

Slowly, her tears dried up and her body quieted and stilled. She scrubbed a hand across her face when her sobs had subsided, wiped her nose, and straightened back up.

It was still too early to resign herself to death quite yet.

She pushed herself up and went back inside the house.

Throckmorton had cleaned up from their failed experiment and laid out dinner in the modest dining room that adjoined the parlor.

The mere idea of eating food turned Cricket's stomach. She took a thick slice of bread, heavily buttered, and fled with it to the sunroom, where she locked herself in. Once that was done, she curled herself up on the faded sofa with her bread and dug her plant journals out of the carpetbag.

Even though she was not the least bit hungry, she forced herself to eat while she refamiliarized herself with fungal spores and what types of fungus best grew on dead leaves, dead wood, or decomposing food scraps.

It soothed her, and she allowed herself not to think of anything beyond her tiny cramped notes on watering schedules as the sky outside the windows darkened and night fell.

She was distantly aware of Throckmorton's heavy tread as he moved about the house outside of her locked door. He did not try to approach her, for which she was grateful.

CHAPTER 5

When Cricket found herself sitting on the stone bench out in the wild garden, she was aware that this time it was a dream.

It was still night, darkness pressing in all around her, cut only very slightly by gray moonlight. She could hear the wind whispering through the leaves of the trees and great unpruned bushes, and a hissing through the long grasses at her feet. Insects filled the air with their buzz and chirp. The stone of the bench was cold under her legs, bleeding through the heavy cloth of her skirt.

She stood, moving through the long silvered grass of the garden. There was no house that she could see, just the garden and the dark shape of the wall. As she moved toward it, she could see the green that grew there, snaking and writhing its way upward in a great reaching mass of vines and leaves.

There were buds of flowers, light and delicate against the dark green of the leaves, but in the shadows cast by the moonlight, she couldn't make out what type they were.

She was close enough now to reach out for it, but when the tips of her fingers touched it, she jerked back. The bloom was too warm. The petal was silken soft, yes, but all wrong for a flower bud, too much like caressing an outreaching hand.

Closing her eyes, she wrapped her arms around herself and wished very hard to wake up.

A wind picked up, rustling through the branches of the trees and long grasses around her, cool against her face and hands.

Below the sound of the wind was something else.

Cricket opened her eyes.

She could hear water running under the ground. She knelt among the tall grass, listening hard. Yes, there was the sound of water over stone.

When she pressed her hands against the cool dirt, she could feel it too—water seeping up around her fingers, bringing the rich scent of decaying leaves, mycelium, and wet stone with it.

Now that she was crouched down, she could see it—a trickle of water running in a tiny stream along the ground and under the garden wall. The constant trickle of water had carved out a little space between the stones and the softer ground below.

It looked small, but as Cricket began to pull away from the dead grass and leaves, the cavity the water had carved was revealed to be much bigger than she had thought. The amount of water seemed to be increasing too, pooling around her and seeping into her skirts.

It smelled different now. Deeper, richer.

Deep in the shadows and green of the garden, a figure moved.

Cricket caught sight of it out of the corner of her eye and whirled, scrambling to her feet.

The woman emerged out of the darkness. The long grass parted like ocean waves as she moved toward where Cricket waited on the bench. Once again Cricket was struck by her pale elegance, the fineness of the dress where it glimmered in the moonlight.

As she came to a stop beside the bench, Cricket realized with a start that the woman looked nothing like what she'd thought. Whereas before she'd seemed all pale blondeness like Cricket's own mother, now her hair was brown, falling around features that were not as traditionally lovely. Her dress was a simpler gray, prim, and quite old-fashioned.

For a long moment, they stood in silence, side by side. The woman gazed out across the tangled mess of the overgrown garden, and Cricket looked at the woman.

Then she turned and looked at Cricket, and Cricket could see that where the woman's eyes should have been were just the dark sockets of a skull.

Yet because this was a dream and not waking reality, Cricket was not afraid. "Why did you look like my mother before?"

The woman smiled. "When people first see me, they tend to mistake me for what they find beautiful. Something they can desire." Her smile grew wider, amused. "Funny that for you, that should be your own mother."

Cricket felt her cheeks heat at the words. It was true enough that her mother had always represented the epitome of feminine charms Cricket both never wanted nor would be able to attain. There was nothing *untoward* about it, though. "That's not true," she said, hearing an unattractively defensive whine under the words. It made her blush harder.

The woman's laugh was relaxed and light. "Don't worry, I can be your mommy if you want me to. I don't mind." Her hand came up, her fingers slipping across Cricket's cheek a little too cool for comfort.

Cricket felt something hot and not entirely pleasant pool in her insides like too warm oil. It made her limbs feel restless as her guts squirmed and she fought very hard not to lean into the touch.

"I don't want that." The words came out too soft, too high and breathy for either of them to believe that.

The woman smiled like a garter snake sighting Cricket's namesake and leaned in closer. Cricket's eyes blinked shut for just a moment. She felt breath ghost across her cheek and the curve of her ear, or maybe it was the wind that still curled through the branches of trees. She couldn't be sure.

When her eyes opened again, the woman was drawing back, and her appearance had changed once more and terribly so, flesh peeled away, leaving only a tangle of wild plants twisted around bones. Creeping honeysuckle fell from her skull like a wave of hair. Her arms and the sharp angles of her torso were clothed in a gown of moss trimmed with twisting ivy.

"I can feel the poison inside you, and the water too." Even though the skull's mouth did not move, Cricket heard the words anyway. "There was no stream here last time I checked. Curious that there should be one now, and you here smelling like fresh water and stone."

"I don't understand." Cricket didn't know whether to be offended or mildly disturbed that her scent was being commented on by someone who was clearly dead.

"No, neither do I." One skeletal hand lifted, her bleached bone fingers brushing against Cricket's cheek. "Not yet at least, but we will see." Each word became softer, dwindling, although the touch on Cricket's face remained strong.

CHAPTER 6

Cricket woke up, flat on her back on the sunroom sofa with weak early morning sunlight on her face, a rather embarrassing ache between her legs, and a strange sort of flutter in her stomach. She could imagine the feel of tapering bone fingers against her cheek and hear the soft lilting voice in her ear. That idea set her heart racing the way the memory of the woman appearing like her mother had not.

The inhuman, otherworldliness of the woman and the dreamland she inhabited reminded Cricket of the books of fairytales she had read as a child but also, strangely, of the deep wooded places around the lake where her father's house sat. The woman reminded Cricket of those dark forested places where life and death, growth and rot intermingled to become the same.

Her spine prickled and a hot, slippery desire curled low in her belly.

Cricket took several deep, steadying breaths and climbed off the sofa, trying to put the woman and the dream out of her mind. She only had one other skirt and shirt in her carpetbag, which meant she would have to do laundry today. She put on new underthings, the clean skirt, buttoned up the shirt, put on her boots, and shrugged on the cardigan folded at the bottom of the bag for good measure. Balling up the rest of the clothes in her arms, she headed for the door.

The house was silent when she unlocked the door and crept out into the hall.

She listened hard for any signs of Throckmorton, but everything was still save for the tick of a clock in the study and the settling of old floorboards.

She brought her clothes into the kitchen and filled the sink with hot water.

When she'd been young, then as a married woman in Walter's house, laundering clothes had always been a task left up to servants, but she supposed it couldn't be too difficult. Applying water and soap and giving it a good scrub seemed to work just fine on dishes and her own body. She took the opportunity to scrub her face and neck in the water before thrusting her armful of clothes into the sink, then grabbed the bar of soap and started washing.

When that was done to her satisfaction, she rang the garments out as best she could and carried the whole sodden mass into the back garden. There was a clothesline close to the back door. She made her way over to it and draped her clothes across it as best she could. There was a pouch of pegs hanging from the line, and she added a few to keep the clothes from being blown off into the yard.

The back wall of the garden seemed very far away, but she couldn't keep her gaze from straying to it as she hung up her clothes. When the laundry was taken care of, she waded through the long grass and twisting brambles toward the back of the garden. There was green creeping its way up the wall here too, but no flowers grew among the green.

Cricket remembered the flowers from her dream last night and shivered, glad there were no blooms here.

There was no stream either. Although she searched the whole length of the back wall, not even a hint of water trickled between the stones.

Cricket squatted in the long grass and remembered what the woman in the garden had said about Cricket creating the water in the dreaming world.

Here, awake, she pressed her hand against the ground, feeling the prickle of dead and dried plants, sticks, and tiny stones under her palm. The ground was dry.

"It's just a dream," Cricket said to the empty air and stood, brushing her hands off on her skirts before turning toward the house.

She went back into the kitchen and rummaged through the breadbox and icebox, unearthing the rest of the loaf of bread and some sausages she thought were from the night before. She gnawed on a cold sausage while cutting herself a thick slice of bread from the loaf. The house was still quiet, and she wondered if Throckmorton was gone or simply sleeping late.

Her stomach flipped uncomfortably when she thought of the day before and the way he'd looked with blood on his mouth.

It was, or at least it should have been, revolting.

Somehow, though, the memory of it kept getting tangled up with Cricket's dream of honeysuckle and bone, the oily desire pooling inside of her. Life and death mingling together again like her blood and his hot breath.

Cricket swallowed the lump of cold sausage in her mouth and put down the knife, suddenly not having much appetite for bread. She was stuffing the bread back into the breadbox when someone cleared their throat loud enough to make her jump and whirl.

Throckmorton stood in the doorway although she had not heard him approach.

"I see you ate." Throckmorton moved into the room, his huge bulk seeming to fill the space between them. "Would you care for coffee?"

"Yes, please and thank you." Cricket watched him as he moved around the kitchen, taking things from cupboards, so absurdly normal when the rest of their time together had been anything but.

Throckmorton didn't speak to her again until the coffee was steeping in the pot. He retrieved the bread from the breadbox again and settled with it at the kitchen table.

"I'm sorry our attempts to lift the curse were unsuccessful."

Cricket took a deep breath and sat on the other kitchen chair. She watched the long blade of the knife as Throckmorton cut himself a thick piece of bread. "You tried at least." She very purposefully didn't look at him as she said it, afraid her gaze might stray to his mouth. "Thank you for that."

Throckmorton chuckled, a rich, low sound that curled around Cricket not unpleasantly.

"I try and keep my word as much as I can."

"You really aren't like them then."

Throckmorton's smile dropped, and he paused in reaching for the butter knife. "If you mean the rest of my blood relatives, then yes, I try very hard not to be."

She could feel his gaze on her like a weight although she kept her own gaze on the table.

"I am sorry," he said, "for the way you were treated."

Her shoulders hunched, tightening as if his kindness were a blow she had to brace for. There was hotness behind her eyes, tears threatening to escape, and she clenched her teeth hard against them.

To have someone apologize, someone actually show any care for what happened to her, well…it had been a long time.

She was distracted from her thoughts when Throckmorton rose to pour them both cups of coffee from the pot.

"Thank you." She took the cup he handed her, casting her mind around for something else, anything else they could talk about. "Do you ever worry about doing magic?" She took sip of coffee, savoring the heat and bitterness on her tongue and against her teeth.

"I don't do magic." Throckmorton settled himself back into his chair. "Not in the way of scholars and rich men with their candles and their sigils. I like to think of myself more as a scholar of folkways than anything else, and of course, I find and sell rare books to collectors—that's how I make my money. So, I've handled quite a few texts on magic and its ways."

He considered for a moment. "But yes, I do worry sometimes. To do magic of any kind, even to come into contact with it, is like traversing a great mountain range. It can be beautiful and mysterious, it can lead to greater intellectual understanding and greater knowledge of self, but it will also kill you. Maybe not the first time or the second, but every time you ascend those treacherous peaks, putting your puny body into the hands of something much greater, you must know death is inevitable eventually. So yes, I worry."

Cricket thought about her own reading into the matter, about poison drinkers, werewolves, and shroud eaters, humans twisted into monstrous mockeries by the combination of strong magics and their own subversive desires. "Doesn't magic corrupt as well?"

Throckmorton paused for a long moment, "It can. I'm not sure 'corrupt' is the right word. Exposure poisons people if it doesn't kill them outright, and the side effects of that can be...*troubling,* to say the least. I knew a very rich man, a collector, who had lost all his teeth and much of his body weight until he looked like some shrunken corpse because of it. And another collector who tried dream walking and ate his own hands because of it, gnawed them right down to the bone. Rich men and their vices." He sighed, shook his head, and took a sip of coffee.

"What about poison drinkers?" Cricket asked, thinking back to a very old book she'd found in her father's library. It had been written in German with woodblock illustrations and had taken her a very long time to decipher.

Throckmorton paused for a very long moment, so long Cricket began to think he wasn't going to answer. "That," he said finally, "is something very different altogether, older and perhaps even more dangerous. But from what I've read, the rewards for those who manage to survive are great indeed."

Cricket thought of the woodcarvings of men who became wolves in order to prey on the unsuspecting, of people who could pass into the spirit realm, who could speak with animals, create storms strong enough to sink ships, and even become deathless, never to sleep.

She shivered.

Throckmorton rose from the table. "And with that, I must leave you for the morning. I have work to do and collectors to contact about book purchases that will hopefully not lead to the loss of their hands." He picked up his half-finished coffee. "I trust you can entertain yourself?"

"I was thinking of going for another walk," Cricket said.

Throckmorton nodded once and headed from the kitchen, leaving Cricket to brood over the remains of her coffee.

Once her cup was empty, she went searching for a basket and found a very old one in the pantry off the kitchen. The wicker was coated in a fine layer of dust that she brushed off with the corner of her cardigan. She fetched one of her field notebooks from the sunroom along with her pocketknife and compass and left the house.

The sun was higher in the sky now, shining brightly and turning the whole world to gold. A cool breeze kept the air from being oppressively hot and made Cricket grateful for her cardigan as she walked.

It was perfect weather to be outdoors in the forest, and on such a beautiful day, she could easily tell herself that the whole incident with the hole had been her overactive imagination or just another dream. Dead animals hardly frightened her, and she knew how to move through terrain that contained holes and other potentially hazardous pitfalls.

As long as she stayed away from people, there should be nothing in these woods for her to truly fear.

Even so, a trickle of unease did tighten her stomach, making her think of ivy-covered bones. She pushed it aside and continued on toward the cow path and the woods.

Today she allowed her pace to slow once she was under the protective cover of the trees. Even though she could rationalize away her fear from the day before, she was not eager to go back to that particular field. Instead, she turned off the path and made her own way through the forest.

Cricket kept her gaze on the leaf-covered ground and the trunks of trees, searching for fungus specimens for her basket. She located a patch of delicate mushrooms only a little way in, nestled at the foot of a tree among the moss. Their tops were a very dark, rich brown folded into complex pleats like little waves. Cricket took out her knife and carefully cut some, stowing them into her basket before continuing on.

She found some gorgeous orange specimens growing all over a fallen log and paused for several long moments just to take in the sight before she cut some to take back with her. There was a fine stepped, white mushroom she was also hoping to find, but she suspected it was still too early in the year for those. Still, she thought she might find a few when they were still small and curled into themselves but no less as useful as the mature plant.

She continued to pick her way through the forest, finding more of the false morels as she went and stopping to carefully cut some for her basket. If she hadn't been looking at the ground, digging at the dead leaves with the toe of her boot every now and then to see what was lying underneath, she might have missed the way the ground dipped off to her left.

It was a natural indentation in the ground, mostly obscured by a large gathering of moss-covered boulders. Such places were excellent for mushrooms to hide and grow.

Cricket squeezed herself between two of the large stones and looked down on what very well may have been a dried-up creek. The area had been carved out into a little cup where the water must once have pooled and become deep. Maybe it still did during the season of high rains.

It was dry now, filled with dead leaves and fallen branches, but she saw that delicate paleness among the leaves and slid down the embankment to examine it. There was the possibility of snakes underneath the leaves, so she used a stick to gently brush some of them aside, then frowned, bending closer.

What she had uncovered was not *amanita bisporigera*, it was bones.

Not a small animal bone or the bones of a deer or even a farm animal who had wandered away and gotten lost in the woods.

It was a small finger bone, if Cricket wasn't mistaken—long, tapered, and not at all animal like.

She took a long breath and began to pick through the leaves more carefully.

It didn't take her long to uncover more. Indeed, the leaves seemed to cover the bones in only a thin layer. Cricket wasn't really an osteology enthusiast, but she didn't need to be to quickly become convinced that all the bones she was looking at were decidedly human.

There were many of them. Cricket stared at them, trying to make sense of what she was looking at. There were no scraps of clothes or items remaining and many of the bones had been savagely gnawed. Unsurprising, given they had been left unburied. Still, it was disturbing to think about.

She climbed back out of the creek bed and carefully wiped her hands off on her skirt, noticing that they were shaking ever so slightly.

A crime had been committed here, that was obvious enough, but of what sort she wasn't sure.

She picked up her basket and headed back the way she'd come, toward Throckmorton's house.

CHAPTER 7

All the way back her head whirled, filled with memories of that hole in the ground out in the field and the dried-up creek bed filled with bones. There was something very wrong with all of this, like a vase had been smashed on the floor and she couldn't quite get all the pieces to fit together.

She quickened her pace back to the road and to the house, flung open the gate, and stalked up the walk to the front door.

Throckmorton was still in his study when she clattered into the hall. He had a ledger open in front of him with several large stacks of books arranged around him. Cricket paced through the house to stow her basket of mushrooms safely in the sunroom before coming back to confront him.

She positioned herself in his study doorway, arms crossed over her chest. "There is something wrong here."

He looked up from his ledger and blinked at her for a long moment. "There are many things wrong here," he said finally, his deep voice a dry rumble. "But what specifically are you referring to this time?"

"I was out in the forest this morning, and I found a pit of human bones."

That got his attention.

"A pit of bones?" he repeated slowly.

"Yes." Cricket was becoming impatient, wondering if she was going to have to repeat everything twice in order for him to grasp it. "A pit of human bones out in the forest. Does that seem normal to you?"

"The forest behind the house?"

Cricket gritted her teeth in frustration. "Come with me. I'll show you."

He pushed his chair back and stood slowly with obvious reluctance, but he followed her.

It was still a beautiful day outside. Cricket paced down the road and turned off into the woods, Throckmorton a quiet yet looming presence behind her. She kept her gaze on the path and her shoulders from hunching at his presence. She didn't want to show nervousness or hesitation, not in front of him. Still, there was already that small part of her mind telling her she'd imagined the bones or had somehow made it seem more than it was.

They left the trail together, Cricket picking her way between the trees, retracing her steps from earlier that morning. In the quiet of the forest, she was very aware of the sound of Throckmorton breathing, the crunch and crackle of his much heavier tread following in her wake.

They came to the stone as last, and Cricket pushed between them. Behind her, she heard Throckmorton grunt as he pushed his bigger bulk through the narrow space after her. Then they were both standing at the edge of the dried-up creek bed, looking down at the pile of bones Cricket had uncovered.

She slid down the bank and began to pick through the bones. "Whoever they were, they must have just been dumped here. Most of these bones are quite badly chewed. It's amazing they weren't scattered farther."

From above her on the creek bank, Throckmorton made a noise that Cricket thought was disgust.

"Do you know what happened here?" She glanced up at him to find him looking down at the bones with a very grave expression on his face.

"I don't know," he said slowly. "I was not aware this was here."

Cricket thought of long-buried community secrets, atrocities committed and then forgotten about. The hairs on her arms and the back of her neck stood up.

But these bones had not been buried very deep. They were barely covered by a layer of leaves, indicating that they hadn't been here that long. If this was something recent, surely Throckmorton would know about it. He'd lived here for some time, after all.

"Come back up here." Throckmorton held out a hand toward her.

Cricket took it and allowed him to help pull her back up out of the creek. "Should we tell someone?"

Throckmorton shook his head. "I think you should forget that you ever found this."

Cricket drew in a long breath and folded her arms over her chest. "This isn't normal," she said, if only to state the obvious.

"I think we should go back to the house."

"Not before I show you the hole." She might as well lay it all out for him, although she was half convinced she'd imagined the business with the hole.

Still, she turned and back and headed through the trees. They found the cow path again, and Cricket led the way down it toward the field where the hole had been. She couldn't quite identify the way her stomach fluttered as the trees gave away to the stretch of field, still sunny and dappled with wildflowers.

"Is this another bone pit?" Throckmorton asked when she paused at the edge of the field.

"It's a hole," Cricket repeated, knowing how unimpressive that sounded, especially when compared to the actual bone pit they'd just seen.

She resolutely took several steps into the field, heading in the direction she thought the hole was. Throckmorton trailed a pace after her, their combined mass treading down a swath in the waist-high grass and flowers.

They were some way into the field when Cricket's foot trod down on something that was definitely not ground or grass.

It gave with such an unpleasant soft crunch that she recoiled back, straight into Throckmorton. His big hands clamped around her arms to keep her from bouncing off him and falling to the ground.

Cricket sucked in a sharp breath and looked down to see the body of a small bird that she'd not been able to see in the grass. Her stomach knotted with painful repulsion, and her hands fisted at her sides.

"What is it?" Throckmorton asked from behind her, his voice tinted with a concerned urgency.

"A bird," Cricket said. "It's dead, poor thing."

Straightening, she stepped out of his grasp, stepping over the bird and continuing forward, but this time with more caution, using the tips of her boots to try and push the grass aside so she could see where she was putting her feet.

She hadn't gone more than a pace before she came across another downed bird, dead among the tall grass, and then another, and another.

"This," Throckmorton said from behind her, his voice low and serious, "this is not normal."

Cricket stared down at the little body next to the toe of her boot and thought of the bones piled up in the forest they'd just left.

A faint breeze ruffled through her hair, pulling at the edge of her skirt, bringing with it the scent of metallic-earthy, rotten, and fecal without being any of those things.

It reminded her of an unused bathroom in her parent's house where she'd run herself a bath once, the wet scene that had come up from the long-disused drain but sweeter, mixing with it the cloying scent of rotten flesh.

"That," Cricket said. "Do you smell that?"

Throckmorton was standing very still too, and she watched his throat work as he swallowed. "We should go back to the house. We should go back now."

Cricket felt a grim sort of determination come over her. "I need to find the hole." She turned back toward the direction where she thought it lay. She started forward again, picking her way slowly through the grass, trying to avoid the now dozens of tiny dead birds she seemed to uncover with every step.

"This isn't right," Throckmorton said again. "We shouldn't be here. Mrs. Mallory—Gertrude, we need to go back."

Cricket ignored him. The hole was just up ahead, she knew it was. She now regretted fleeing from the field the last time she'd been here.

The hole seemed to come out of nowhere.

One moment there was nothing but grass stretching out in front of her, and the next she was right at the edge of it, looking down, far down, at the shape of a carcass lying at the bottom.

Even from the edge, she could hear the buzz of the flies as they crawled across the remains. The smell of rotting meat wafted up from the hole in huge waves, strong enough to make her gag. That other scent filled up her sinuses again, mushing itself deeper into her skull and down her throat with every breath. Her mouth filled with a dirty bitterness like chewing on toadstools, their fleshy denseness turning to pulp in her mouth. There were things growing on the carcass now, she thought, although she was too far away to make out what kind of plant life it was. Mold, fungus, or something else entirely. She could imagine it pushing down into the crevices of the carcass, winding out from the dirt to push mycelial fingers into the meat of it...

Something heavy slammed into her side, throwing her back.

Her vision was abruptly filled with a whirling smear as all of her breath was shoved out of her lungs and her head hit the hard ground.

There was the long, low growl of a large animal quite close to her, the heavy, panting breath of a beast.

CHAPTER 8

Suddenly, very human arms were around her, pulling her up and dragging her back. She thrashed, fighting against their hold out of reflex. Hadn't she heard the panting of an animal? There seemed to be noting here now.

"We are going back to the house right now." Throckmorton's voice was low and furious in her ear as he bodily hauled her through the grass.

"But the hole," Cricket panted, struggling against his grip. It just made him tighten his hold on her until it was as unbreakable as iron.

"To hell with the hole," Throckmorton said. "If that's far enough, which I doubt it is. Do you even realize how close you came to death just then? Unless of course, that was the plan all along. In that case, I'd thank you to throw yourself down a very deep hole sometime when I'm not there to witness it."

Cricket blinked, trying to clear her head and pull her scattered wits together.

They arrived at the forest again, and she regained her footing as Throckmorton hauled her onto the somewhat even ground of the path.

"I wasn't going to jump," she said finally.

"Well, you were most certainly going to fall," Throckmorton snapped. He hadn't let her go completely; one strong hand still curled around her upper arm.

She was increasingly aware of how close they were, the bulk of him, and the way his body gave off heat.

Her treacherous mind conjured up the memory of him kneeling in front of her, licking her blood from his teeth. Her entire body suddenly flushed impossibly warm, her palms breaking out in a prickling sweat.

She ruthlessly stamped down on any and all emotions she might have been wanting to feel in that moment and willed her mind to blankness as he continued to pull her down the path toward the house.

Throckmorton didn't break his stride until he was pushing open his own gate and didn't come to a halt until they were back inside the front hallway of the house with the door locked behind them.

He let go of her then, sliding the key to the door back into his waistcoat pocket.

"Stay out of the forest," he said, his expression grim and voice brooking no argument.

Cricket opened her mouth to argue anyway. "I can't stay locked up in the house forever," she pointed out quite reasonably.

"Then go out into the garden if you need to get out of the house," Throckmorton said. "But stay away from the forest, and in particular, do not go back to that hole."

Cricket stared at him, feeling the walls of the house closing around her.

She knew on one level he was right. Whatever was going on there seemed sinister and dangerous, and the most sensible course of action probably was to forget any of it had happened and stay out of the woods—for the time being, at least. At the same time, it felt so limiting. She already could not leave Throckmorton's proximity, a fact that even on a good day felt impossibly caging. Taking away her ability to roam even a short distance was almost intolerable.

She turned from him and headed back to her little sunroom.

The basket of mushrooms she'd picked that morning was still there waiting for her, and she set about sorting through them. She divided out the ones she wanted to clean and dry. A few she set aside to try and propagate. The sunroom itself got too much sunlight for fungus, but perhaps the pantry off the kitchen would work for it, or the cellar.

She abandoned her mushrooms again and lit the lamp on the table by the sofa, picking it up and carrying it out. It was large and heavy, not really intended to be carried, but Cricket still managed to hold onto it and get the cellar door unlocked and opened.

The wooden stairs creaked alarmingly under her meager weight but held as she descended.

Her lamp illuminated a small space at the bottom of the steps. The floor was packed earth, the walls stone, and she could feel the added moisture in the air as it settled against her skin.

It would be perfect for her purposes.

Rejuvenating from scraps was probably her safest course of action, which she'd successfully done before. Growing from actual spores was more of a difficult and uncertain process. Tomorrow she'd search through the garden to find what she'd need to start trying to cultivate, and perhaps if she was very lucky, she'd be able to find more fruit bodies to work with.

It would give her something to do within the house and gardens for a little while, at least.

She climbed back up the cellar stairs and snuffed out the lamp at the top before going to find Throckmorton again. He was back in his study, bent over his ledger.

She leaned against the doorway, arms crossed over her chest. "Is there anything we can do about this?" she asked. "Or is your advice to ignore it and stay away from the forest indefinitely?"

Throckmorton glanced up at her and slowly closed the leger, steepling his fingers together. "And what would you suggest we do? The closest constable is a good half day's travel by train over in Brookhaven. And I know from long experience that no officer of the law would come here unless we had a fresh body with a bloody knife sticking out of its back, and maybe not even then. So, shall I tell the preacher about this? See if he can pray away bones in the woods and mysterious holes in the ground?"

Cricket clenched her teeth at the mocking edge in his voice. "I'll remind you that I don't want to be here either, and I never asked to be involved in whatever this is."

"I haven't forgotten." He drummed his fingers against the top of the desk, then looked back down at his ledger. "Now if you'd excuse me, Mrs. Mallory, I need to finish this."

Don't call me that, she wanted to tell him. She did not belong to Walter any longer and didn't want to have anything to do with his name. Besides, she had only one true name, and that was neither "Mrs. Mallory" nor the dreaded "Gertrude," but she held all those words back.

He didn't deserve her true name any more than he deserved a glimpse at her true self.

Instead, she turned, leaving him to his work and fetching the lamp again so she could descend once more into the basement and begin her preparations.

CHAPTER 9

Cricket dreamed again that night.

She was standing in the garden, everything cast in dark gray shadows and silvering halos as it had been before. Once again, she made her way through the tall whispering grass toward the back of the garden.

She encountered the water before she even got close enough to see the pink buds growing from the strange creeping vines. The ground became marshy enough for her boots to sink into rich soil and cold water, the air becoming pungent with the smell of wet rotting grasses.

Cricket lifted her skirts up in her fists to keep them out of the mud as she waded forward. Now she was close enough that she could see where the water was coming up and under the wall.

Where it had been a trickle, now it was a strong stream that had plowed up the ground, carving a hollow out of the ground, the stones of the wall itself eaten away by the flow of water.

How much time had passed here? It felt as if she had just been here, and yet the wall now looked like the water had been flowing under it, slowly wearing it away for years and years.

Maybe time didn't matter here.

Cricket traced her fingers around the cool, smooth edge of the worn stone, slippery with the fine lichen that liked to live on river rocks. Crouching down, she let her fingers trail in the water, feeling the pull of its eddy around her hand, the coldness of it against her skin. The tips of her fingers went numb after only a few seconds, but she didn't mind. All around her was the stillness of the night and the faint murmur of the stream. Cricket let her eyes slide shut, inhaling and exhaling the scent of plants and wet rocks, glorying in it.

After a few moments, she opened her eyes and idly thought the hole in the wall looked big enough for her to squeeze through now.

She hesitated for several moments, not sure what would be on the other side of the wall or if she cared to find out. She half expected the ghostly woman to appear again, but all was quiet and still.

She shuffled forward like a spindly crab and carefully waded into the water of the little stream. Although the stream bed it had carved for itself was large, the water barely covered the tops of her boots as she moved through it.

Not that it mattered much; she still had to get down into it once she reached the wall and wriggle her way through the hole. She could feel the cold water seeping through her skirts, blouse, and other things as she pushed herself through the small space, digging into wet soil on the other side with her fingers in order to pull her way through.

With one last kick, she was clear of the wall and climbed to her feet, wiping the mud off her hands onto her wet skirts.

The woods stretched out in front of her, a ghostly pale copy of the woods behind Throckmorton's house. A thin mist snaked between the trees, making the world feel even grayer.

There was a strong humming in Cricket's bones, a weird jitteriness that seemed to crawl out of the forest along with the mist, making her skin prickle, her stomach flip, and her entire body feel on edge.

The last thing Cricket wanted to do was set foot into that stretch of gray woods.

The stream crept along the side of the wall instead of flowing toward the trees, and Cricket decided to follow that instead. She made her way through the water, one hand on the garden wall for balance as she felt for one foothold after another on the slippery stones at the bottom of the creek bed.

She wasn't afraid of drowning in this little water, but she could still turn her ankle on a stone or fall and injure herself badly, even if she didn't hit her head.

The stream turned the corner of the wall, and Cricket could see where the house would have been in the waking world was just more stone wall, this side crumbled away, overtaken by creeping vines and tall grass. Beyond it, where Throckmorton's front garden and the road should have been, was just more forest.

The trees were thicker here than they had been behind the house, and greener too somehow, the mist almost blue where it lay thick and low to the moss-covered ground. It was as if whatever was leeching the color from the moon-pale trees behind her had yet to reach this part of the woods.

Cricket hesitated, looking up at huge, towering pines and thick undergrowth, but the stream ran down between the trees, so she followed it.

It was dark under the trees. The moonlight that had painted everything in silver was only a faint glow here, throwing everything into shadows of browns, greens, and blues so intense and deep in their colors they appeared almost black.

The water of Cricket's little stream flowed into a wider and obviously older stone stream bed here, becoming deeper and quicker the farther under the trees she traveled. Soon she'd never to get out, Cricket thought, feeling the tug at her boots as the water slowly rose around her.

The banks on either side of the stream were thick with dark green moss and the roots of trees twisting through rich burnt-umber soil. The farther into the forest she got, the more Cricket felt herself relax. The strange vibration that had gripped her ebbed away, leaving only a faint ache in her back teeth.

The wind whispered through the great trees all around her, clicking their fur needles together, but no birds called, not even the solitary night hunters, and no small animals rustled their way through the underbrush.

There was just the sound of the wind, the water, and Cricket's own breathing.

She could smell wet soil, fir trees, and rot, but as she walked on, the wind began to carry another scent—sweet, heady, and nectarous.

Cricket climbed up out of the water, pulling herself up on moss-covered rocks and fallen branches.

Up ahead of her and a little to her right, there was a house. It was not a big house, but a small stone farmhouse of the sort favored a few generations earlier. There was smoke curling from the chimney and a well-kept little home plot around it, the ground worn down from chickens scratching and what Cricket thought was a tidy kitchen garden behind it.

When she set foot onto the hard-packed earth of the home plot, however, the scent hit her again, strong and almost cloying. The unmistakable smell of honeysuckle.

Cricket pivoted slightly and wasn't at all surprised to see the ghostly woman in her plain gray dress watching her from the shadow of one great tree.

"Was this your house?" she asked.

The woman moved forward with her slow, gliding movements that still reminded Cricket too keenly of a hunter snake.

"The memory of it," the woman said, hands folded primly in front of her. "I was happy here to spin, weave, and sew, tend to my brewing, my hearth, and my garden. Patient, obedient, and never idle as a good woman should be. I lived with my mother, but the fevers came in the winter and she died. Then in the summer, a man came and killed me in my garden."

She raised one hand, long-fingered and elegant, and honeysuckle burst from the ground. Its green web of vines and leaves heavy with perfumed blossoms covered over the house until the green had completely swallowed it up. Still, the vines pushed deeper, digging into the small places between the stones, pulling them apart with great scraping crunches. The stones were pushed by a great wave of green, rearranged. It was like bones being articulated into something completely different that looked more like the ruins of some castle or tower of legend still enrobed in green and flowers.

"I find the longer I am dead, the less I want to be patient, obedient, and never idle."

When Cricket turned to look at the woman again, her skin was gone, her head, neck, and hands now nothing but white bone although she still wore her plain gray dress.

"My patience and obedience had worn nothing." Once more when she spoke, her skeleton's mouth did not move, but Cricket still heard the words. "And all I want to do is be free of here and rest." She turned abruptly away from the green-covered ruins. "Maybe I could if I hadn't died here, but magic is inside me now. It poisons everything it touches here." She wrapped her skeletal arms around her wasted chest.

Cricket didn't know what to say. "Please, what is your name? What do I call you?"

The woman paused and looked back at her. "Rosaleen," she said. "My name was…is Rosaleen."

"Cricket." Cricket stepped forward, hand outstretched.

"I know." Rosaleen did not reach for Cricket's hand, and after a silent moment, Cricket let it drop to her side.

Rosaleen's gaze was on her. Even with the illusion of flesh stripped away from those empty sockets, Cricket could still feel the weight of her gaze.

"There wasn't a creek here before you came," Rosaleen said cryptically. "No water at all, in fact—not a brook or a stream, and now there is."

"I don't understand." Cricket's brow furrowed. The stream she'd followed had been deep and wide, the sort that only existed if water had run there for years if not far longer.

"Neither do I."

Cricket was seized by the sudden desire to reach out to her, take her hand or touch her in some way. Some tiny act of comfort in this lonely place.

She clenched her hand tight into a fist in the folds of her skirt instead and looked away at the huge dark trees all around them.

When she looked back, the woman was gone.

She spun in a tight circle, but she was all alone again although the stone house was still contorted into its ruined state and weighed down by greenery, the air heavy with the cloying scent.

Cricket looked back at it again and felt a chill creep up her spine, suddenly far more aware of the presence of death than she had been with the dead woman by her side.

She firmly turned her back on the ruins and headed back for the stream bed.

Once there she half climbed, half slid down the rocky bank back into the cold water.

The sound of it against the rocks, even the little bit of cold damp that soaked into her boots was a relief of sorts. She inhaled the scent of wet stone and rotting vegetation that almost eclipsed the still lingering scent of the flowers. She turned back the way she had come, slogging through the water, listening to the sound of her own breathing and movements in the dark stillness of the night.

There was a blue-black mist hanging low to the forest floor, but as Cricket walked, she became aware of a change. The mist grew paler somehow, thicker too. When Cricket glanced down, she saw her hands looked unnaturally silvery pale, although whether that was a trick of the light, she wasn't sure.

The mist felt heavy and wet against her face, matting down her hair to stick to her neck and forehead.

There was the snap of a branch breaking so loud in the eerie silence, it might have been a gunshot.

Cricket jumped, stumbling in the water. She sunk her fingers into the rocky, muddy slope of the side of the creek bed and craned her neck, looking for the location of the noise in the mist and the gloom.

A huge shape moved between the trees.

Cricket pressed herself against the creek bed, trying to quiet her breathing as her heart raced. The mist was so thick now, it was hard to make out what exactly she was looking at, but she thought she saw a flash of horns, the great curving rack of a huge stag in the moonlight.

Then the mist was moving not at all like mist should, or to be more correct, things were moving through the mist.

There were suddenly hands reaching out from the fog. Cricket could see them now, shockingly human as they crawled along the misty ground.

All those sickly white hands were on the stag before it could flee back into the woods.

Then Cricket saw the first spray of blood, shockingly bright among the dark shadows and silvering mist.

The stag bellowed a deafening scream that felt as if it went on without end.

Cricket crouched, frozen in the creek, terror closing her throat and locking her limbs in place.

Gray human shapes swarmed over the stag, mouths open. There was the wet rending of flesh, the iron stink of blood, the stag's bellowing screams that ended far too soon.

Cricket pressed her face against the dirt on the side of the creek bed, feeling every tiny stone and spiderweb root where they pushed against her cheek. She did not close her eyes, but she did not, could not watch either.

Finally, there was silence from above her on the bank.

Cricket's body shook, and she stared into the darkness, willing herself to wake up.

She didn't wake up.

Slowly and carefully, Cricket raised herself up against the bank, just enough to see over the edge. The…*creatures*—Cricket couldn't bear to think of them as people—were gone and the great carcass of the stag lay on the forest floor, picked clean save for a scrape of fur or flesh still clinging to pinkish bone.

The fog was thickening again, ghastly pale as if bleaching away the rich darkness from everything it touched. No, not true fog, Cricket thought somewhere in the back of her head, it was like the fine filaments of spider web or cocoons, the silken threads of new and tender roots reaching out and twisting around the bones. It rolled over what was left of the stag, the carcass vanishing like a stone sinking into water.

The wind picked up, and into the silence came a new sound—the scraping of bone against bone.

The mist heaved around the carcass as if something unimaginably huge, maybe the very ground itself, had inhaled deeply.

It took Cricket several heartbeats to realize it was the mass of bones itself that were moving. The grinding scraping noise came again, and slowly the stag climbed to its feet, all blood tinted-bones with scrapes of sinew still clinging to the ribs.

It began to walk, spindly legs clacking as it moved back toward the garden and the gray wood. Back where Cricket had intended to go.

She was no longer sure she wanted to. She sank low into the creek, grounding herself with the feeling of cold, wet dirt under her hands and water against her boots. So little water. She dearly wished for the deep stillness of a lake, the taste of brine and mountain air in her mouth. A cold, welcoming darkness she could sink into and be gone from here.

She groped her away along the side of the creek and almost fell when her hand met a thin veil of roots with nothing underneath. She staggered again and reached out, fingers catching on those roots before they pulled away in her hand and she could make out the hole underneath.

A sort of cave, carved out by erosion, underneath the twisting roots of the trees.

Cricket thought of the hole the water had carved under the garden wall and figured she had nothing to lose. The last thing she wanted to do was continue walking toward where the remains of the stag had gone.

She knelt and began crawling to the hole.

Roots and rocks caught at her hair, and her senses were suddenly filled by the overwhelming scent of soil and something else, something deeper and older somehow. It wasn't the scent of well water drawn up from the depth or the scent of the incense from church or the scent of very old undisturbed bones, but it made Cricket think of all those thing as she crawled deeper under the ground.

She had a moment of absolute clarity that she had made a mistake.

CHAPTER 10

Then she was awake, back in Throckmorton's dusty sunroom with morning light streaming across her lap as she all but threw herself out of bed.

It took her several seconds to compose herself and shake off the last of the dream. She scrubbed her hands across her face and told herself to get a grip. It had just been a nightmare, and she'd had plenty of those before.

Still, her stomach felt unsettled, and her senses pitched a little bit too high as she pulled open the door to the rest of the house.

Like the mornings before, Throckmorton was gone by the time she made her way into the kitchen to scrounge a breakfast of leftovers and the remaining coffee in the pot, far stronger and cooler than she would have preferred.

After she ate, she decided fresh air and some vigorous exercise was what she needed to shake off the last vestiges of fear. She'd found some gardening supplies in the basement during her explorations there: a shovel, rake, and hoe along with a very large, wickedly sharp knife made for cutting back brush. Armed with this, she went out into the garden to begin working on the overgrown space.

There were many evergreen bushes that had grown to three to four times their preferred size. Cricket considered them to be useless plants and personally detested them, but she cut them back as best she could, keeping plans to dig some of them up in the back of her mind if she was going to stay here for any great length of time. There were also wild roses everywhere, their long, sharp canes twisting around every available surface. Cricket cut cane until her hands were bleeding from trying to handle the dangerous things and her dress and shirt were smeared in dirt and green sap.

She paused several hours into her vicious assault and sat on the stone bench. She rubbed a hand across her sweaty forehead, probably leaving streaks of blood behind and not really caring. She'd made good progress on the roses and bushes, but there was still a great deal to be done. At some point, she'd need to get a scythe for the grass and other weeds.

Depending on how long she was here, of course.

She didn't really want to imagine still being here for the spring when she might dig beds and do some planting of her own. Her gaze roamed across the space now, picking out the shape of leaves, the beginning buds of flowers not yet ready to bloom.

She frowned as a distinctive leaf shape caught her eye. She stood and waded through the tall grass toward the now more accessible back of the garden.

There was a large bushy plant with a heavily veined three-pointed leaf. She stood in front of it and rubbed one of the leaves through her fingers.

Now that she'd seen it, she could see others. There were big patches of black henbane throughout the garden. There was nightshade too, now that she was looking for it—*atropa belladonna*, the deadliest kind not yet sporting its distinctive berries. There was monkshood too and lots of it, unassuming and green now, but it would bloom vibrant purple by late summer.

She went from one plant to another examining them, tracing the dense patches of them all across the garden space from the kitchen door straight to the back wall of the garden.

These plants were not indigenous, she knew that well enough. They must have been planted here. Some of the deadliest plants in existence. It was very clear that at one time, this had been a poison garden.

A shudder went through her body. She stared, unseeing, at another patch of monkshood.

Who had planted these? Had it been Throckmorton?

That was a disquieting thought. Her mind instantly went to the mushrooms she'd picked and carefully cleaned, laying them out in the sunroom to dry. She'd used fungus very similar to the ones she currently had in her possession in small doses to sedate Walter throughout most of their relationship, particularly when it became clear that he had no respect for her and would not let her go. Just enough to make him feel sluggish and unwell enough to never put his hands on her throughout the course of their years under the same roof.

She had only seriously poisoned him once, to see if the curse would lift if he were to die, but a doctor had been fetched in time, and shortly after she'd learned it did not matter if he lived or not. His illness had been blamed on bad food, and she hadn't dared another serious attempt after that, afraid that if he died under suspect conditions, the suspicion would fall to her.

Walter had threatened to send her to an asylum enough times that she feared that was the natural course of action for the Mallorys to take if he were to perish, even if she wasn't arrested for murder.

It was that fear that had driven her onto a train when he had actually died in that boating accident.

Far better to fall on the kindness of strangers—in this case, Throckmorton—than to resign herself to whatever prison or asylum Mrs. Mallory would lock her up in.

If Throckmorton showed any signs of danger, she had assumed she could do to him what she'd done to Walter for all these years. But if he knew poisons well enough to grow his own poison garden…well, that changed things.

Her fingers clenched around the handle of the knife still in her hands.

The garden was so overgrown it could very well have been the previous inhabitants who had cultivated all these plants, and Throckmorton could have no idea they were even out here. She might even be able to harvest them and use them for her own devices.

Still, her gut churned with sickening fear. If she tried to poison him and he outsmarted her, she'd have no more cards to play. She'd be truly vulnerable.

The memory of her blood on his teeth swam through her mind again. This time it was not accompanied by a heady, squirming rush deep inside of her, only cold dread that made sweat break out on the back of her hands.

Part of her wanted to believe he'd never be a real threat to her, but she knew better than to listen to that. Everyone was a threat under the right circumstances, and they didn't really know each other.

Her gaze went back to the plant in front of her, the deceptively delicate curve of the monkshood.

Cricket thought of him and the blood on his teeth again. There was something niggling at the back of her mind now, a thought just out of reach.

She only had *his word* for the fact that he couldn't remove the curse, she thought suddenly. He'd said it hadn't worked, and she'd believed him. Right before he'd forbade her from leaving the house, tying her even tighter to him than the curse already had.

She swallowed thickly.

It was unclear how far she needed to be from him before the curse took effect. Did she really need to reside in the same house as him, or could she simply stay nearby until she had located a witch or mage to help her? She didn't know, but it was worth finding out.

Cricket went back into the house. Throckmorton was not back yet. She washed and bandaged her hands in the kitchen before going to the sunroom to gather up her few possessions.

Her experiment in laundering clothes had not gone well, she'd discovered when she'd brought them in from the garden the night before. Her fine morning dress was ruined, but the rest of her clothes were still usable if more bedraggled than when she'd had a maid who knew what she was doing. She stuffed everything back into her carpet bag along with the mushrooms that still needed to dry a little longer.

There had to be a farmer in the area who might take her in. She might not have many practical housekeeping skills, but she could garden and work in the fields. She could find a way to mail a letter to her father's banker and pay them off if she had to.

She didn't let herself think about what she'd do if this plan triggered the curse. Maybe she'd be able to find a witch or mage before that happened.

Lastly, she cleaned the knife she'd been using in the garden and stowed that in the bag before leaving the house and making for the woods again.

This time, Cricket walked with purpose down the cow path and off into the trees, hoping to skirt around the field without having to go through it. There might be a farm on the other side, and it might be close enough to pull this entire plan off.

At least she hoped so.

She trekked through the forest, hauling her carpet bag with both hands as she went, and purposely not looking toward where she knew the creek bed full of bones was located. A good ways beyond it she found another cow path. It led her along the edge of the woods with fields on the other side, and she was grateful no mysterious voices called to her from these fields.

Her day was already starting to look up.

She finally came to a set of wooden hitching posts. Beyond them a slate stone path led through a neat yard up to a large, whitewashed farmhouse with a kitchen garden off to the side and a barn behind it.

Her spirits lifted at the sight of it, and she quickened her step up the path. She climbed the steps to the well-swept porch, feeling more than a little bit grubby after her morning's work in the garden. Squaring her shoulders, she wrapped on the door, readying herself to do some quick and persuasive talking with whomever opened it. Maybe she should have put on her ruined mourning dress. People tended to be more sympathetic to a young widow in full morning attire, and she would have looked more moneyed and less like a vagrant.

She didn't need to worry about that quite yet, though. No one came at her first knock. She raised her fist and banged again, then again.

Still, no one answered.

Unease prickled up her spine. She told herself she was overthinking this. Most of the household was no doubt out working, and the rest could have gone into town. The house was clearly not abandoned.

She climbed back down the steps of the porch and circled around toward the carefully tended kitchen garden. A well had been dug some ways from the house and there was a bucket lying beside it. She walked closer and saw the bucket had fallen onto its side and the water had spilled out and seeped into the ground some time ago.

Cricket looked at it for a long moment, her stomach flipping over unpleasantly. She turned back toward the house.

There was something lying in the grass between the garden beds, long and pale against the green.

She took a step toward it, one step and then another until she could see the body stretched out on the ground.

The body wore a plain work dress and apron. Its feet were in study work boots pointed toward where Cricket stood. She could also see the bright shape that had originally caught her eye—one pale hand flung out and curled in the grass like a dead spider.

It was hard to tell much more about the body beyond that. Whoever it had been, their throat had been ripped out and was now a mess of flesh, bone, and blood. The face was also mostly gone, bitten and torn away in large, gut-churning hunks Cricket could barely look at. The blood on the body had congealed and gone dark around the edges, but the inside of the wounds still shone wetly in the hot sun.

Cricket breathed slowly through her mouth, trying not to smell anything, trying not to look past those work-worn boots.

Her mind flashed back to the stag from her dreams dying in the forest.

Very slowly, she lowered her bag to the ground and knelt beside the body. Her legs shook, hands trembling as she fumbled with the clasp on the bag and drew out the knife. She gripped it as tightly as she could, trying to think of what to do next.

Might there still be people alive in the house? If there were, they must be injured since they hadn't come outside yet.

On the other hand, whatever had done this might still be there or somewhere else on the farm.

Or in the forest.

Cricket could feel the cold sweat prickling up her arms, sticking down the hair on the back of her neck.

She wasn't an expert on murder, but the body had been mauled by something big, not stabbed or shot. Clearly, a large animal with very strong, sharp teeth had done this, and it could be in the trees right now.

The fact that she'd made it out here this morning could have simply been luck, or it could have been stalking her.

Her gaze strayed to the house again. The beast might be in there, but it was more likely to be in the forest or roaming the farm grounds. If so, she was safer in the house than out in the open.

She set her sights on the house's kitchen door, just at the edge of the garden, judging the distance as she wrapped her skirts in her free fist. Then she ran as fast and hard as she could, skirting around the body without looking at it again.

There was a high buzzing sound in her ears, and her breath came in big heaving pants as she propelled herself across the garden and grass and hurled herself bodily against the kitchen door. There was a moment of fumbling with the door handle, then it gave under her weight and she staggered into the house.

The kitchen had been utterly ruined. Cricket had a brief impression of smashed dishware, everything pulled from the shelves and spread all over the floor. She turned and slammed the door close behind her anyway.

Leaning against it, she held her knife out in front of her, panting hard.

Around her the house was silent.

Quiet enough to make her heart drop and her gut clench. Her hands shook harder, and she gripped the smooth wood of the knife handle tighter to keep them steady as she moved into the kitchen. The cuts from the rose cane earlier that morning stung and ached under the pressure, but Cricket didn't loosen her grip. If anything, she was grateful for the sharp pain, which cut through some of the haze of panicky fear that was threatening to engulf her with every step she took.

She inched forward, slow and quiet, trying not to step on or kick any of the mess covering the floor for fear that the sound would give her away.

There was a lot of broken crockery, splintered wood, and broken glass but no food. There was a smear here and there of something that could have been food—sticky molasses, flour, grains, and even the hint of blood clinging to a cleaver on the table, but it was as if the food had been hastily cleared away while the pieces of broken glass and pottery had been left among a few stray smears.

On the other side of the big kitchen table, she found the second body.

They were lying in a pool of their own slowly congealing blood. Whatever had savaged the person in the garden had killed and partly eaten this one as well. Cricket could recognize the bite marks now, the…*chunks* missing.

She averted her gaze again, edging around the blood until she came to the kitchen doorway. There she paused, unsure if she actually wanted to go deeper into the house.

She stood as still as she could, her entire being straining for any hint of breathing beyond the kitchen door, any sounds of movement. Any hint of the click of claws on wood or the heavy panting of an animal.

There was nothing. Nothing moved beyond the kitchen door. Nothing breathed.

Cricket crept forward as slowly and quietly as she could, still holding the knife out in front of her.

The hall leading from the kitchen was clean, at least—no debris or blood, worn but well cared for rugs on the floor, pictures still on the walls. There was even a small side table with a vase of cut early spring flowers that had not yet begun to wilt.

Beyond the side table was another doorway to what Cricket could only imagine was a sitting room or parlor of some sort. Her heart hammered hard enough for her to feel lightheaded as she approached the doorway, pausing just before she rounded the corner to take a two-handed grip on the knife as if it was a sword.

She took a deep, deep breath, inched around the doorway into the room, entire body tense and fully ready to hack apart the first thing that moved.

There was nothing there.

Cricket stood in the middle of a very neat and orderly parlor, her pulse racing for all it was worth as her gaze swept the empty room. Like the hallway, it seemed untouched by the carnage from the kitchen. There was no blood, nothing out of place. The grandfather clock in the corner ticked slow and steady, and golden sunlight spilled through the windows onto the floor.

There were also no doorways aside from the one she'd just burst through.

Cricket turned in a slow circle, her knife still held out in front of her, looking for any sign of danger or survivors. The slow and steady click of the clock in the corner was almost more unnerving than the silence had been.

Then she heard the heavy tread of footsteps on floorboards.

Her heart immediately leapt into her throat, although the steps sounded human enough. In a brief moment of panic, she considered hiding behind the sofa or one of the chairs.

It was too late.

She only had time to turn and face the doorway, knife held in both hands before a dark shape loomed up in it.

CHAPTER 11

For a moment he seemed impossibly huge in the dimness of the hallway before Throckmorton stepped into the sunlit room.

They stared at each other in silence.

She'd always been aware of his heaviness, and bulk but never like she was now as he stood there, a black-clad presence filling up every inch of space.

His expression was closed and impossible to read as he looked at her, frozen in front of him, still holding out the knife.

Unbidden, her mind recalled the blood on his teeth, the feeling of them sinking into her flesh. She remembered the low guttural growl of an animal as she was pushed backward in that sunlit field, and the golden eyes and huge jaws from her dream the first night she'd slept in his garden. There was the slow, stalking presence outside her window on the second night, and he'd forbidden her from going back into the woods once she'd found the bodies with bite marks on their bones.

Then there was all that deadly nightshade, black henbane, and wolfsbane growing rampant throughout his garden.

Cricket remembered a woodcut from one of the books she'd read a long time ago. It had depicted the contorted body of a man changing from human to beast as he ripped at the mangled body below him, consuming it.

She knew him then. She finally knew what he truly was.

"You," she said, her voice shaking and her whole body numb.

"We need to leave," he said, his voice low and urgent. "We need to leave right now."

He took a step forward, and she watched the way he moved, focused and deadly. It was something part of her mind had noticed a long time ago but had then discounted. She'd been so desperate for him to be the answer to her problems, a safe place for her to run to.

Cricket saw him now, the calculation in his gaze, the strength in his massive arms and shoulders and loosely curled hands. She knew if he smiled or opened his mouth, she'd be able to see his teeth, far too sharp to be human. Another thing she'd noticed and discounted in her desperate willful ignorance.

Now she was going to pay the price.

He could kill her. She had no doubt he could if she let him close enough.

She wasn't going to do that.

The knife was still in her hands, still held out before her, the blade not even shaking in her grasp anymore.

If he went for her, she'd aim for the face and neck. It would probably be more effective to try and drive it into his gut, but he'd be within biting distance then. Slicing an artery was her only hope, provided that could kill him.

"You did this." Her voice sounded like it was coming from very far away, but at least it was steady now.

His brows furrowed. "I did not," he said, mildly offended.

She bared her very human teeth at him. "I know they were eaten. Isn't that what you do, *wolf?*"

He went very still at that, and it was enough to tell her she'd been right. Even though she'd known since he stepped into the room, the confirmation was enough to make her heart leap into her throat. She took several steps back without really being aware that she had moved until her back bumped into a doily-covered side table.

He didn't move toward her again, but his gaze didn't leave her either. "Mrs. Mallory—"

It was too much. "Don't call me that!" Cricket's voice rose in a shriek, cracking on the last word.

"I am not what you think I am."

"Aren't you?" She took one hand off the handle of the knife and snatched a small object off the side table, a little silver cross. She threw it at him as hard as she could.

He flinched from it, trying to twist out of the way. He was fast when he wasn't trying to be human, faster than she'd expected.

He wasn't fast enough.

It hit his shoulder, and there was the sizzle of flesh against hot metal.

As he bellowed in pain, Cricket lunged at him, swinging the knife as she went.

His hand closed around her arm with brutal force, and he slammed her against the ground hard enough to knock every last ounce of breath out of her. Pain jarred up her spine in the same instant her head hit the floor and pain exploded behind her eyes.

The knife clattered to the ground, and Throckmorton kicked it farther across the floor without letting go of her arm. He twisted it, and she yelled at the pain that shot through her shoulder.

At least he was panting, not completely unmoved, when he knelt over her, although that was really no solace.

"You need to stop and listen to me," he said between clenched teeth. "Gertrude, please just stop."

"That's not my name," she spat. If she was going to die, she wasn't going to die as someone she wasn't.

"Take a deep breath," he said as if he was trying to soothe her, "and listen to me for a moment. I did not kill those people. I followed you here when I got back to the house and found you and your possessions gone. I was worried about you, for my sins."

"If you're so concerned for my welfare, you'd let me up and give me back my knife," Cricket panted.

"Oh yes, I'm sure you'd love to slit my throat." Above her, Throckmorton rolled his eyes. "Although maybe it would serve me right for not leaving you in the garden that first night. But right now, I am primarily concerned with whatever did kill those people and where it is."

"You killed them!" she bellowed at the top of her lungs, incensed by how calm he seemed while her entire body was tensed and ready to fight for her life.

His mask slipped then, the calm cracking under real anger. He bared his teeth at her, a low deep noise vibrating in his throat. It was the noise of an animal and the expression of an animal in a human face, shocking and horrifying enough for her to go completely still on instinct, her heart hammering so hard he could probably feel it. She was like a wild rabbit pinned under a wolf. Every part of her hated it, her hands curling uselessly into fists where he had them trapped.

Then the mask of humanity and civility snapped back into place.

"I didn't," he said again. "I did not kill those people, which means whatever did is still out there hunting us." He changed his grip on her so he could shake her a little bit, her head thumping against the floorboards. "You have to listen to me. I am trying to save your life."

He looked down at her silently for a moment. "If I was planning on eating you, don't you think I would have done it already? When we were in the forest together or maybe while you slept? Sometime when I could have taken you unarmed and unawares."

She took a long slow breath at that. "How do I know you won't kill me now to protect yourself or preserve your secret?"

Throckmorton pressed his lips together in a thin line but slowly sat back, letting go of her and standing in one fluid motion. He took several paces away from where she still lay and picked up her knife, examining it as she pushed herself up and scrambled to her feet.

He turned back toward her and held out the knife. "I'm not going to kill you. I'm not going to eat you or any of the other things you are imagining."

Hesitantly, she reached out, still expecting a blow to come until her fingers slid around the polished wood of the handle. They brushed him, just the merest hint of skin sliding against skin before he let go and stepped back a pace.

Out of easy stabbing range, she noticed.

"We need to leave," he said again. "The sooner the better."

"My bag," Cricket said, thinking of where she'd left it in the garden by the first body.

"To hell with your bag. We are very likely running out of time. I don't know if I can protect us both if whatever killed these people comes back."

Cricket clenched her jaw, thinking about her field guides. "It has everything I own in it."

Throckmorton's own jaw clenched visibly. She thought he was going to fight her on this, but instead, he nodded once. "Fine. We'll go out the back."

They headed out of the room together, both very careful not to turn their back on the other. Although in the narrow hallways this meant they had to walk shoulder to shoulder.

They picked their way back through the destroyed kitchen with the body still on the floor, and Throckmorton eased open the back door, scanning the yard before gesturing it was all clear.

The sun was still deceptively bright outside. Cricket could hear the hum of insects, the rustle of the breeze through the leaves of the trees making everything seem normal and peaceful in stark contrast to the mutilated corpse still lying among the garden vegetables.

She could see her bag just a little way beyond the body and headed for it.

The first scream came when she was within a few paces of it. Both she and Throckmorton's heads snapped around at the sound, far too loud in the quiet. It was definitely a human scream but not like anything Cricket had ever heard before—a long, low wail of pure, hopeless anguish.

Every hair on her body stood on end. For a moment she was rooted to the spot, unable to move.

Run, her body said. *Run and don't look back.*

Then she was running, barely aware she'd started moving until she could hear the wind whistling in her ears and her blood pumping desperately through her body as she propelled herself.

Not back toward the trees and Throckmorton's house, but forward toward the screaming.

Behind her, Throckmorton yelled and swore, but Cricket didn't stop.

The screams came again, definitely from the barn behind the house.

Cricket ran, knife still clutched in one hand, her skirts bunched in the other, hair flying, boots slipping on the grass. The barn loomed up ahead, coming too fast, big doors open and gaping like a dark maw in the weather-worn building.

Cricket skidded in front of the barn and almost fell, catching herself in time. She brought up both hands to hold the knife out in front of her and advanced on the doorway, clearing enough of the door to see in.

There was blood on the packed earthen floor. Lots of blood, seeping into the dirt.

It was hard to say how many people had died there. The corpses around the house had been badly mauled but were still mostly intact. These bodies were different.

There was far less left.

There was a woman kneeling in the blood and the gore in the center of the barn. She was covered in blood, her dress soaked in it, her hair matted in clumps, her face streaked dark. She was screaming, a long gut-wrenching sound that came over and over again as she rocked herself back and forth on the bloody mud of the floor.

Cricket tightened her grip on the knife, inching forward, opening her mouth to call out although she had no idea what she'd say.

The woman saw her. The scream died on her lips as their gazes met.

Cricket saw the expression on the woman's face change, saw her eyes change, watched all the humanity leech out of them as they became something else completely.

She knew then that she'd made a mistake.

The woman came at her in a staggering run. Cricket had a glimpse of pale lips pulled back from blood-stained teeth before she was knocked aside. She hit the ground with a jarring pain up her side, and her knife skittered from her hand.

At the same moment, an overpowering scent hit her—rich soil, moss, wet fur, and something else that reminded her of standing at the mouth of a cave.

She looked up to see a monster standing between her and the blood-covered woman.

It was a wolf in name only.

If glimpsed between the trees in the dark, it might be mistaken for that animal. Up close it was huge, its fur black, eyes golden and shining like lamps in the dark. Its body was misshapen as if each bone and pull of muscle had been created by something that knew the idea of a living, breathing animal but had never actually seen one. Its skin pulled too tightly over bone and sinew, its jaws too wide and slavering.

It was a wolf of fairy tales and legends, a monster of nightmares and half-remembered dreams, not a creature of science and facts.

The wolf opened his mouth and panted, red tongue lolling past far too many teeth. He growled, and Cricket could feel the sound in her own chest as much as she could hear it, the low throbbing warning before the bite.

The blood-covered woman opened her own mouth and screamed a noise of blinding rage and anguish coupled together, then she turned and ran away from them, toward the back of the barn.

Cricket sucked in a shocked breath and scrambled for her knife. Her hand closed around it, and she glanced back up in time to watch the woman clumsily scale the ladder up to the hayloft, nearly slipping with boots still slicked in blood.

"Why is she going up there?" Cricket climbed to her feet, untangling her skirts so she'd be able to run if she had to.

The wolf growled in warning, not looking at her but moving his great bulk enough to keep her from following the woman.

"What if there's someone hiding up there?" she snapped at him. "Maybe she's gone to look for weaker prey."

There came a noise from above them, a soft rustling whistle that Cricket couldn't quite place but still made her stomach flip painfully inside of her, followed by a loud crack from outside.

Cricket froze, but the wolf turned and padded back out of the barn. After a moment she followed him.

A body lay crumpled on the ground on the other side of the barn, surrounded by an ugly pool of dark blood.

Above them, the hayloft door stood open where the blood-covered woman had thrown herself out.

Cricket stared at the body as the wolf sniffed it before turning away in seeming disinterest.

She supposed she should be grateful that there hadn't been anyone hiding up in the hayloft, or at least if there was, that the woman hadn't harmed them. She didn't feel grateful, though. She felt numb.

A cool wind rustled the leaves on the trees around them, pulling at her hair and the edge of her skirts.

Cricket stared at the body on the ground without so much as blinking until the wolf padded close.

The scent of him, the heat of his huge body, the puff of moist breath against her skin, and the gut-level awareness of his huge mouth too close to her body snapped her out of whatever trance she'd fallen into.

She took a stumbling step back, hands starting to shake around the handle of her knife again.

"Do you—" Her voice petered out into nothing, and she swallowed several times, trying to work moisture back into her mouth and throat. "Do you think she was the one who killed all those people? Or do you think there are more like her?"

The wolf growled again, a low warning noise. Cricket nodded jerkily, then turned and headed back the way she'd come.

Now it was well and truly time for them to leave while they still could.

CHAPTER 12

Cricket didn't really remember crossing the lawn of the ruined farm. She didn't remember picking up her carpet bag or heading for the woods.

When she thought back on it, it all felt too foggy, like a dream.

She barely remembered stumbling through the forest, sure of every tiny sound; every snap of twigs or crunch of a leaf under the heel of her boot signaled sudden, horrible death. She couldn't seem to stop her body from flinching at every shadow or play of light through the branches of the trees.

It felt like a very long way across that sweep of forest, back to the road and Throckmorton's front gate.

It wasn't until her hand touched the cool, smooth iron of his gate that she was aware of him again, looming up behind her.

She turned her head enough to glance over her shoulder, half expecting to see the wolf standing in the road.

Instead, he was just a man, hair completely disheveled, carrying his coat and waistcoat instead of wearing them. His black shirt was open at the collar to expose his throat.

She jerked away from him as if he could burn her and stumbled through the gate and up the path to the house.

He herded her along in front of him until they were both inside again with the door locked behind him.

Cricket dropped her carpet bag onto the floor of the front hall and staggered forward, still holding onto her knife for all she was worth. "What the fuck is going on here?"

"That's a very good question." Throckmorton pushed around her to stalk into the sitting room.

She followed him, hands still trembling, her entire body feeling like a wire stretched too tight for far too long.

He was standing by the cluttered sideboard, pouring dark liquid from an unmarked bottle into two tiny crystal glasses. "Put the knife down." He said when he saw her. "Unless you're planning on trying to murder me again, after all that." He waved one of the glasses at her. "And sit, before you fall down."

She sat, or more like *collapsed* onto one of the armchairs but didn't let go of the knife as she took the glass he offered her and threw back its contents. The taste of bitter herbs exploded across her tongue, followed by the burn of hard liquor down her throat. She gagged slightly, doubling forward.

"I was going to tell you to sip it." Throckmorton sounded at least a little amused. "It's quite strong."

Cricket straightened back up once she was sure her stomach was not going to heave itself up through her throat. "So." She licked her teeth and held out her glass for a refill. "Have your neighbors always been cannibals?"

"Not to my knowledge." Throckmorton filled her glass for her. "Although I can't say I socialize much with the neighbors. I have historically kept to myself and not strayed too far from my house, the grocers, and occasionally the post office. I don't walk in the woods as you do."

Not even in wolf form? Cricket wanted to ask, but she kept those words firmly inside. The last thing she wanted to think about right now was the wolf with his jaws and teeth or the fact that he was standing *right there* with a sherry glass in his hand, looking far too human.

"Which is to say," Throckmorton went on, "something could have been happening for a very long time without me even noticing." He sounded not at all happy about that admission.

Cricket thought about the bones in the forest, the way they had been gnawed, and her stomach sank. Some of those bones had looked old.

Was Throckmorton telling the truth? She watched him over the rim of her glass, sipping carefully this time, savoring the taste of smoke and bitter herbs on her tongue.

Or was he in on it? Part of whatever this was, this…*hunger*. A wolf ate human flesh; Cricket had never read anything else. Wolves were created by ungodly desire and ungodly appetites, the unfettered need to experience and consume no matter how dark and horrifying that path got.

He was haloed in golden afternoon light here in the parlor, still in his shirt sleeves, hair disheveled although he'd run his fingers through it several times to push it back from his face. His collar was still open, revealing a pale slice of throat, seemingly fragile against the unforgiving blackness of his shirt.

In complete and sober black, he looked like one of the preachers or otherwise respectable men from the old stories she'd read as a child, the ones who were tempted into the woods by witches, demons, or spirits. Destined to be tricked, ravished, or simply murdered.

Except that she knew better now.

He turned to meet her gaze, and she realized how dark his eyes were, brown and deep as the richest earth after a heavy rain, threaded through with the wolf's gold.

What appetites had he been hiding from her all this time? What hungers drove the wolf? Her skin prickled and her hand tightened on the handle of her knife.

"I'm going out to the garden," she said abruptly, setting her now empty glass aside and only fumbling it a little bit. "I need to clear my head, to think."

She didn't wait for him to reply before she was up and out of the sitting room, down the hall, and through the kitchen at a near run.

The air was at least cooler outside, and she took several long, gasping breaths of it once the back door slammed shut behind her. Her face felt flushed, her whole body too hot and on edge.

The bushes on either side of the bench still needed to be cut back, she thought critically. She'd done her best that morning—it felt like a lifetime ago—but they still surrounded the bench, near engulfing it in green. She rather liked the effect when she was sitting on the bench among the green, although perhaps a trellis would be a better choice. A trellis with some kind of creeping flowering vine, that would fit right in.

She still felt vaguely hazy from the drinks she'd had. Just enough to take the edge off the jittering fear that had been filling her up since she'd started back through the woods. It was pleasant to sit here, surrounded by green, feeling the cool breeze on her face.

The kitchen door banged open, causing her to startle.

Throckmorton gestured at her from the doorway, looking tense and perhaps a little angry, although she had no idea why. He beckoned for her to come into the house. She shook her head, starting to feel a tad annoyed herself.

It was nice out here in the garden, where she'd be able to have some peace and quiet and might actually be able to relax. That was, if he'd go away and leave her alone.

He beckoned again, and she shook her head sharply, turning half away from him.

Next thing she knew, he'd crossed the space between them with quick strides and grabbed her by the shoulder, dragging her off the bench and onto the ground.

He knelt beside her and leaned in close so she could feel his breath ghost across her ear. "There are people in the woods, just on the other side of the garden wall. I don't know who they are or what they want, but given this morning, I would suggest you stay very quiet and very still until they go away."

She froze, carefully adjusting her hold on the handle of the knife while her ears strained for any hint of sound. She heard nothing behind the rustle of the leaves in the garden around them. Finally, she leaned close to him, far closer than she really wanted to, and whispered, "How do you know?"

He let out a soft huff. "I can smell them," he said, which was about as unsettling an answer as she could imagine.

She couldn't see his full expression this close, just his jawline and part of his mouth curved into a frown. His jaw had very fine, dark stubble across it, and his lips were pink, full, and a little bit pouty. She jerked her gaze away from them, but that allowed it to drop down to his exposed throat again.

Cricket took a breath of cool air, her head still swimming more than she liked. She remembered the feel of his lips on her arm, his teeth biting into her. What would he do if she were to bite him in return? Just lean forward and let her own teeth sink into that tender, pale skin at his neck or the soft roundness on the underside of his jaw. Would he…*let her?*

She abruptly realized she'd been leaning forward into his shoulder, closer to that tempting curve of his throat, and jerked herself back before she did something truly unforgivable.

Some doors weren't meant to be opened. She needed to remember that.

His gaze had been fixed on the back of the garden and the trees beyond it, but something in her sudden movement caught his attention. He turned just a little bit to look at her where she knelt beside him. "What is your name?" he asked, his voice still pitched in a low murmur.

She blinked at him. "Excuse me?"

"Your name," he said again. "This morning you said that Gertrude Mallory wasn't your name. So, what is it?"

She bit her lip, silently cursing herself. She'd been so sure she was about to die on the floor of that parlor, she hadn't carried what she said, but now she wished very much she'd kept her mouth shut.

She supposed she could lie and tell him that he'd misunderstood and to call her Gertrude. Instead, she sighed. "It's Cricket. Gertrude Mallory is just my legal name."

He looked at her silently while she braced for him to tell her that "Cricket" was a child's nickname.

Finally, he nodded. "Cricket, then." He was quiet for another long moment before sitting back on his heels. "May I tell you something? About why I became the wolf?"

She nodded, curious despite the tiny shiver of unease that pricked at her, wondering if she really wanted to know what he was about to tell her.

"When I was younger," he said in that low deep murmur, the words coming slowly as he obviously chose each of his words with care, "I lived as a woman. Not by choice, you understand. It was a lie started at my birth, perpetuated by my family, and, probably worse of all, my bodily anatomy. But I knew the lie of it from a very young age. At first, I thought I could keep the truth to myself." He grimaced. "That did not go well. So, I left the community I had grown up in, cut myself off from my family, and reinvented myself as a man from the ground up. It was not, of course, as easy as that makes it sound, but I survived. My flesh and bones, though…that was not so easily changed.

"But the wolf changes flesh and bone. That is the purpose of it. It forces the body to rework itself, and through that, I can have a voice that is as deep as I want it to be, grow hair on my jaw and chest, gain muscle and even height. A body that fits the man I have always seen myself as is what the wolf gives to me, and I have never regretted that."

He paused again, watching her carefully, his dark eyes calculating and intent. "I tell you all this because I think in some way you may understand. Because I think you are like me. You aren't a woman, are you?"

She stared up at him, opened her mouth to deny it, to lie, to hide, to protect herself as ever.

But instead, she said, "Yes, you're right. I'm not a woman. It's what I was raised to believe I was, but I'm not. I'm not a man either, I'm pretty sure. I'm something else entirely."

He smiled at her, a genuinely soft smile that caused the corners of his eyes to crinkle. Then he stiffened, his smile dropping off his face as his head snapped around toward the back of the garden again. "Quiet."

Cricket hunched closer to him again, low to the ground, her gaze also going to the far garden wall, or as much of it as she could see around the bench and the bushes. She tried to breathe calm and quiet as the minutes ticked by.

Finally, Throckmorton straightened up. "They're gone," he said, his voice more normal now. "Come on, let's go back inside."

She did take his hand this time and followed him.

He locked the door behind the two of them. "I think it would be best for us both to stay away from the neighbors and townsfolk until we know what's going on."

Cricket nodded. She was suddenly exhausted, her body weighed down to the point where she thought she might collapse right there on the kitchen floor. She sat at the table instead, putting her knife down across the clean white tablecloth. She looked up to find Throckmorton studying her.

"Is there anything else I should call you?" he asked, "Asides from Cricket."

Her brows furrowed. "Like what?"

"Should I call you 'him' or 'her,' or something else?"

"I've always gone by 'her.'"

"And you still can if you want," he said easily enough. "But you don't have to, not with me."

Those words lodged underneath Cricket's ribs, hard and painful like a stone jabbing her in the side. Ridiculously, she felt tears prick at her eyes and blinked them back.

"I'm going upstairs to bathe." She pushed herself up from the table and grabbed the knife more on reflex than anything else. Indeed, her shirt and blouse were caked in dirt, blood, and even some green sap left over from that morning.

More than that, though, her entire body felt filthy and worn out.

Throckmorton didn't try to stop her as she made her slow and stumbling way out of the kitchen and down the hall. He did watch her, though. Even without turning, she could feel his gaze on her all the way to the stairs.

She trudged to the bathroom, locked herself inside, and ran a bath before finally stripping her clothes off and climbing into the hot water.

Steam rose from the tub, the heat of it turning Cricket's skin pink but also soothing her, easing just a little bit of tension from her limbs. She leaned back, staring up at the ceiling and trying to force some of the exhaustion away so her head might clear.

She'd left the knife on the floor beside the tub, and her hand strayed over the edge to brush against the handle, soothing and familiar. At this point, she wasn't sure she'd ever be comfortable with it out of her sight again.

Her mind kept jumping back to the farmhouse, the bodies, the blood, the sound of the woman jumping to her death out of the hayloft.

Cricket screwed her eyes shut, trying to force it all back. Pressing her free hand against her chest, she counted her breaths in and out, concentrating on the rise and fall of her ribs under her hand, the feeling of her skin against her palm. She forced herself to think only of the way the hot water felt, slippery smooth against her skin, lapping gently at her legs and across her hips. Slowly, she breathed, waiting for her mind to settle. It felt an almost impossible task, like finding her way through an unfamiliar forest at night, her thoughts like so many trees rising up before her.

After several long moments, she let her hand rise from her chest and reach for the bar of soap, sitting up and setting about washing herself. She soaped up her hair and thought about the question Throckmorton had asked her, it being preferable to the constant memories of horror.

"Ter." She tasted the word on her lips. To be something that was neither "he" nor "she," not just inside her own head but to others… She'd never thought it possible before.

Cricket straightened up as much as she could and turned so she could see her own dim reflection in the mirror over the sink. Her dark hair appeared almost black when it was wet, tumbling in a wild mess around her shoulders and into her face. The rest of her was all pale, skinny limbs and bony angles dripping with water. Her dark eyes peered out from the mass of dark hair.

For the first time in her life, Cricket thought about what it would mean to be truly seen and perceived. Not even her father had known. Her father had been the only other person who she had wanted to know anything about herself. Everyone else would get only the most superficial and easily manipulated details from her.

To be truly perceived felt like taking one of the most fragile parts of herself and offering it up to a world she knew would do its very best to crush it to death. Like throwing a tiny baby bird directly under the wheels of a cart. It would be better to keep it secret and safe inside of her as she had done for so many years.

Yet she could still feel the flutter in her stomach from when Throckmorton had looked at her in the garden and *known*. It was like jumping from a great height into cold deep water—exhilarating, terrifying, but ultimately powerful.

She slid underneath the bath water, rinsing the soap off, and shoved her hair away from her face when she sat up.

What if this part of her was not a baby bird, but like the wild roses in the garden, able to be cut and cut again only to grow back stronger, bigger, more vicious, and beautiful.

She could feel it growing inside her even now—ivy, no longer a young budding thing, but strong enough to work itself between every brick and into every crack of her body and soul if she would allow it.

She rather thought she might want to allow it.

That Throckmorton had been the one to offer it to her…

When she had first come here, she'd been far too aware of her own vulnerability and of the way others could prey upon that vulnerability. The way Walter had preyed upon her inexperience, naivety, and youth. She shut her eyes as if to block out those memories. Her nerves were far too on edge; if she thought too much of Walter right now, she'd break apart.

Throckmorton had been different, though. He was kind, and she hated to think that kindness had been a mask for another sort of predator.

She thought of the wolf, its hugeness and its mouth. She thought of his teeth stained in blood, and her stomach flipped, her body softening into the water.

His monstrousness, much like Rosaleen's, spoke to a desire deep inside of Cricket, the wild part of her that wished to disappear into the forest and the mountains and never return.

In them she could see a different path from the one she had been raised to believe she had no choice but to follow: to be a wife, a mother, a lady—a woman.

She had been fleeing that when she'd left Walter's house as surely as she had been fleeing the Mallory family's clutches. The idea that she might not need to do it alone was as terrifying as it was relieving.

She could not let herself hope like that, especially when she still had so many doubts about Throckmorton's true nature. If she allowed herself to trust him, to answer his carefully contained wildness with her own, and he turned out to be a murderer…

Cricket thought of the dead bodies at the farm, and her stomach turned over with nausea this time.

Trusting Rosaleen was just as risky; Rosaleen didn't even pretend to be human, and she passed through a world Cricket did not really understand.

There were still so many parts of Cricket, broken and newly scarred over. How could she trust when the possibility of being hurt in ways she could barely even imagine where so great?

The water around her was cooling, so she climbed out.

There was a knock at the door just as her feet touched the bathroom floor. She startled and grabbed her knife.

"I thought you might need fresh clothes," Throckmorton called through the door. "I'm leaving some on the floor just outside in the hall if you would like to change into them."

Cricket's gaze went to the pile of filthy, bedraggled clothes she'd changed out of. She cleared her throat. "Thank you."

He made a low noise that was hard for her to interpret, then she could hear his heavy tread heading back down the hall and down the stairs.

She didn't move until she could no longer hear him, then she went and unlocked the door, picking up the pile of clothes from the floor. Underclothes, her one other skirt, and a shirt she'd never seen before. A man's shirt, the cloth thin and worn with age but still perfectly usable.

She shrugged it on along with the rest of the clothes. It was almost comically too large for her, but she gamely tucked it into the skirt and rolled the sleeves up so they wouldn't fall over her hands.

There had also been a pair of boots placed next to the clothes. They were old, the leather creased from wear and the soles worn, but like the shirt, they were perfectly usable and a good deal sturdier than the ones she'd been wearing. They were also, she found with pleasant surprise when she slid her feet into them, not too terribly large for her. Fully dressed again, she picked up her knife and went back downstairs.

For the first time since she'd been there, Throckmorton had actually spread food out across the dining room table. Most of it was cold leftovers—bread, butter, cheese, sausages, part of a roast chicken, and some various pickled vegetables.

Cricket sat. Throckmorton poured them each a glass of wine and sat as well.

Cricket's stomach growled in hunger, although she wasn't sure how keen she was on the idea of putting any food into her mouth quite yet. Her mind was still muddy, churned up water with the promise of a nightmare just under the surface. It made her feel just as queasy as she was hungry.

She reached for the bread and cheese, thinking it must be safe enough, and nibbled it. "Thank you for the clothes," she said once she'd swallowed her mouthful of bread.

Throckmorton shrugged, buttering a piece of bread for himself. "I looked through your clothes. I apologize for the intrusion, but I thought you might like to change after you bathed. I noticed you've ruined most of them. Next time you need to launder clothes, tell me and I'll show you how to do it properly. You can keep the shirt and the boots. They're old and no longer fit me." He looked back up again. "Although it doesn't seem as if the shirt fits you much better. Still, I can show you how to take it in if you'd like."

Cricket reached for her glass, feeling that strange jabbing pain right below her ribs again. "I…thank you."

He made a gesture as if to dismiss the need for thanks and continued portioning food onto his plate.

She watched him bring a piece of chicken to his lips, those too-sharp teeth biting into it.

Her fingers tightened on her wine glass, and the bite on her arm ached and throbbed. She realized that she'd never seen him eat before, and something about that fact disquieted her and sent prickles down her spine.

He was eating perfectly normally now, taking polite bites of mundane food like chicken and pickles, but it was too easy to remember her blood on his lips and the stench of blood from that afternoon.

Over the last few horrible hours, he'd been kind to her, protected her, and listened to her, but he was still a wolf by his own admission. Cricket knew the only way to become a wolf was to eat human flesh and that once one became a wolf, that person could not stop the cravings or curb their appetite.

He reached for his wine glass, and she watched his throat move as he drank. His shirt was still unbuttoned, and it gave her an unobstructed view of the column of his throat as it worked around every swallow.

She remembered the feel of his mouth on her skin again, the pain of his teeth sinking into her flesh.

Her fingers tightened compulsively around her glass.

She had a sudden clear fantasy of his mouth on someone else, but this time his lips pressed against their throat, not their arm. She could imagine the beat of their pulse against his lips, desperate and wild, the way he would smile against their skin before opening his mouth and letting his teeth sink in deep…

Her whole body jerked this time, the wine spilling out of the glass down her wrist and onto the tablecloth.

"Are you all right?" Throckmorton was watching her with a concerned frown.

She jerked her gaze away from his, feeling her face flushed hot. "I'm fine."

She thought of that afternoon, the body stretched out among the plants of the garden with its ruined face and throat, the other torn apart in the kitchen.

A sudden hot rage laced with a good amount of fear boiled up inside her.

That's what it would be like to actually hunt a person like an animal, she told herself, corpses mauled and mutilated, not whatever overwrought erotic fantasy her mind wanted to inflict on her. What had been done to the woman in the garden was what Throckmorton did to people, and she needed to remember that.

But when he'd bitten her arm, that was…something else entirely.

The bite throbbed again, a hateful reminder.

She pushed herself away from the table. "I'm tired. I'm going to lie down."

"All right," Throckmorton said, although he still looked concerned. "Good night, then. Stay out of the garden."

She gave him a short nod before turning and fleeing toward the sunroom.

She knew he watched her go. She could feel his gaze follow her the entire way.

CHAPTER 13

Cricket didn't sleep right away, afraid of what her dreams might be. Instead, she sorted through her drying mushrooms. She picked the assortment she wanted, sealed them into an envelope, and slipped it into her skirt pocket before she finally allowed herself to drop down onto the sofa.

Once she was actually sitting down, the exhaustion took hold of her again. She allowed herself to curl up on her side on the sofa, her knife on the floor but still within easy reach.

It was still not completely dark outside the windows, but she drifted into a restless half-sleep anyway.

At first, all she could think of was mouths open wide, their teeth streaked in blood, coming at her out of the darkness inside her own eyelids only to vanish every time she blinked her eyes open.

She imagined several times that she could hear something large moving through the house, the click of claws on the wood floors, and the heavy breathing of an animal. He paused outside her door, and she jerked awake, ears straining for any hint of sound, and her gaze locked on the closed door even through the growing dark.

She could hear nothing, and the handle of the door did not move.

Eventually, pure physical exhaustion forced her down into the darkness of full sleep.

There was cold water pulling against her legs, weighing down her skirts. For a moment Cricket imagined it was the lake water pulling her down into its depths, all gray blue and green where the light hit it, smelling of stone and rot and secret places deep inside the mountains themselves.

Then she opened her eyes and she wasn't sinking at all, no water tangling her hair or moving through her fingers.

Instead, she stood in the creek, the cold water barely covering the tops of her boots. All around her was dense green forest, the trees stretching impossibly high above her head.

Instantly she remembered hands and teeth in the mist, now overlaid with the stench of blood and the memory of a body stretched out in the grass.

Fear churned in the pit of her stomach.

Wherever this was, this dreaming world, was inhospitable for people like her, living people of flesh and blood. She could feel that down to her bones now.

There was magic here. Magic was like the ocean—vast and powerful and useful at times, but every time you set sail, you became one voyage closer to being pulled down into the realm of endless sleep. Those who dared push into uncharted depths became the stuff of terrible and frightening legend.

Cricket knew all too well the power of even a small lake against the frailty of the human body. She could not imagine what destruction the ocean itself was capable of.

She turned in the creek, looking back in the direction the garden, but she remembered the spiderweb-like fog and that the body of the stag had gone that way after it had died.

So instead she turned back toward the forest and started to make her way down the stream, deeper into the woods.

The cold water ran over the rocks and around her boots, never a lot of it but fast moving and cold when she bent to brush her fingers through it. She wondered where it was running; it seemed to be no ordinary stream, having sprung from nowhere inside the garden.

She'd followed it a few minutes more when she heard a scrapping noise, then the soft thump of something being dropped.

Still, any noise at all was enough for Cricket to flee, pressing herself against the deep bank of the creek bed. Slowly, she pushed herself up to peer over the edge.

The mist had rolled in again between the trees, although it did not extend to the creek where Cricket was. It seemed to bleach everything it touched gray and colorless like old bones. Within that mist figures crouched, moving and scrabbling at the ground.

Cricket squinted at the figures in the mist. She could make out the sweep of skirts and bowed heads covered in old-fashioned hair scarves. They were digging, she realized, digging into the soft, mossy ground with their bare hands, scooping up handfuls of rich soil and tossing them aside only to reach back down for more.

The closest woman, the one Cricket could see the best in the mist, paused in her digging, holding up a large dark beetle that squirmed between her long bony fingers. She brought it to her shawl-shrouded face, and there was a loud crunch as Cricket realized she was devouring it with the intensity of the starving.

Cricket ducked back down into the creek bed and tried to keep very quiet as the sounds of digging continued above. She crouched in the water for several minutes, pressed against the wet bank of the creek, wondering if she would need to wait until the women went away or she woke up.

Minutes crawled by excruciatingly slowly as Cricket counted her breaths, too aware of the beat of her own heart.

The women continued to dig.

There was a pain starting in Cricket's right thigh as the muscles began to cramp from not moving. She was going to have to press forward and hope she wasn't heard.

Right as she was preparing herself to move, the sounds of digging stopped.

Cricket stayed very still for a few more moments, then pushed herself up to have a look.

The women were gone, the mist cleared from the forest ground. Only the hole they'd dug remained.

Cricket waited for several more seconds, but nothing moved or made a sound. Slowly, she climbed up the bank of the creek and onto the forest floor. She crept toward the hole the women had dug.

It wasn't large, but it was deep. Far deeper than it should have been considering the women had been using their hands. It was a rift in the green ground, a jagged-edged wound in the earth.

Leaning over it, Cricket didn't think she could see the bottom.

A soft whispering floated to her on the breeze like fingers brushed against the nape of her neck. It sounded like a sort of keen, but higher and sweeter and soft as if very far off.

A hand slid into Cricket's, small like hers but cold as ice.

"Run," a voice said in her ear as the thick scent of honeysuckle enveloped her senses.

Cricket stumbled forward, pulled in Rosaleen's wake.

The sweet keening rose, higher and higher until it was a long scream, the same scream the woman in the barn had made, a sound completely devoid of hope.

Cricket didn't look behind her, but she knew they were pursued. She could sense with every fiber in her that if she did look over her shoulder, she would see those hands and hungry mouths reaching toward them from out of the mist, ready to devour her as the woman had devoured the beetle she'd plucked from the hole.

Cricket ran, stumbling over rocks and roots, branches pulling at her skirts. The fingers around hers were strong like a vice, and Rosaleen's pace did not slow. Cricket gasped in great lungfuls of air as she was propelled along.

Rosaleen swung suddenly to the left, and Cricket found herself stumbling down the embankment back into the stony stream bed.

The stream had dug out most of the ground underneath the tangled roots of a large yew tree, and Cricket found herself tugged into the space between those roots, pushed up close to the dirt, rocks and bark at its base.

Rosaleen pressed behind her, her hands encircling Cricket's waist like an embrace.

Cricket's breathing sounded too loud in her own ears, rattling the silence of the forest.

Thankfully, she could no longer hear that horrible keening scream. Behind her, Rosaleen did not breathe.

Cricket strained for any sound, any trace of what pursued them. Her own hand strayed down to the clasp of Rosaleen's hands, grasping at her fingers without realizing it.

Around them the silence of the forest pressed in, broken only by the whisper of yew leaves overhead, the sound of water running over the rocks at their feet, and Cricket's own frantic breath.

She became aware of those cool fingers under hears, of the press of another body against her back, the brush of skirts tangling in her own.

There was that frantic fluttering of fear, a tiny toothy creature deep inside herself that said to fight and run, to push those hands off of her and get away.

There was something else tangled up inside of her too, like shoots of ivy just beginning to put tender vines into the cracks of a very old, high wall.

That ivy was the hands under hers and the fact that she could not make herself raise her own and let go.

She turned her head very slowly to look back at Rosaleen behind her, trying to ignore the brush of cool skin against her jaw and neck as she moved. She turned until they were facing each other, so close she would have felt breath across her lips if Rosaleen breathed at all.

"Are they gone?" Cricket asked, the words so low, it was only the faintest murmur against Rosaleen's skin.

"They are never really gone," Rosaleen said just as low. Her hands still rested on Cricket's waist.

Those hands rose suddenly, cupping Cricket's face. Her senses were overwhelmed by the nectar-drenched scent of honeysuckle mixing with the tang of brushed leaves and the deeper smell of rot underneath.

She clutched at Rosaleen's shoulders for a long moment, frozen like a frightened rabbit, sure Rosaleen would kiss her and not at all sure what she would do in return.

The kiss didn't come, though, just a creeping sort of haze that made Cricket's vision darken and her body go numb.

When she blinked her eyes open, there was early morning sun slanting through the windows of Throckmorton's house and spilling onto her. Her body felt stiff and uncomfortable from having slept fully dressed, and she was not nearly as rested as she would have liked.

Fragments of the dream still lingered in her mind: those shadowy figures in the mist scrabbling and digging at the ground, the fear as she ran through the woods, a cold hand clasping her own…

Cricket staggered out of bed, picking up her knife and taking it with her out into the kitchen.

Throckmorton was already up. She knew that because there was hot coffee in the coffee pot sitting next to a freshly baked loaf of soda bread.

From the kitchen doorway she could see down the hall to where his study door was closed. A good indication that unlike the other mornings she'd been here, he hadn't left the house today.

It sent a prickle of unease across her skin, both because it meant he might not think it was safe to leave the house, but also because she could still remember that deep animal breathing coming from the other side of her door the night before.

How long could he go without fresh meat? How long before he decided she was the only available source?

Cricket's stomach heaved and turned over. She turned away from the food on the table without touching it. She did pour herself a cup of coffee, though, and she carried it with her into the sitting room. There she curled up in one of the armchairs to brood.

Throckmorton had said to stay out of the garden and inside the house, and as much as Cricket hated to do something because Throckmorton had told her to, he was probably right. The memories of the day before were still too vivid in her mind, wrapped up in the dream from the night before. Until they knew what was going on and who to trust, it was probably better to stay away from other people.

Maybe she could work on her mushroom plantings in the basement. Right now, though, it all seemed like too much trouble.

Her eyes drifted shut and she dozed in the chair, her knife across her lap.

As her mind drifted in that hazy half-sleeping space, she became aware of humming. Someone was sitting beside her, singing very softly in a high, clear voice. Maybe she was imagining it. She drifted off, listening to the voice, to the soft rustle of skirts, to the even softer shushing noise of the pages of a book being turned.

It was easy to think that she was back in her parents' house, safe within the cold embrace of the mountains and the lake. She was sitting in one of the genteelly moldering parlors with a woman beside her, enjoying a quiet afternoon reading in each other's company.

Cricket longed for that with every fiber of her being.

A hand brushed across hers with long, delicate fingers, but it was so cold.

She turned her hand over on instinct, her own small fingers closing around those longer ones, trying to warm them with her touch.

She could see Rosaleen in her mind now. She smiled at Cricket, who felt her own lips turn up in return.

Cricket was still so tired, her body heavy with it, her mind foggy. She didn't resist when Rosaleen moved toward her until she was leaning over Cricket, her hand still caught in Cricket's grasp.

Rosaleen's hair hung free in dark waves around the two of them. Cricket wanted to surge up and kiss her with a strange coiling desire verging on desperation. Their mouths would press together, hungry and hot, and Cricket would sink her free hand into Rosaleen's hair, tangle her fingers in it and hold her close at the same time. Yet her body felt too heavy with drowsy half sleep for her to move.

Rosaleen's hand came back up to cup Cricket's cheek. "Let us fix what is broken here."

Her face so close to Cricket's own didn't change, but Cricket felt the shift in the fingers still braided through her own, lighter, slimmer, harder. She knew between one breath and another that if she looked down, she would be holding only bone.

Cricket made a choked sound, perilously close to a moan.

A hand slammed down onto her shoulder, large, warm, and far too real.

Cricket's entire body jerked as her eyes snapped open and she thrashed in the chair, her knife clattering to the floor.

Throckmorton loomed over her, a huge dark shape frowning hard. "Were you having a nightmare? You didn't look at all well."

Cricket straightened up and ran her tongue over her teeth. Her mouth felt stale, like she'd been sleeping far deeper and longer than she'd thought. "I don't know. It was definitely a dream." She wasn't sure it qualified as a nightmare.

"Have you eaten anything?"

"Not yet." Cricket slid out of the chair.

"You didn't eat much last night either," Throckmorton said, still frowning. "You need to eat sooner or later."

Cricket just pressed her lips together in a thin line. "Let me make us some tea," she said to distract him. She picked up her now cold cup of coffee and carried it into the kitchen.

It was easy enough to find the teapot and tea things. Cricket put the kettle on the stove and waited for it to boil. She rinsed out the teapot with hot water and measured the tea leaves, then pulled the envelope from her pocket and measured its contents as well. She'd done this so many times over the years it felt routine, almost soothingly so. She watched the darkening liquid swirl in the pot and waited for it to steep before going to get two cups. Not enough to kill, just subdue. To take away the niggling worry that Throckmorton might not be telling her the truth about the extent of his hunger.

The Rosaleen's touch still lingered around her. Clinging to her skin. It left her feeling off kilter and vulnerable in exactly the way Cricket hated. She needed to take control of something so that she could feel as if her plans mattered anymore.

As if she had *any* power to keep herself safe.

She strained the tea into the cups when it was dark and strong enough, added sugar and cream, and poured the rest of the contents of the teapot down the sink drain. She washed out the sink and the teapot and carried the cups back into the parlor.

Throckmorton was no longer there, so she walked across the hall and knocked on his study door.

"Tea is ready," she told him when he opened it.

He followed her into the sitting room and settled himself onto the small sofa while she curled back up in the armchair.

"Do you think whatever happened at the farm is spreading?"

"Like a disease?" Throckmorton reached for his cup and sipped it while Cricket nibbled on the pad of one thumb.

"I suppose it could be some sort of conspiracy or secret society of cannibals."

Throckmorton made a deep rumbling noise in his chest as he took another sip of tea. "That woman didn't seem to be part of a secret society. She seemed out of control to me."

"So maybe it's a singular occurrence," Cricket said without much hope. Her mind kept flashing to the creek of bones in the forest. Something or someone had eaten those bodies. She'd love to believe it was wild animals, but that was seeming less likely by the hour. "It could have been a horrible tragedy unrelated to anything at all."

Throckmorton looked as unconvinced as she felt. "I wouldn't discount both being true."

Cricket didn't know what she found more likely, that there was a demonic force out there gripping people or that this was some sort of cannibalistic secret society.

"You seemed to think that your neighbors posed a threat to us last night," she pointed out.

"I was more than a little bit on edge last night," Throckmorton said dryly. "And I have no idea if they do or not. There is clearly something very wrong going on here. I think it's only wise to treat everyone as a potential threat until we've gotten to the bottom of it."

She swallowed hard and reached for her own cup, although she only allowed the liquid inside it to wet her lips and not actually enter her mouth. Over the rim she watched Throckmorton finish off his tea and set the cup back in its saucer.

"Speaking of which, do you want to tell me why you've decided to poison me, Cricket?" His tone was just as soft and conversational as it had been before, but his words caused her heart to beat wildly in her chest and her throat to close just as surely as if she'd been the one poisoned.

She'd forgotten in all the fear and revelations of the day before that there was a very good possibility that he knew poisons just as well as she did.

The sugar and cream in the tea should have concealed the taste, but there was still a chance...

She schooled her expression to polite blankness. "What are you talking about?"

He rolled his tongue around the inside of his mouth as if tasting every last drop that might still be lingering there, then stood with that inhuman, graceful ease.

When she forced herself to meet his gaze again, she saw the wolf clearly in his eyes as he prowled toward her. She couldn't help but shrink back, hands gripping the arms of the chair so tightly her fingers hurt.

Run, every instinct she possessed screamed. *Run, run!*

She'd never been caught before, and maybe that was her mistake. Maybe she'd grown too sure of herself.

He leaned over her, well into her personal space, and her heart leaped straight into her throat at his closeness. She could smell him like the forest at night.

"Oh yes," he murmured, his voice very low and deep. "You see I am very familiar with the taste of poison and its effects on my body, but you are out of luck if you think you can kill me that way."

They were so close together now, close enough that she could feel his breath against her throat. She thought suddenly of cool lips pressed against her own, a hungry mouth against hers. His mouth would be searing hot, no doubt just as ravenous if not more so.

Once again, she felt like a rabbit in the grips of a predator. She hated it even as her whole body pulsed hot and very much alive.

She sucked in a long, slow breath. "What am I supposed to do? You are just as much a cannibal as that woman was. Am I just supposed to accept it and wait for you to kill me?"

Throckmorton drew in a long breath of his own. "I'm not a cannibal."

"You're a wolf," Cricket said sharply this time. "I know you only become a wolf by consuming human flesh and once a wolf, that hunger only worsens."

Throckmorton opened his mouth and closed it again, seeming to gather his thoughts. "That's not the only way," he said finally. "It's the most common way, yes, but not the only one. I am not a cannibal. I'm a poison drinker."

He pushed himself away from her and left the parlor, returning a few moments later with a slim leather-bound volume in his hand. "There is a combination of nightshade, black henbane, and wolfsbane that, while it kills most people, can trigger lycanthropy in a very few." He held the book out to her. "Here, this is one of the few accounts that exist of poison drinking as a means to lycanthropy. I generally don't give this information out or even let others know I own it, but I doubt you'll believe me without proof."

Her hands closed around the slim volume and opened it. *A Treatise on Poison Drinking: the Methods Used and Powers Conveyed into Those Who Partake In This Wicked Practice. A Study Conducted by Right and Honorable Reverend William Snell* was handwritten, not printed, across the front page.

Cricket glanced up at him and found she didn't know what to say. She cleared her throat and looked back down at the volume in her hands.

"I didn't intend to kill you," she said into the silence gathering between them. "The tea is supposed to make the drinker ill and lethargic but not kill them. I used it quite often when I was married as a means to protect me from my husband. It's not like I could leave him after all." Her jaw clenched. "Or leave you, for that matter."

Throckmorton's expression shifted, and Cricket's hand tightened on the volume.

"Don't you dare pity me. I just tried to poison you, remember?"

"Oh, I do. Just like I remember that you tried to stab me yesterday." He took several heavy steps closer to her. He was a massive and heavy form so very close to her, not leaning over her now but definitely looming. "What do I need to do to prove that I am not planning on ripping your throat out or eating you alive?"

She hated the way her stomach tightened when he said "rip out her throat," the way her pulse fluttered even now. She didn't want him to be a cannibal and hated thinking he was responsible for those bodies in the woods.

The idea of him pinning her down like a hunted thing, though, biting her with those sharp teeth, watching her out of those wolf eyes…she hated how much that aroused her.

He didn't have a face built for care, but there was something about his expression as he looked down at her. "It was never my intention for you to feel like a prisoner here. But you are right in that I think you leaving now would be inadvisable for many reasons. So, how can I convince you that you are at least marginally safe here and that you can perhaps stop trying to kill me for at least one full day?"

She shifted a little uncomfortably under his gaze. She really wished he'd go back to looking at her like she was a threat, someone almost as dangerous as he was. The gentleness in his voice was too close to pity, too close to kindness.

If she stopped to dwell on it, she'd remember all the other little things he'd done for her over the past few days. The ways he'd tried to make a bad situation easier on her when he hadn't needed to or taken her fears seriously even when they seemed all too far-fetched.

Strange, it had been so long since she'd been faced with someone who she thought might actually care one wit for her. It felt a little like dipping her hand into water she expected to be warm and quite shallow to find it far deeper and colder, with secrets and depths she wasn't prepared for.

Plus, there was desire still coiled inside her like a snake, and the two emotions were threatening to entangle in such a way that Cricket knew she was not prepared to deal with.

He moved away from her as if sensing her intense discomfort bridging into emotional turmoil. "Well? How can I convince you?"

She wet her dry lips with the tip of her tongue. "I don't know." She hated admitting it. "You can't just demand my trust."

He sat across from her again, putting his hands in his lap where she could see them. She didn't think that was unintentional. "Then let me try and earn it. What would a good first step be?"

Her fingers curled around the book in her lap once more. "Let me read this," she said. "And then maybe show me how you do this poison drinking you claim can change you into a wolf."

He hesitated for a moment but nodded. "If that would help you believe that I don't eat people, then all right."

"All right," she echoed.

"I'll leave you to your reading." He stood but did not move close enough to loom over her, which made her stomach twist in a strange sort of loss. Instead, he turned away from her altogether, moving toward his study again.

She waited until she heard the door of the study close behind him before sighing and turning her attention back to the book in her lap.

CHAPTER 14

She dreamed too much that night, her mind leading her down dark and twisted paths with no clear end in sight. They were not the dreams she had been having of Rosaleen and the dark ancient forest.

Instead, she dreamed she was submerged in deep cold water. With her eyes closed, she could feel the chilliness and depth of it, the pull of the current through the sodden weight of her morning dress.

Even without looking, she knew it was the mountain lake of her childhood. She smiled as she sank deeper into its unforgiving depths, but when she opened her eyes, she could see trees—a forest stretching above her, not so far away at all, and she realized that instead of sinking into the depths of some huge deep lake, she was floating quite close to the surface surrounded by the soft, quiet green of the woods behind Throckmorton's house.

A dark shadow fell across her, then the man himself was standing over where she lay, frowning at her. He reached down and grabbed her arms, his grip strong and burning hot against her deathly cold skin. He dragged her out of the water and onto the bank.

Cricket gasped and choked as soon as the warm air of the woods hit her, filling her senses with the smell of fir trees and rich soil. She lay face down, pressed against the mossy forest floor and retching up cold lake water in a way she was sure was frightful to look at, but Throckmorton just knelt beside her.

"Here." He pushed the sodden hair out of her face. "We need to hurry. We aren't safe here."

She looked up into his eyes, which were completely gold now without a hint of the human man left in them. Despite his words, he didn't seem to be moving with any real haste as his hands slid lower on her body, undoing the buttons of her dress as his mouth pressed against the curve of her throat, too hot against her chilled skin. She felt the rake of his teeth, and it went through her like fire with the memory of his bite.

Cricket woke up stretched out on the sofa in the sunroom, her heart hammering in her chest. Taking several deep, ragged breaths, she pressed her face into the scratchy upholstery of the sofa she had been sleeping on, feeling a scream churning up inside her.

Her entire life, she'd counted sexual desire low on her list of priorities. She'd found her mother's collection of erotic materials quite early in her teenage years and had been rather relieved that they did not stir that much interest inside of her. Certainly, her marriage to Walter had never aroused anything within her.

Now her desires seemed to have a life of their own.

She turned over so she could stare up at the ceiling in the dark, refusing to pleasure herself to the phantom sensation of Throckmorton's hands and mouth on her.

It took her quite a long time to fall back asleep.

When she did, she dreamed she was back in the garden, the night air cool against her face. This time things were different; she could feel it deep to the core of her.

She was sick of being toyed with, sick of being afraid and besieged on all sides.

This time she had her knife with her. The handle felt as heavy and solid in her hand as it did in the waking world. She stood among the wilderness of poison plants and waited.

The dead woman came to her out of the green.

She was humming softly to herself as she moved, the same song she'd sung as she'd sat beside Cricket in the parlor. Now her long fingers trailed through the leaves of the plants as she sang until she caught sight of Cricket standing there, waiting for her.

"Cricket," she said, her voice low and amused.

Cricket didn't reply, but she did bring the knife up between the two of them.

The dead woman stopped, looking from the knife in Cricket's hands up to Cricket's face.

A smile spread across her own features. "You don't really think that would stop me?"

Cricket felt the touch of fear up her spine. She knew it wouldn't. After all, you couldn't kill what had already died long ago. "I don't want this," Cricket said, her voice tight and too high in her own ears. "Whatever all this is, whatever your role in it is, I don't want any part of it. I just want to be left alone."

"And you think I don't?" Rosaleen said, all amusement gone now. She flung out her arms, gesturing around her. "I don't pretend to know what should happen to us after we die, but I know this isn't what I wanted. The forest I could come to love, but the creeping grayness, it twists and destroys everything it comes into contact with the way poison withers a healthy limb."

"What is wrong here?" Cricket asked. "The people at the farm, the people in the mist? What is this?"

Rosaleen didn't answer, she just turned away from Cricket toward the end of the garden.

Where there had been nothing but ruins the last time Cricket had been here, there was now a house— Throckmorton's house, as ghostly pale and shadowed as Rosaleen's cottage had been.

Cricket remembered what Rosaleen had said then, that it was the memory of a house.

She wondered whose memory this house was—hers, Rosaleen's, or Throckmorton's.

Did the dreaming world itself remember?

There were too many questions spinning through her head, but Rosaleen was getting farther away now, drifting toward the house with her unearthly guiding tread.

Cricket took a long deep breath and followed her.

The house was dark and silent in this dream space. Cricket wondered if they went upstairs, would there be a dream version of Throckmorton sleeping in his bed?

The idea of that set her on edge.

Rosaleen's hand closed around the doorknob that led down into the cellar, and she drew it open, the door completely silent in a way Cricket knew it wasn't in real life. She drifted down the stairs, the shimmering sort of moonlight still reflecting off her as she moved even though they were now inside the house. It shone pale and ghostly in the darkness of the cellar.

Cricket followed her down.

The cellar looked as it did in the waking hours, dark and empty, the walls and earthen floor giving off the faint scent of wet and musty dirt.

Rosaleen waited for Cricket to join her, shining dimly in the center of the room, then nodded to the dark corner of the shadowed space. "There."

Cricket looked at the corner too, but it was far too dark to see if there was anything there. She took a firmer grip on the knife and moved slowly forward.

There was a shape on the floor she could make out as she got closer. Round, flat, and obviously manmade. She bent and placed one hand against its cool, smooth surface and realized it was a stone cover, probably placed over a storm drain.

Rosaleen drifted to stand beside her. "You'll need to remove the cover." Her voice was still more of a sigh brushing against Cricket's senses than actual words.

Cricket's stomach twisted with a twinge of real fear. She knelt on the cool earth and set aside her knife, putting both hands on the edge of the stone cover and pushing with all her might.

At first, nothing happened, but then the cover moved with a scraping scratch that echoed loudly around the complete silence of the cellar.

A hole was revealed, not wide but going deep.

"There is a powerful wild magic that threads through this land like a rich vein of metal through rock," Rosaleen said, kneeling beside Cricket now. "It used to be that it very rarely touched the surface and almost never affected those outside the world of dreams and visions, but then we came. The settlers. We dug wells and mined ore and rocks, and in doing so, tapped into something meant to stay deep underground, a magic humans were never meant to encounter at all. Like arsenic or lead, it seeps into our bodies, into our flesh, hair, and bones and we change."

Long cold fingers suddenly closed around the back of Cricket's neck, and she was being pushed forward with terrible strength, her face directly over the hole. She could feel the cool air rush up at her and smelled the scent of dirt, stone, and rust-tinted water far below her.

"Listen," Rosaleen said.

Cricket heard it then. A whispering from deep under the earth with that pungent all-consuming smell both vegetal and sweet. Cricket recognized it as the scent of colonizing fungus. Something was down there, slowly and steadily creeping toward the surface, leeching up from the depths like spring water, like roots growing in reverse.

"If you let it grow inside of you, it will fill every space and every hole, remaking you until you become something different entirely," Rosaleen sighed.

Cricket tried to rear back but the skeletal hand on her neck was strong as any iron and it kept her in place. Her fingers bit into the edge of the hole, soil crumbling under her grip, her nails leaving gouges in the floor.

"Will you fall, little Cricket?" Rosaleen whispered low against her ear. "Or will you fight?"

Cricket woke twisted in the blankets, crying out in fear.

CHAPTER 15

Cricket dressed in the gray light of dawn. Fear still twisted inside of her, its roots planted deep in her guts. Her skin felt too cold and clammy to her own touch, and she ventured up to the second floor of the house so she could wash her face and arms in the sink, scrubbing at the skin until it went pink and blotchy.

None of it erased the memory of the dream or did much to assuage her fear.

Cricket knew what she was going to have to do, and the dread that filled her at the mere idea was a terrible thing. It didn't change the facts, though.

Outside the sun was rising, and for once Throckmorton wasn't up yet, the door to his bedroom still firmly shut. Cricket stood in the hall outside of the bathroom and looked at it for a long time until the palms of her hands began to sweat.

She very much wanted to knock on the door. She wanted to see him solid before her, very much wanted him at her back for what she was planning on doing. Despite that, the idea of seeing him warm and newly roused from sleep made her insides cramp with an unpleasant mix of emotions that kept her rooted to the spot.

Would he interpret her showing up at his bedroom door as a request for intimacy? If so, would he mind?

She spun away from the door in question and resolutely marched back down the hall and to the stairs without looking back.

In the kitchen, she made herself some coffee and drank it while watching the sun rise above the forest behind the garden. She did not go outside, even though she would have loved to feel the cool morning air on her face.

Cricket dumped her cup in the sink when she was finished and went to fetch her knife from the sunroom. She sat at the kitchen table and carefully sharpened its long blade. Realistically, it probably wouldn't do her much good, but it felt even more unwise to go unarmed.

When the knife was sharpened and cleaned, she lit a lamp and carried them both to the cellar door.

Fear turned inside her, causing her heart to beat too hard in her chest as she undid the latch and started down the old wooden staircase. Unlike in the dreaming space, these stairs creaked and groaned with each step. Cricket's mind clutched at the difference, reminding herself that this was the real waking world.

The air smelled the same, wet earth and must, a smell she hadn't minded a day ago but now just made the dread inside her mount. She descended slowly, one step at a time. One hand held tight to the solid handle of the knife, the other held the lamp high, the light illuminating the earthen walls and floor of the small space below her.

Shadows danced and jumped in the flickering light of the lamp. Cricket ground her teeth together, holding her body tight and stiff so she wouldn't jump at any hypothetical movement that caught the corner of her eye.

At the bottom of the staircase, she took a moment to steady herself and take a firmer grip on the handle of the knife before she approached the corner of the room where she'd knelt only hours earlier in her dream.

The stone drain cover was there, just as it had been in the dreaming world. Cricket half expected to see marks in the floor where her fingers had gouged into the dirt.

There were no marks there, of course. The cover was heavier and more solid than it had been in the dream, and it looked like it had not been moved in a very long time.

Cricket stared down at it. There was still time for her to go back. She could go back upstairs and wake Throckmorton, make him come down here. It would probably be safer to have someone with her just in case anything happened, even though she wasn't sure *what* she expected to happen or what Throckmorton would be able to do about it.

It's a small hole, It was too small for an adult person, even one as slender as Cricket, to fall into.

Or to get pulled into.

Her hands were clammy and her knees were weak with the fear of the unknown and what could happen, but she had to know whether last night had been just a dream or the real root of all the horror and chaos of the last few days.

Slowly, she put the lamp down on the ground and knelt next to the drain cover. The stone was shockingly cool against her sweating hands and covered in a fine layer of dust and grime that had no doubt built up over the course of years.

She took a breath and pushed with all her strength.

The stone didn't move.

Cricket braced herself against it, curling her fingers around the cold, smooth edge as much as she could. She heaved again, trying to push it up and over, throwing all her strength and bodyweight against it as she did.

There was the unholy noise of stone against stone. A deeply unpleasant scraping, grinding sound filled the small cellar as Cricket pushed.

The stone cover moved—not by much, but just enough to uncover a thin sliver of complete darkness.

The air that hit Cricket's face smelled just as it had in the dreaming space, and nausea rose up in her throat. Despite that, Cricket forced herself closer until she was fully leaning over the exposed opening.

Her eyes strained, trying to see down into the darkness for any hint of movement. She stilled her entire body, barely breathing as she leaned over the hole in the ground, bending closer until her face was almost pressed up against it.

Then she smelled it, the waft of sweetness and rot tinged with something completely unknown and alien drifting up from deep, deep below.

She jerked back, half falling in her need to get away. Her fingers closed around the handle of the knife although they were shaking badly enough that she was afraid she'd drop it again. She scrambled back across the dirt floor as far as she could from the hole until her free hand touched the stairs.

Cricket froze there for a moment, heart hammering in her chest, breath coming in ragged gasps.

It was down there.

She twisted her skirts up into her fist and ran up the stairs. She did not pause until she was back in the hall and had heaved the cellar door shut, throwing the lock with fingers that were trembling so hard they felt numb.

She leaned against the locked door and focused on trying to get air into her lungs until she no longer felt like she might faint on the spot. Once the terror had receded enough for her to actually think, she realized she'd left the lamp in the cellar, but even her very real and sensible fear of house fires could not compel her to go back down there to fetch it.

Her entire body was still shaking, and nausea kept trying to rise up her throat. She stumbled into the sitting room and collapsed into one of the armchairs. There she curled herself up as small and tight as she could.

It was all real: the too-vivid dreams, Rosaleen and her skeletal fingers against Cricket's skin.

For several long minutes, she sat there frozen, her mind jumping from one fearful image to the next, memories that parts of her hadn't wanted to fully believe until now. She could almost feel the touch of bone against her throat, hear the soft whispering voice through her mind.

She closed her eyes finally and sucked in air through her teeth.

When she opened her eyes again, her gaze fell on the slim book on the table beside the armchair.

She'd read it the night before while Throckmorton had worked in his office. It had left her convinced the author of the book truly believed that what Throckmorton had said was true. There were people who, through the ingestion of powerful and poisonous plants, could induce lycanthropy.

There was still a voice in the back of her head that said the ideas laid out in the book would make a convincing cover story for anyone who happened to be feasting on human flesh to give themselves the ability to become a monstrous creature. At the same time, Throckmorton had not given her any reason to think that he was doing that and had at least tried to produce proof that he wasn't, albeit imperfect proof at this point.

Still, she needed to trust him at least a little bit. He was the only ally she currently had among a growing sea of threats.

Cricket pushed herself up from the chair and went back upstairs.

Throckmorton pulled the door to his bedroom open when she knocked on it. He wasn't fully dressed yet, just in trousers and shirt sleeves. His half-buttoned shirt showed a long stripe of his bare chest, heavy swells of breasts covered in a tangle of dark hair.

She averted her gaze immediately to the faded green wallpaper of the hall wall.

"Yes?"

"There's something I need you to see." She risked looking at him again and found he'd thankfully buttoned his shirt all the way up and was frowning at her.

"In the basement," she clarified, which only made his frown deepen.

"This better not be another attempt to kill me." He disappeared back into his bedroom and came back wearing shoes and shrugging on his jacket. Joining her in the hall, he straightened his cuffs and nodded to her with a small gesture as if he was about to escort her into a ballroom. "Lead the way."

This time it was her turn to frown at his mocking tone, but she straightened her back and led the way down the stairs and through the hall to the cellar door.

There she hesitated, her hand on the latch. A terrible, primal fear froze her in place and made her heart pound. At the same time, she was very aware of Throckmorton standing behind her, huge, solid, and very real. What would he think if she lost her nerve after she'd dragged him down here?

She pulled the door open. The staircase lay shrouded in deep shadow before them, but Cricket could make out the flicker of the lamp far below. "Remember when we were in the field?"

"When you almost jumped into that hole?" Throckmorton asked from behind her. "How could I forget?"

Cricket took a long breath. "There was something down there. Something besides the carcass of that dead animal. Did you sense it too?" She turned to look over her shoulder at him and saw the way his expression had closed off, every trace of half-mocking humor gone.

She knew then that he had.

The fear that had been simmering away at the bottom of her stomach rose up like an ocean wave, threatening to engulf her, and she fought hard against that undertow.

"It's in the basement." She forced her voice to come out steady and calm. "It's coming up from under the ground."

Throckmorton was very quiet for a long moment. "Show me."

Cricket took every ounce of courage she had in hand and led the way down the cellar steps into the dark.

CHAPTER 16

In the cellar, all was as she had left it. The lamp still sat on the ground, the flame inside it flickering slowly. The stone lid was pushed partly off the storm drain, still revealing that long gaping space leading down into the earth.

The cellar felt eerily quiet and almost uncomfortably small with both her and Throckmorton standing in it. If Throckmorton had been a slightly taller man, he would have had to stoop. As it was, he hunched his shoulders forward in a futile attempt to make himself smaller.

There was something about being in such a confined space with him. The dimness and the smell of dirt made Cricket think of being entombed. It was all she could do to not bolt back up the steps to the relative safety of the house.

"There." She pointed at the drain. "It's coming up from that."

"Do I even want to know why you were in the cellar peering into the storm drain in the small hours of the morning?" Throckmorton asked, approaching the storm drain with a certain amount of caution. He just stood over it for a moment before sighing and kneeling beside it. "At least it's too small for you to push me down it."

"Shhh," Cricket hissed at him, standing a good few paces back, as close as she wanted to come to the hole. "Listen! You have to be quiet to hear them."

Throckmorton went still beside the hole. Cricket half-held her breath, her gaze darting between that slash of darkness and as much of Throckmorton's face as she could see.

In those long silent moments, she didn't know what she dreaded more: him not hearing anything and thinking her mad or him hearing them and confirming all over again that this was real.

She was studying his face so intently as he bent over the hole that she saw the exact second his expression froze and his whole body went rigid.

He reared back from the hole so suddenly that it caused Cricket to stumble back too.

Throckmorton put a few paces between him and the dark slice of opening, as much as he could in the small cellar. His shoulders heaved as he stared at the hole.

"You heard it too." It was not a question, at least not anymore.

"We should go upstairs," Throckmorton said slowly. He hadn't looked away from the hole yet.

This time Cricket did take the lamp with her when they both went up the creaking stairs. The back of Cricket's neck prickled the entire way up, and she didn't think it was because of Throckmorton behind her. It was as if the hole watched them both, that whatever seeped up from under the ground knew of their presence here.

You're being paranoid. Cricket's hands shook as she put out the lamp in the kitchen. Beside her, Throckmorton was still and quiet.

"Did you…" Cricket hesitated, not looking at him, then forced herself to continue. "Did you ever have dreams of a woman made out of bones? Here in the garden?"

Throckmorton pinched the bridge of his nose. "When I first came to this house I did but they stopped after a time, and I assumed they were only dreams."

Cricket let out her breath in a sigh. "I've dreamt of her nearly every time I've slept since I got here." It felt good to say it out loud to someone. "She showed me the storm drain in the cellar. She talked about a wild magic coming up to the surface and changing people. Like the woman at the farm."

She thought of tapeworms and other parasites that lived inside their hosts, draining them of their nutrients before the host's own body could process it. Or worse, parasites that attached themselves to their hosts' brains or spinal columns, making them living puppets, nothing but a meatsuit for the parasite squatting inside of them.

Throckmorton paced back and forth across the kitchen. "And you believed her?"

"These aren't like normal dreams," Cricket said. "But I did go down to the cellar myself this morning to confirm it while I was awake. And..." She hesitated, thinking of parasites again. "It fits with what we've seen."

"So if we've both been exposed, are we going to start...trying to kill and eat people?" Throckmorton pressed the tips of his fingers against his temples as if he could feel a headache coming on.

"In my dream, Rosaleen said I wasn't affected because of the curse," Cricket said slowly. "And you might be because of the tonic you drank to become the wolf. The poisonous magics already inside us act as an inoculant to the wild magic."

Throckmorton sat and drummed his fingers on the top of the kitchen table, his gaze fixed on the ceiling for several long moments before he said, "I am going back to the farm."

"Why?" Cricket stared at him.

"I want to look at the bodies again." Throckmorton's expression was grim. "Whatever is left of them, at least. I should have looked more closely the first time, to see if there was any sign of what happened. Whether this magic leaves marks on its victims or has symptoms. Something we can go by to tell who is affected and who isn't."

Cricket could feel a headache coming on too. "I think I liked it better when our working theory was this was a cult."

"Don't worry, there is still time." Throckmorton pushed himself up.

"I'll come as well." Cricket's stomach did a nervous sort of squirm at the idea of going back to the farm and looking at those corpses again, but she was interested too. If there was a way to tell who had been affected by this parasitic wild magic she wanted to know what it was.

Throckmorton looked down at her. "It will be harder for me to protect us both. It may be more practical for me to go alone and you to stay here."

Cricket thought about staying in the silent house alone. She thought about the hole in the cellar, the strangers roaming through the woods on the other side of the garden wall. She thought of Rosaleen whispering in her ear, her bone fingers wrapped around Cricket's neck.

"I'll bring the knife," she said with finality.

Throckmorton looked like he wanted to argue but he didn't.

Cricket got the knife and followed him out of the house.

"Stay close to me," Throckmorton said as they walked down the road.

As if Cricket was likely to go haring off by herself. She stayed close to him and let him go first when they entered the cool shade of the woods.

Throckmorton moved with uncanny silence through the forest, fast and sleek like a predator in his own territory. Cricket was not silent, but she'd spent enough time in wooded areas that she knew how to walk without making much noise. Her steps were light and quick but purposeful. Her gaze scanned the forest around them as they moved, looking for anything out of the place, any signs of other people or something that had once been a person.

They made it all the way to the edge of the woods without her having seen anything more than birds and a few squirrels. The farm lay before them as they stepped out from under the trees, still as it had been when she'd first come across it.

Still in death, she knew now.

They made their grim way across the wide expanse of grass toward the garden where the first body had lain.

It wasn't there.

Cricket and Throckmorton stopped short once they were in sight of where the body should have been.

The body was gone, although there was still a long smear of blood where it had lain, each fragile blade of grass matted down with drying, rusted red. The smell of dirty iron and meat still hung in the air.

Throckmorton knelt by the dried patch of blood, staring down at it. He did not touch it.

Cricket watched his head lift as his gaze swept their surroundings, alert and watchful.

"She was moved," Throckmorton said. "I can smell that others were here—living people, and they smelled…" He pressed his lips together, frowning unhappily. "Acrid."

Cricket's fingers tightened on the knife. On one hand, it would be slightly relieving if the scent Throckmorton was picking up on indicated the people were affected by whatever the voices were. On the other hand, the idea of more afflicted people roaming the woods snatching bodies was hardly a happy thought.

"I've smelled this before." Throckmorton shook his head and straightened. "More often than I'd like. This scent always seemed strange to me, wrong, but I thought…" He fell silent for a moment, then shook his head. "Well, I'm not from here. I don't do the sort of work most of the locals do. I don't live similar lives to them. And there have been so many reasons to keep myself to myself."

Cricket felt her heart sink into her stomach, which churned up her guts in protest. "How many people have you smelled this on?"

Throckmorton took a long slow breath instead of answering, which was in its own way answer enough. "We should see if they left any of the bodies."

They crept across the farmyard. Cricket's senses strained for any sign of movement by the house or in the woods that surrounded them. In silent agreement, they headed to the barn to see if the body of the woman who had attacked them was still where she had fallen.

Cricket's heart sank even lower when they rounded the corner to find the body gone and only a strain of blood where it had once been.

Throckmorton knelt over the spot in the dirt where the blood had seeped into the ground. He went to his hands and knees over it, bending until his face was almost pressed against the earth.

Cricket watched with a strange fascination. His body was so normal and human in the bright sunlight, but everything about how he held himself crouched over and snuffling at the ground was so very wrong. It sent a cold touch of fear up her back, but at the same time, she could not draw her gaze away from him.

"I can smell it in her blood too," he said after a long moment. "Like coal dust and stagnant water at the bottom of an abandoned well or the rain collecting in the gutter outside an abattoir."

Cricket's hand felt cold and her lips were numb. "I've smelled it too. In the hole. Like black mold and spoiled food but…worse."

He pinched some of the blood-clotted dirt and rubbed it between his fingers. "Like all of that together but also like something completely different. Something I've never smelled before." He shook his head. "I think the woman in your dreams was right—this is a sickness, a slow leeching poisoning."

"Or like a parasite," Cricket said what she'd been thinking earlier. "Like a larvae or fungus." She swallowed, her tongue feeling thick in her dry mouth. "Horsetail worms infest crickets and grasshoppers, feeding off them as larvae and taking control of their nervous system, causing them to drown themselves in bodies of water where the worm can then swim free of the corpse. *Ophiocordyceps unilateralis* is a fungus that infects its host, manipulating its actions until it's in the best conditions for the fungus to grow, then it paralyzes the host and eats it from the inside out."

"Jesus," Throckmorton said succinctly, his gaze flicking back to the blood smears on the floor.

"Let's check the house," Cricket said, "then leave this place as quickly as possible."

"Agreed."

They moved as one back across the yard, quickly and quietly toward the kitchen door. Throckmorton went first, pushing the door open and scanning the destroyed kitchen. "It's gone," he said before his body went very still, his head lifting.

Cricket froze too, her entire body straining for any signs of movement deeper in the house.

After a moment, Throckmorton said quietly, "There's no one here, but there was. I can smell fresh dirt tracked onto the floor. It wasn't here last time. We should go."

Cricket nodded without protest and let him lead the way out again. They moved back across the farmyard and into the woods just as fast and silently as they had come. Cricket kept her steps light and her senses watchful as she followed Throckmorton into the shadow of the forest.

They were almost in sight of the road and the house when Throckmorton stopped, causing Cricket to almost collide with his large, solid back.

"What is it?" The words were almost more breath than anything.

"People." His voice rumbled just as low.

She watched his posture change, his shoulders roll forward and his back bend, no longer a man but a slinking thing in men's clothing that prowled slowly forward between the trees.

She followed slowly after him, trying to move just as silently. Up ahead the trees thinned, and there was a high stone wall much like the one at the back of their own garden.

Throckmorton stopped again, and Cricket pressed close to his side.

Cricket's lips parted to ask what exactly Throckmorton had heard when there came a scream like nothing she had ever heard before.

Regrettably, Cricket had heard the sound animals made when they died, and she'd heard the way well-bred ladies shrieked. Most recently she'd heard the woman in the barn make that horrible high wailing keen, but there had been grief and hopelessness in that.

This sound was completely different. This was pure terror, the cry of a human taking their last breath.

Cricket's entire body locked in response to that noise. Every thought was blown out of her mind with the single primal need to get as far away from whatever was happening on the other side of that wall as she could.

She was distantly aware of Throckmorton growling beside her, that deep, inhuman warning, but she was no longer truly cognizant of anything aside from the need to run that was filling up her entire body now.

Then a form came up and over the wall.

CHAPTER 17

The form was half crawling, half falling, all long blood-drenched limbs and far too human noise.

It fell onto the ground, leaving a long smear of blood against the stone.

The sound choked off. Everything around them seemed too quiet in its wake. More than anything, Cricket wanted to close her eyes, but self-preservation kept them wide open. She wasn't sure she'd be able to even blink.

The body on the ground moved slowly, painfully crawling toward where Throckmorton and Cricket stood together just inside the tree line.

Then it stopped moving.

Cricket stared at it, willing whomever it was to move again, but all she could see was the dark blood-covered shape crumpled on the ground.

Throckmorton made that noise down in his chest again, a deep, inhuman, dangerous sound, then he moved, crouched and prowling. He stepped out from under the trees. One big hand closed around the body on the ground, and he dragged it back into the forest. When he reached where Cricket still stood, he laid the body carefully across the leaves and moss of the forest floor.

She was caked in blood. Tangled dark hair that had been yanked out of whatever style it had been made up in now fell across her face, and her pale dress was soaked in blood almost beyond recognition. There was a huge wound across her torso, slashing open her belly. Cricket half expected to see the pale fleshy petals of fungus or the undulating bodies of worms filling up her insides, but there was just the deep red and pale purplish-whites of the woman's organs.

Cricket swallowed down the acid that had risen to the back of her throat and quickly fixed her gaze on the woman's face instead. Her lips had gone blue, but she still breathed in shuddering, short, wheezing sighs.

Throckmorton knelt beside her, his hands hovering over her body as if unsure where to touch or if it could do any good at this point.

It caught them completely off guard when the body suddenly reared up suddenly with truly impossible speed.

Cricket saw her lips pulling back from too long, sharp-looking teeth as the injured woman half fell onto Throckmorton and bit him on the arm.

He cried out, a yell of pain and shock.

Cricket moved without thinking. She grabbed the woman and hurled her back away from Throckmorton with everything she had in her. "Get up!" she yelled at him. "Run!"

Throckmorton was already climbing to his feet, and together they ran back into the forest without any attempt at silence.

Speed was all that mattered, and Cricket allowed all of the fear and panicked desire to flee carry her faster than she'd known she was capable of moving through the forest, out onto the road, and slamming through Throckmorton's front gate toward the house.

She finally came to a skittering halt on the front step while Throckmorton got the door open, her heart hammering so hard she was afraid she would collapse before they made it inside.

His hand clamped around her arm, yanking her back inside before he threw the bolt behind them.

They stood in the hallway, gasping big lungfuls of air, staring at each other.

"Are you all right?" Cricket asked finally, not even caring that her voice cracked halfway through the words. Her eyes filled with tears very suddenly, and she blinked them back hard.

Throckmorton's hand fell onto her shoulder, heavy and real. She leaned against his side, shuddering and gasping against him.

Very carefully, his hand came around her shoulders, holding her there. She could feel him trembling against her.

"Are you all right?" she asked again.

"I think so. I don't think she broke the skin, but there will probably be a bruise." He let go of her and stepped back, pulling off his jacket.

"Come into the kitchen and let me take a look at it," Cricket said.

He followed her down the hall and sat at the kitchen table while she found a basin and filled it with hot water from the tap. Her hands still shook as she did, but she ignored them, searching until she found a clean dishcloth and turned back to him.

He'd stripped his shirt off, and she could see the bite on his arm already turning a livid purple-red ringed in white, tooth marks clearly visible.

"It looks bad." She dipped the cloth in the water and pressed it against the wound. The fact that someone so weak, injured, and close to death had been able in a moment to bite so hard and violently was terrifying. She felt like she was going to be ill.

He let out a soft hiss as the wound was touched. "It doesn't look good."

She cleaned it carefully until she was satisfied he had been right and the skin wasn't broken. Then she returned to the sink, soaked the cloth in cold water, and pressed it against his arm to try and bring down the swelling.

There were so many questions tumbling through her head right now, too many things they needed to discuss.

She was not unaware of his closeness and state of undress. She was in fact *acutely* aware of the thickly corded muscles in his arm, the dark curling hair across his chest, and the solid weight of his stomach. His skin was soft and very warm under her fingertips.

Her hand was shaking again. He reached up and covered it with his own, which shook ever so slightly as well. "Thank you."

Cricket wet her lips before she could make any sound come out. "Ah, well…" She looked away from his intense golden-flecked gaze. "Think of it as making up for trying to poison you yesterday."

He snorted and let go of her hand.

She wished she didn't feel a little bereft at that.

She set the cloth on top of the kitchen table. "What is going on here, Throckmorton?" She wasn't sure what part of the day she meant at this point. It all felt like such a confusing tangle inside of her, so much fear and uncertainty mixing unpleasantly with the ghost of his touch against her skin.

"Gabriel," he said, watching her although she didn't meet his gaze now. "Call me Gabriel. I think we're past any formality at this point."

Cricket crossed her arms over her chest, tucking her hands under her arms and away from him. She finally met his gaze, frowning hard. "That woman," she said, "and the bodies disappearing."

Throckmorton—*Gabriel* raised his uninjured arm, propped his elbow on the table, and massaged his temples. "There has clearly been something very wrong here for a long time."

She watched him, her eyes narrowing.

He wore a heavy silver signet ring on the hand currently pressed to his forehead. It was worn, scarred with age and more than a little bit tarnished, but when she looked closely, Cricket could make out the snarling head of a wolf.

"Yet you've somehow missed it," she said. "How many years have you lived here again?"

"I moved here because I wanted somewhere I could keep to myself," he said with a note of irritation, but he mostly just sounded tired. "I sell rare volumes through mail order. I have never made it a habit of mingling with the local population, and one of the things I very much enjoyed about living here was that they never showed any interest in me. No nosy neighbors bothering me or older women pushing their young daughters on me. No one coming around to inquire about attending the local church or town dances."

"Probably because they were all eating each other and didn't want you to find out."

"Well, that's obvious now." Gabriel pressed his hand to his face, then let it fall to the tabletop. For a long moment, he stared vaguely at it. "This wild magic is coming up from underground?"

Cricket nodded.

Gabriel's fingers curled slowly. "They just started a pit mining operation not far from here."

"Yes, I read about that in the paper." It had been one of the few pieces of information Cricket had been able to find about Berwick prior to traveling there.

"Perhaps digging things like wells and drains released the magic slowly, but the mining may have accelerated things greatly. That might be why it was more easily hidden until now."

"You said magic poisons people. That's what Rosaleen said as well. That it seeps into your skin and bones like lead or arsenic. Like that collector you knew—what did you say? Didn't you say the magic he'd dabbled in drove him to gnaw off his own hands?" She thought of what Rosaleen had said about the ghostly women and how the magic drove them to a hunger that was never satisfied.

They looked at each other.

Gabriel's brows furrowed. "Either way, we need to assume everyone in town is complicit in this."

"Anytime someone digs a new hole, more is released." Cricket thought of the hole in the field, of the bucket left upended by the well on the farm where she'd found the bodies. "And whenever anyone goes near a hole in the ground—a drain, a well, even a backyard latrine—they run the risk of being poisoned a little bit more."

They stared at each other for a long moment.

"We should leave," Cricket said finally. "We need to leave this place. My father's house is up north, very far from here. It is still technically mine. We could go there and let whatever is happening here take its course."

"That's very cold-blooded of you." Gabriel didn't sound like he disagreed, though.

Cricket scoffed. "I am responsible for my survival, and these townsfolk are not my people to worry about."

"Hm." Gabriel ran his hand across his jaw again, where the faint outline of dark stubble was showing. "But this is my house, my home. I've worked hard to make it what I wanted it to be, and I'd be loath to lose it."

Cricket looked around them. "I could fit this entire place in one wing of my father's house. Whatever it is you like about it, I can give you that tenfold once we leave here. Trust me about that."

Gabriel propped both elbows on the table now, watching her with a sort of curiosity. "It is also interesting to me that I seem to have become one of your people."

Cricket froze at that, a mortified heat slowly rising inside of her. "I need you," she said finally. "Because of the curse, unless you've forgotten. If I left by myself, I'd die. I must take you with me, or trust me, I'd be gone first thing tomorrow morning regardless of what you decided to do."

She forced herself to meet his gaze and found him smiling, his eyes crinkled at the corners. He was laughing at her.

"Good to know that I'm not special after all."

"You are most certainly not." Cricket bared her teeth at him, which just seemed to amuse him more. She snatched up the cloth and stalked to the taps, slapping it into the sink with perhaps too much force.

"You should eat something."

When Cricket turned, she saw that his expression had sobered somewhat.

"I don't think I've seen you truly eat anything in days, and we should both rest before we decide what to do."

"I'm not hungry." She crossed her arms over her chest again.

"I'm sure you're not," he agreed easily. "But if you don't eat at least a little bit, who will be there to pull my bloodthirsty neighbors off me next time one of them goes for my throat with their teeth?" He stood and shrugged his shirt back on, buttoning it before he went to the icebox and began carrying food into the dining room to create an odd sort of spread across the table.

Cricket noticed he'd left his collar open again. She followed him, her stomach cramping at the idea of putting anything into it even as she knew he was right. She hadn't eaten much of anything in far too long. She'd start losing strength soon, becoming dizzy and nauseous, then she wouldn't be of much use to anyone.

She sat at one end of the table and let him put a plate, cutlery, and a glass in front of her. He filled the glass with wine and put food on the plate. It reminded her of the last time they'd drunk wine together. She felt a strange fluttering in her chest at the memory, like something trapped there was trying to get out. She pressed one hand to her chest as if to hold it inside herself as Gabriel settled at the other end of the table.

Cricket watched him spear a slice of cold ham and put it on his plate, slicing into it before placing the first piece into his mouth.

"Where does the meat you eat come from?"

Gabriel swallowed and tilted his head. "The butcher in town. If you are wondering if it's human, it isn't. I know the difference between what flesh I put in my mouth."

He smiled with too many teeth in it, and she felt that pounding in her chest again—fear, revulsion, and desire all mixed together with something else she couldn't quite name.

"Does the wolf crave human flesh?" she asked before she lost the nerve.

"I told you, I don't eat people." He frowned, reaching for his wine glass. The heavy signet on his finger caught the afternoon sunlight spilling through the window and gleamed dully.

"I know, but that's not the same as the wolf not wanting it."

He took a sip, considering her over the edge of the glass. "First off, there is no wolf—not in the way you mean. No separate creature lives inside of me, no monster that only comes out when the moon is full, none of that rubbish. There is only me; I am the monster every moment of every day. And I don't crave human flesh. I crave other things but not that."

She leaned forward, fingers curling tight around the smooth edge of the table. "What other things?"

He leaned toward her, elbows on the table, studying her over his laced fingers. "Lycanthropy isn't possible for those without appetites, hungers, but mine are terribly prosaic—knowledge, independence, and to a lesser extent, food and sex, although neither is more necessary for me than anyone else." He smiled that predator's smile. "I just enjoy them."

"Oh." Cricket swallowed hard and sat back. After a moment of silence, she dropped her gaze to her plate and picked at the assortment of pickles, cheeses, preserved fruit, and cold meats Gabriel had put there.

"Are you disappointed?" His deep voice made her gaze lift to him again. "Did you want me to try and eat you?"

His tone was nothing but teasing, dry, and amused, but her mind flashed back to his mouth against her arm, his teeth sinking into her flesh, the feel of his hot tongue against her skin.

Cricket swallowed hard. She wasn't sure what emotions showed on her face, but his own expression changed in turn.

His eyes, pure gold as the afternoon sun across the forest floor, narrowed. "Oh, you did?" He pushed his chair back.

As if frozen in place, Cricket watched as he came around the table, looming over her, too large and too close, his bulk blocking out too much of the light from the windows.

Two big fingers crooked under her chin, tipping her face up to his.

She could see it now, the hunger in his gaze. She could feel it through her entire body.

Cricket drew in a long ragged, gasping breath, slapping his hand aside with all her might. The legs of her chair screeched across the floor as she stood fast enough for her skirts to whip around her ankles.

They stood facing each other.

Cricket's chest was heaving as if she had just run through the woods again, pursued. "I don't." Her hands balled into fists at her sides. They both knew she was lying, and it made her want to flee from him and this entire situation without looking back. "When you bit me to try to alleviate the curse, I may have felt some…things."

His mouth curved into the beginnings of a smile. "Things?"

She lifted her chin, her gaze not wavering from his. She did not dignify that question with a response.

He leaned forward very slowly until his lips hovered over hers and their breath mingled.

It felt like the longest second of her life, like there was a chasm stretching out between them and no space at all. She knew that she could fall or fly or simply walk away; it was her choice to make.

She reached for him at the same moment his arms slid around her waist, pulling her up onto her toes.

Their mouths met, a hot wet slide, a fight to the finish and a comfort so deep and familiar it was as if she'd known it her entire life. She gasped into his mouth and kissed him harder, both drawing in him and pushing forward harder than she had known was possible.

His fingers sank into her hair, cupping the back of her head as he kissed her, devouring her mouth like the beast he actually was deep inside.

He finally pulled away and put her back down on her feet.

Cricket ran the tip of her tongue across her bottom lip, tasting the faint traces of wine from his mouth.

His eyes shown golden in the light, definitely the eyes of a wolf as he looked at her. "I would be more than happy to bite you anywhere you desire," he said. "Anytime you want it."

It was a promise that made her throat go dry, her stomach flip over, and her knees lock.

She had a sudden blinding image of him spreading her out across the table among the cut glass and silverware, his teeth sinking into her flesh, leaving marks across her arms, chest, the soft inside of her thighs.

She took a very deep breath, not trusting herself to speak.

Gabriel circled the table once more and seated himself again, giving them both some space. He rested his elbows on the table and steepled his fingers together, waiting for her.

Cricket briefly considered her options. She could storm off and avoid the situation or sit back down and actually talk about her feelings for once.

She very much wanted to storm off and lock herself in the sunroom, never to emerge again, but self-preservation and perhaps a certain amount of wisdom made her sit. She wasn't going to wither away to a mummified husk in the sunroom no matter how tempting that option sounded.

"I don't know what I want," she finally said into the silence. "I've never desired anyone before, you know. Certainly not my husband." Resolutely, she picked up a piece of cheese from her plate and ate it to distract herself so she didn't have to look at Gabriel. Her stomach turned over unpleasantly, but she forced it down. "I know that I want you and I like you. I just..."

"I understand," Gabriel said. "And when you are ready, *if* you are ready, I am here."

Cricket nodded, feeling that ridiculous hot prick of tears behind her eyes again.

She picked up another piece of cheese. Her stomach only turned over a little bit this time, then hunger hit her in earnest and she found herself ravenous for the food in front of her. She ate everything on her plate like it was the last food she'd ever see, desperate for it until there was nothing left and her stomach groaned from being so full.

After dinner she curled up in one of the armchairs in the sitting room, her feet tucked up under her and a half-full wine glass cradled between her hands. Around her, the house was still except for the small sounds of Gabriel cleaning up before joining her.

"What's your house up north like?" he asked as he settled himself across from her.

Cricket sighed, a small wistful sound of longing that she couldn't help. "It's the most beautiful place on earth," she said. "My father's house sits atop a high ledge overlooking a lake deep in the mountains and forests. It's very remote, you understand; we had all the household supplies shipped to us monthly because the nearest town is some ways off and the roads are not always passable, particularly in winter.

"The house itself is a great stone thing, built maybe forty years back by a rather eccentric friend of my father's. It was modeled on a Scottish castle, I think, but very loosely. I've been told my father's friend was a great collector of things and a lover of secrets. My father was much the same." Her words trailed off as she thought of him.

She very rarely allowed herself to dwell on more than a fleeting memory of him, remembering his laugh or smile from time to time, the way he'd held her close when she'd been a young child and easily frightened.

"When I was very young, we lived in New York City. My father was ill for my entire life, but as time went on, it got worse. He decided when I was about eight to move us to the house in the mountains. The fresh air was supposed to help."

She stopped again, remembering the way his hand had felt in hers as he had slowly grown weaker and sicker.

"It didn't, ultimately. He was consumptive, and people don't generally survive that, but he had good days along with the less good ones, which was why we stayed. My mother never liked it; she liked the city, going to parties, and being part of society. Without people around her she...*withered* inside, I think, but I loved it there—the mountains, the forests, the lake, and secrets of the house. When my father died, he left the house to me by name in his will. I always intended to go back there, but Walter insisted once we were married that we move closer to the city. In the beginning, I thought I'd at least try to humor him, and after I did...well..." She frowned down at the wine glass in her hands. "But we've already talked about Walter. When I lift this curse, I'll go back there and live as I please without being interfered with."

Gabriel made a soft noise. "I'd like that too. It's the dream, ultimately, to be left alone with my books to just be."

Cricket looked across at him. "Then come with me. Let's go north. We could be on the train tomorrow. Or do you want to stay here and see how long it takes the townsfolk to decide we'll be their next source of meat?"

Gabriel stared down at his hands, clasped loosely together. "You're probably right. Knowing what we know now, it would be unwise to stay here longer than we have to." He looked up around him at his little parlor filled with his books and comfortable, worn things. "But it will be hard to leave this behind. I worked so hard for so long to have it."

On impulse, Cricket set her wineglass aside and stood, moving over to where he sat. She knelt next to him and took his big hands in hers. "We can arrange for all your things to be moved out of here once we are safely north. We'll pay to have all this packed into boxes and shipped to us."

Gabriel still looked unconvinced by this plan.

CHAPTER 18

The house felt too small with little to nothing to do. Cricket paced through the downstairs rooms while Gabriel went back to his study.

She no longer dared to go down into the basement, and the still-fresh memory of the bloody woman in the woods kept her from going out into the garden.

Her body felt both exhausted and keyed to an almost fevered pitch at the same time. She searched through the kitchen until she located a tin of tea and brewed herself some before taking it into the sitting room. She curled back up in the armchair and brooded over the volume on lycanthropy that Gabriel had given her. Eventually, she fetched her notebook and made notes on herbs and tinctures, although many of the descriptions discussed in the book were frustratingly vague. It did make her wonder how Gabriel had reconstructed the poison when he had first tried it. Maybe he'd experimented over time with various doses. He must have been extremely brave to have tried it or extremely desperate, possibly both.

Eventually, between the warm tea, the golden afternoon sun on her face, and the rather dry prose she'd been picking over, Cricket found herself nodding off.

She'd been half dreading the next time she went to sleep, but part of her also welcomed it. She *wanted* to see Rosaleen again, was itching for the chance to confront her after she'd all but pushed Cricket on top of that drain and held her there.

Cricket felt her dreaming self awaken as her physical body pushed deeper into sleep. She was dressed in her mourning black again, the same way she'd been when she arrived here.

While she had no fondness for the heavy dress or dresses in general, there was a certain symmetry to being dressed the same way she'd been the first time she'd dreamed of Rosaleen.

This would be the last time they'd meet like this.

Rosaleen was waiting for her. Her arms were crossed over her chest, her hair and the hem of her dress pulled by a wind that rustled through the leaves on the trees and the long grasses around them.

"You're leaving," she said as soon as she saw Cricket. Her tone was flat and upset, the words a statement, not a question.

"Of course, I am," Cricket snapped. "I don't know what pushing me over that hole was supposed to prove aside from that I need to get as far away from here as possible."

"But I think we can fight this." Rosaleen held out her hands palms up. "We might be able to contain the magic, you and I. I am not strong enough on my own, but you…your curse protects you from the magic's effects in ways I don't truly understand, and you change things here. You created the creek where there was none before."

"So has this all been about manipulating me?" Cricket felt a tightness in her chest at that thought. "Using me?"

"I am not using you," Rosaleen snapped. "I need your help!"

"I can't fight whatever this is." Cricket shook her head. "I'm sorry, I can't."

"If you don't, if no one does, I'll be stuck here," Rosaleen said, desperation replacing the anger in her voice now. "Held eternally in this gray place. I should be the trees, the ground, the small things in the roots of plants by now. Instead, I am a shadow thing, a movement always just out of sight." She stopped talking and just looked at Cricket. Her anger was almost completely gone. She looked helpless, no longer confident, powerful, or seductive. Just a person only a little older than Cricket was.

"I want to be free," she said. The words cut into Cricket as sure as any knife, wrapped around her throat more tightly than Rosaleen's bone fingers ever could.

"I can't fight this for you," Cricket said one last time. Even though it lacked the conviction she'd had before, it was still true.

Rosaleen took yet another step closer to her until they were very close indeed. Close enough that if Cricket drew her hand up between them, she would be able to press it to Rosaleen's chest and feel if she breathed or not. They were close enough that all Rosaleen would need to do was lean down to press her lips against Cricket's.

Cricket found herself tipping her head up, her lips ever so slightly parted.

"If we were one," Rosaleen said, her voice low, sweet, and hot like the scent of flowers on a summer's night air. "If you were to take me inside of you, we could fight this together. I have been buried here so long, I am a thing of magic now, magic in its purest form. Magic from the earth formed into the shape of a memory of a woman, reaching from beyond the veil to you, Cricket. I have the power, but you have the will."

Cricket moistened her lips as Rosaleen watched her tongue touch soft skin. "Why should I trust you? Why should I do any of this at all?"

Rosaleen smiled and cupped her cheek. One of her fingers stroked along Cricket's bottom lip, and Cricket felt her mouth open slightly without meaning to. "I would hope that you would do it out of care for me."

Cricket drew in a long breath.

"I will make you a deal," Rosaleen added. "Help me and I'll lift the curse off you."

Cricket froze at that. She remembered Rosaleen making some reference to lifting the curse before, but she'd always assumed that was just part of the dream, part of her own wishful thinking. "You can do that?"

"Yes." Rosaleen tilted her head to the side. "For a price."

"Prove it."

Rosaleen reached forward, drawing one finger down Cricket's throat to her clavicle and down farther to rest against her breastbone.

Then Rosaleen pushed and sank her entire hand into Cricket's chest.

It was not a nice experience. Rosaleen's hand was no ghostly apparition. It felt solid to Cricket—bones, skin, and muscle. The pain of it entering her body was excruciating.

She screamed, the sound alien in her own ears, trying to twist away, but Rosaleen wrapped her other arm around Cricket's waist and held her fast, thrusting her fingers deeper into Cricket's ribcage.

There was blood on Rosaleen's hand and arm, blood on Cricket's own hands where she had reached up, trying to physically claw Rosaleen's hand away. Her knife lay on the ground, dropped and forgotten.

Even through the pain, she felt it when Rosaleen's fingers closed around something deep inside of her and pulled. It was like she was trying to pull up a particularly difficult weed or scrape hair out of a clogged drain.

Cricket gasped, choking as she felt the twisting, knotted, growing thing inside her move and shift as if fighting back, but Rosaleen was stronger. Cricket could sense that now Rosaleen would be able to drag whatever it was out from her body, roots and all.

Then Rosaleen let go. Her hand came free of Cricket's chest with a wet sucking sound, and she stepped back.

Cricket staggered and fell to her hands and knees. She gasped there for a few moments before bringing up one shaking hand and pressing it to her chest. She expected to touch ruined flesh and blood, but there was nothing there. Her breastbone was whole, her skin unmarred, and the only blood left was a few dried smears crusted onto her own fingertips.

For a long moment, she stared at those flecks of blood before letting her hand fall again.

"You've made your point." She forced herself up. "So tell me, what would I need to do?"

CHAPTER 19

Cricket and Rosaleen left the garden together and went into the gray wood.

In the waking world, the forest behind Gabriel's had been ordinary enough to look at, though far less ordinary in what happened there.

In the dreaming world, it seemed different, the trees growing thicker and closer together. As they drew closer, Cricket noticed that the bark of each tree seemed strangely gray, almost silvery regardless of the type of tree it was. Even the leaves looked grayer than they should have, she noticed as she tipped her head up and back. It was as if the entire swath of forest had been slowly leeched of color, leaving every plant inside a sun-bleached pale gray, except for some places which looked far darker than they should have. It made Cricket feel as if she was moving through a badly developed photograph.

Rosaleen led the way between the trees of this shadow wood with Cricket following after. She seemed unusually gray, her plain work dress blending in with the tree trunks, her hair and skin far paler and duller than they had looked before in Cricket's garden.

It made Cricket long for Rosaleen's skeletal form draped in lush green and flowers, bathed in the scent of honeysuckle. Here Rosaleen truly seemed like a ghost, dead in a way she never had been before, even when she'd appeared to Cricket as nothing but bones.

Rosaleen stopped when they were deep inside the wood, tipping her head up as if searching for something. "Do you hear that?"

Cricket stopped and tried her best to listen.

The wind had died down as their emotions had settled, and the air around them was still. The wood was unnaturally silent, devoid of the waking sounds of life moving through it.

There was still that smell hanging in the air, though, thick and clinging to the bath of Cricket's throat.

"So close to the surface," Rosaleen said. "It's been getting worse and worse." One of her hands pressed against her chest as she listened. "They don't stop, digging deeper and deeper."

They'd gone on for several more minutes, traveling through the unnaturally still and colorless forest when Rosaleen froze. "Get behind those stones," she said, her voice low but urgent, gesturing at a group of large moss-covered boulders.

Cricket didn't wait to argue, just picked up her skirts and hurried behind the rocks, crouching down so she'd be hidden from sight. Rosaleen crouched beside her, her expression tense and watchful.

Through the still air came a kind of shuffling, scraping noise of dead leaves and sticks being crushed under foot. It sounded like something large was moving through the wood, half walking, half dragging itself as it went.

The fine hairs at the back of Cricket's neck stood up on end.

She dared to peak around the rock and saw shambling shadow figures as gray as the forest around them herding huge shapes between them. Animals of a sort, but like no animals Cricket had ever seen. They were huge and dark as if swathed in deep shadows that did not touch the forest around them as they moved. Cricket could make out only long limbs, misshapen backs, and curves of bone like antlers from their heads.

Her mind instantly went to the devoured stag, and she felt fear prickling up her arms. The figures that led the creatures were much more human in shape and far too familiar in their long skirts with bent heads veiled with shawls.

Rosaleen had said she was magic in the shape of a memory of a woman. Cricket had an awful rising sense that this was what these creatures were as well. That the magic had eaten away at them, ever spreading like fruit that rotted from the pit outward. Was that what the people devouring each other were? People being eaten away from the inside by wild magic like rot in the cavity of a tooth? Were they already dead, their corpses being used as puppets much as parasitic fungi did with grasshoppers and ants?

If the townspeople in the waking world were nothing more but husks, corpses, their insides filled up with a root-mat web of parasitic magic, here in the spirit world—the dreaming world, the world beyond the veil—were they nothing more than that raw magic in the half-remembered shape of humans or beasts?

Cricket ducked back around the boulders and pressed herself against Rosaleen's side.

They waited until the women and their strange misshapen creatures had passed them, then Rosaleen slowly straightened up and stepped back out onto the path. "All right, let's keep going."

"Who are they?" Cricket asked, pitching her voice low as she hurried to keep up with Rosaleen.

Rosaleen's expression was grim. "I am not the only ghost trapped here. Those poisoned by the magic in life remain bound to it after death. As in life, it drives these ghosts to great and terrible hunger."

It took them several more minutes of walking through this dead and gray forest for Cricket to realize where they were going. When she did, she froze. "No. I am not going back there."

"Did you think we would be able to do this without going underground?" Rosaleen asked. "We need to go to the source, Cricket."

Cricket's pulse had picked up, and now it hammered in her ears. She took several deep breaths trying to calm herself. "Is there any other way in?" she asked in a voice sounding pleading in her own ears.

Rosaleen just shook her head. "Not as easily." She turned away and started to move through the forest again.

Cricket took several steadying breaths, gathering all her courage around her before she started after Rosaleen.

Soon enough the forest thinned in front of them, then Rosaleen stepped through the tree line into the field of tall grass and wildflowers where the hole lay.

Cricket followed slowly after, although she truly wanted to be just about anywhere else.

Here too, it seemed strangely pale and devoid of color. The greens and yellows of the grass and the once-bright colors of the flowers were drained and muted.

At least this time, Cricket thought as she moved through the long grass in Rosaleen's wake, there weren't any dead birds on the ground. There seemed to be no animals at all in this dreaming place, and Cricket was grateful. She knew the hole was ahead of them, and dread knotted her stomach tight with every step she took closer to it, her palms clammy with sweat where they gripped the handle of the knife.

Ahead of her, Rosaleen had stopped. She was looking down at what must be the hole.

Cricket crept forward, every step feeling leaden. Her body felt strangely heavy as if she was pulling herself through mud.

Rosaleen slowly stepped aside and Cricket saw the hole, huge and black, cleaved into the ground.

It seemed so much larger than she remembered, so very much darker here.

Every breath was a struggle as if the air itself had become thick, and she fought to pull enough of it down into her lungs.

The hole filled up her senses, seeming to grow before her very eyes until it took up the entire field.

She stood at the edge, and it felt as if she was standing at the crumbling edge of a cliff. As if the ground itself were slowly sliding into the hole or the hole was rising up to swallow it even as she and Rosaleen stood there.

She looked down and jerked into the waking world with a sensation of falling.

Cricket flailed desperately, barely aware of her surroundings.

There was a crash of china as her abandoned teacup was knocked onto the floor. Cricket sat bolt upright in the armchair in Gabriel's sitting room, gasping for breath.

A door opened and slammed shut, then Gabriel was in the doorway. "What happened?"

"I knocked over the cup." Cricket's head felt muzzy, her body heavy as if she'd been sleeping for much longer than she had. She slid to the ground and started gathering up the broken pieces.

Gabriel briefly left and returned with a dustpan and cloth and helped her mop up the rest of the mess.

"I dreamed again," Cricket said, pushing herself up off the floor. "Rosaleen—the woman—was in it. We…we talked." She rubbed her fingertips over her temples. "She can lift the curse."

"The woman from your dreams," Gabriel said slowly. When Cricket, nodded he frowned. "Are you sure you aren't, well, *dreaming* that part?"

"It's not that sort of dream." Cricket collapsed back into the armchair. "More importantly, I told her I would help her stop whatever it is that's happening to this place."

Gabriel crossed his arms over his chest, looking down at her. "Earlier this afternoon you couldn't wait to get away. You were perfectly fine leaving everyone in this town to their fate, in fact. 'Not your people,' wasn't it?"

Cricket looked away, not willing or able to meet his eyes. "Is that what you want, to fight for these people?"

"While I'm not known for my boundless generosity, I do think that, left to my own devices, yes, I'd at least try to help. Both because whatever is going on here is very, deeply wrong, but also because this has been my home for over a decade now."

"Well, good," Cricket said, finally managing to meet his gaze squarely. "We are on the same page. All three of us."

"And what do you get out of it?"

Cricket glared at him. "Rosaleen will lift the curse for me in exchange for my help."

"Will she?" Gabriel raised his eyebrows, tone dubious.

Cricket chewed fretfully on her thumbnail, mulling over the course the dream had taken. Rosaleen had said she would show Cricket what they needed to do, but Cricket had awakened at the edge of the hole none the wiser.

Maybe she needed to go back to the hole in the waking world.

The idea of it made her whole body tense up, but even putting her fear aside, it didn't quite make sense. The two times she'd been in the field in the real world, she'd seen the bottom of the hole.

Here it was just a hole, an unfinished and abandoned well in a field.

In the dreaming world it had been far more sinister.

"I think I need to go back to sleep and stay asleep this time." She drummed her fingers on the arm of her chair and looked up at Gabriel. "I think you need to sleep too. Whatever it is Rosaleen thinks we can do, I don't think it's possible in the waking world. She's not powerful enough here, and it is…shallower there."

"Me entering your dreams sounds a lot like magic to me," Gabriel said, crossing his arms. "Which neither of us could do last time I checked."

"Maybe not. Show me where you keep your dried herbs."

Gabriel led the way through the kitchen and into the pantry where shelves of jars lined the walls.

Cricket picked through them, reading labels and daring to reach back into the far and dusty corners to pull unused jars into the light and shake them to inspect their contents. "Is this all?"

Gabriel pressed his lips together, hesitated for a moment, then shook his head.

He left the pantry. Cricket listened to him move through the house, then there was the creak of his heavy tread on the stairs. Several minutes later she heard him come back down. She gathered up some of the more promising jars and carried them to the kitchen table just as Gabriel returned carrying a plain-looking wooden box with a lock firmly holding the latch shut.

He wordlessly set the box down on the table, fished the key out of his pocket, and unlocked it.

"Ah." Cricket leaned forward as he opened the lid. "I wondered where you were keeping them."

The box was filled with tiny glass jars and a few silk pouches of dried herbs. Cricket took the bottles out one at a time, carefully turning them in her hands as she read their neatly printed labels. They were tinctures and dried mixes made from herbs and mushrooms, most of them so poisonous that one of the tiny bottles could easily kill an entire household of people. She set aside ones they'd need, tinctures that, in small enough doses, would act both as sedatives and powerful hallucinogens.

Gabriel watched her work. "Whatever it is, you'll have to make it quite strong for me. I have a very high tolerance."

"I'm surprised it hasn't destroyed your body, quite frankly. Isn't that the great drawback to poison drinkers?"

"Misjudging a dose and dying the first time you try is the great drawback to poison drinking," Gabriel said. "But no, true poison drinkers—people who can walk between worlds, see the future, extend their natural age, or take on a monstrous form from the practice—have generally moved beyond the point of being truly physically harmed by too much nightshade. Although it does tend to make even us mildly ill, and the hangover the next day can sometimes feel life threatening."

Cricket mulled all that over as she filled their two wine glasses with water.

"If the plan is to put both of us into a drugged sleep, we are going to be awfully vulnerable." Gabriel looked around them. "I don't know what has happened in your dreams, but I for one am very aware that out here the threat is real. Perhaps you should take this draught and I'll stay awake to make sure you still have a body to come back to once you want to wake up."

Cricket shook her head. "I'm not going back there alone. Whatever this is, I'm still not convinced I can face it, and to say I don't fully trust Rosaleen would be putting it extremely mildly. I need you there. For us both to go under will be a risk, I know, but I think we stand a far greater chance of doing whatever it is Rosaleen thinks needs to be done with the three of us working together rather than separately."

For a moment she thought Gabriel would argue, but then he nodded slowly. "Let me secure the doors. When we take this tonic you're making, we should do it in my room upstairs." He went to the back door that led out to the garden and bolted it before dragging a heavy wooden cabinet across the floor to barricade the doorway.

Her deep-seated fear of fire caused Cricket's throat to close as she watched him block any possibility of retreat out of the house. At the same time, she knew he was right. This process would leave them in a vulnerable position regardless of if it worked or not. Just the idea of the townspeople breaking into the house to find their drugged and unconscious bodies sent a chill up her spine.

Cricket didn't protest when Gabriel left the room, presumably to barricade the front door as well.

She filled a bowl with water and added some of the dried herbs and mushrooms, timing their steep against the ticking of the clock in Gabriel's study. The steep swirled through water already colored by the few drops of tincture she'd added, turning it a deep amber color with the faintest of green undertones where the sunlight hit the crystal glass. When the time was up, she strained out the leaves and caps and slowly added the brew to the wine glasses.

Cricket took a deep breath and set the bowl aside. She repacked the bottles into Gabriel's little chest and washed the bowl in the sink.

"Are you ready?" she asked him as he reentered the room.

"As ready as I am going to be." His gaze swept from her to the glasses on the table and back, then he reached for one. "We should go upstairs."

Cricket did not like the idea of going. She very much did not want to enter his bedchamber, but there was a certain practicality to doing this where there would be a bed.

She choked down her complaints and followed him.

Gabriel had not only dragged a solid oak side table across the front door but had gone through the house and drawn all the drapes as well. The house felt darker and far more closed in. Everything felt stifled and quiet now, even their footsteps as they climbed the stairs, each carrying their glass in one hand. The only sound that seemed to pierce that deep muffling quiet was the steady tick of the clock from Gabriel's study, which became fainter as they stepped onto the landing at the top of the stairs.

Gabriel led the way to his room and pulled the door open.

Cricket braced herself and stepped through. The room on the other side of the doorway was normal enough, she found to her relief. It was smaller than she'd expected and narrow, the ceiling slanting with the shape of the roof. At the far end of the room was a window that looked out onto the garden and the forest beyond. There was a wardrobe off to one side, a chair draped with clothes partly covering a stack of books, and a bedside table bearing another large stack of books. There was a bed too, a very large bed with a deep red coverlet.

When they were both inside the room, Gabriel closed the door and locked it with a normal door key before drawing not one but two bolts across it as well.

Cricket stared at it. "You have three locks on your bedroom door?"

"I do." The words were clipped enough to not invite further questions on the topic. He slid the key into his pocket.

Cricket's gaze lingered on those locks, wondering if they'd been installed to keep him in or something else out.

There were many things about him she had yet to discover. Looking at the locked door, the only feeling pooling up inside her was relief at another level of security between them and the outside world mixed with a healthy dose of curiosity.

She was not afraid to be locked in a room, even this room, with him. And that realization felt…strange, a kind of aching tenderness inside of her as if she'd brushed her fingers across a slowly healing bruise.

Cricket shook her head sharply to bring herself back to the matter at hand and walked over to the bed, sitting on the edge.

They would have to lie on it side by side.

Just thinking it made her insides squirm like snakes trying to escape up her throat.

"We should drink these sooner rather than later," she said to distract herself. "They'll get stronger as they sit, and I for one don't want to risk doing something permanent."

She picked up her glass before she could convince herself this was all a terrible and downed its contents as quickly as she could. It was a bitter and murky brew, but she managed to force it down before her body could try choking it back up.

Her stomach churned as the mixture hit it. She gritted her teeth and willed herself not to vomit.

The intense feeling of nausea rose up like a wave but ebbed after a few moments, and Cricket felt comfortable easing herself down onto the bed, although she did take the precaution of lying on her side. Heaviness gripped her limbs, not sleep as much as a cold numbness that crept upon her.

The bed dipped as Gabriel sat on the other side. He must have drunk his glass as well, but she could no longer turn her head to watch him do it or move any other part of her body, for that matter. She did feel him lie down beside her after a moment.

Cricket realized she could no longer even force her eyes to close. She lay there unmoving, unblinking as her vision slowly blurred. Despite the warmth of him beside her, she felt a chill creep up her back.

They were the cold fingers of death, she realized with sudden, startling clarity. She felt them slowly reach into her chest and wrap fingers around her heart as surely as Rosaleen had.

I've made a mistake. It was the last thought she had before there was no more breath in her lungs and no more thoughts to think.

CHAPTER 20

Cricket expected there to be water, the cold embrace of the lake filling up her lungs and pulling her down into its dark depths.

Instead, she lay on the forest floor. She could feel twigs, pine needles, and stones under her body and pressing into her back, feel dried leaves and moss against her fingertips. The branches of the trees stretched up above her, a green so dark it seemed almost unreal against an overcast sky. She could smell the forest around her: dirt, tree sap, and wet leaves, things growing and things decaying.

Lying there on the ground, she was unable to move, unable to breathe, unable to even blink. Her skin felt cold. Her lips were parted but no sound could pass between them, and her chest did not rise and fall.

A trio of tiny ants crept their slow way across the back of her hand, and she could not brush them off nor even twitch a finger. She was still as a corpse lying beneath the trees.

At least it was not the gray wood. The trees were too large and tick, too vividly green for that. Still, her mind was filled with the memories of the mist and those hungry searching mouths.

This time there would be nowhere for her to run or hide.

Her vision was abruptly blocked as someone leaned over her. It was Rosaleen as Cricket had seen her last, wearing hair and skin and her plain linen dress.

"What did you do?" Her voice was harsh with anger, but Cricket fancied there was some fear there too. Rosaleen knelt beside her, and Cricket felt her hand slide underneath her head, cradling it.

"What are you doing?" A voice snapped suddenly through the quiet of the woods, a deeper voice threaded through with a chest-deep rumble of a growl.

"You?" Rosaleen jerked back from Cricket's body, rising in one fluid motion to stand between Cricket and Gabriel. "What are you doing here?"

"I came with her." There was definitely a growl in Gabriel's voice now. "I'm here to protect her, since you're either unable or unwilling to." Cricket could hear the heavy crunch of his boots against the ground and feel the huge, ominous presence of the wolf.

"You are one to talk of wellbeing; look what you've done to her." Rosaleen either didn't sense the wolf as Cricket did or, more likely, did not care. "You should have known that, despite everything, she is still human. Look at her—she has not fully come here with you. The poison you foolishly allowed her to ingest has damaged her who knows how much. For all we know, she could be dying. We see how little your *protection* is worth."

Cricket saw Gabriel's boots come into view for a moment before he knelt beside her.

His fingers felt warm and alive where they pressed against her face, gently cupping her jaw before sliding to the back of her head.

"Oh Cricket," he said, his voice so low that Cricket almost missed it even with him leaning over her.

His eyes were gold, she noticed, and there was something about the way his bones pressed up against the underside of his skin that made the shape of his face seem far less human than it had in the waking world.

He slid one arm firmly under her neck and the other under her knees and picked her up in one easy motion.

She hung completely limp in his arms, and he adjusted his grip on her carefully so she could be cradled closer to his chest and he could support her head instead of allowing it to hang loosely from her neck. This entire process treated Cricket to a truly dizzying view of the forest landscape as her head was tipped backward and forward without her control.

Rosaleen's hands came into Cricket's view suddenly, passing over Cricket's eyes, her lips, and down to where the pulse at her throat should have been.

"Honestly, she'd be more useful if she were dead," Rosaleen said.

Gabriel snarled, a bone-chilling sound of pure rage that made the soft animal part of Cricket freeze in pure fear.

Not that she actually *could* freeze any part of her body or react at all.

Rosaleen didn't recoil at the sound, but her hands did pause where they still were pressed against Cricket's throat.

"I would take a step back if I were you. While you still can," Gabriel said, his voice pure menace and barely contained violence.

"Planning on dropping her on the ground so you can go for my throat?" Rosaleen asked, but her hands did leave Cricket as she stepped away from the two of them. "I have no plans to hurt her, you know. We aren't going to make it very far if we don't trust each other."

Cricket wished she could move, say something, or even just roll her eyes. If she wasn't dead, she wished they'd get on with fixing her or at the very least talk about what they were planning on doing to stop the wild magic—the thing they were *actually* here to do, not whatever pissing match Rosaleen and Gabriel had gotten into.

"Do you suppose the paralysis will wear off?" Rosaleen asked as if she could sense Cricket's thoughts.

Gabriel was silent for far too long before he said, "I don't know."

Rosaleen reached out toward Cricket again. This time Gabriel didn't say anything or try to stop her, although Cricket could feel his body stiffen.

Rosaleen's long cool fingers touched her cheek, skimmed down the side of her jaw, and rested on her throat again. "The poison is too dispersed throughout her body for me to draw it out," Rosaleen said after a moment. "I suspect it will either kill her or it will wear off with time."

"Should we leave her here?" Gabriel asked. "I don't like the idea, but surely it would be safer."

Rosaleen's fingers curled loosely against Cricket's skin until Cricket could feel the delicate scrape of her nails against the fine hairs there. "I doubt we can do it without her."

Gabriel sighed. "So do we wait, or do we take her with us and just hope?"

A chill wind blew up, rustling the leaves above their heads in a long, low hushing noise. Cricket could feel it bite cold against her skin, tangling in her hair and pulling at her skirts.

"We shouldn't stay here," Rosaleen said. "We should keep moving. We'll become a target if we stay in one place too long."

"I have some idea," Gabriel said, his grip on Cricket tightening.

Then they were moving. Cricket watched the trees and sky change with each of Gabriel's strides, felt the weight of his steps jolt through her entire body. Above her, the tree branches swayed, rustling together like waves lapping at the shore. Her head jostled a little to the side as they walked, giving her glimpses of the forest ahead. She was almost sure that they were going deeper into the forest in the opposite direction from the gray wood and the hole.

Cricket had no idea where they were going and could not see the stream she had always followed, but Gabriel's stride seemed sure. He turned suddenly, heading in a direction she'd never been before, away from where she thought the creek bed might lie.

The trees seemed to close in around them, growing thicker and darker the farther they went, seeming to become even bigger, towering above their heads. Cricket could feel a flutter of anxiety in her own chest.

Up ahead a shape loomed in the darkness of the forest. A house, old fashioned with a thatched roof, and a fenced-in house plot.

As they drew closer Cricket noticed that the walls of the house were completely covered in a twisting blanket of thick brambles. She suddenly realized that the fence, which she had first thought was made out of sun-bleached fallen branches, was instead made out of bones so large they must have belonged to elk.

Indeed, when Gabriel carried her over the threshold of the bone fence, she could see the skulls of elk, still bearing their antlers, hung from the branches of the trees closest to the house.

This close, Cricket could see how deeply matted the brambles were across the stones of the house. They crept up the eaves to twist into the thatch as well. She could tell from the dead leaves and bone-white skeletons of past cane that the new growth had grown up to cover year after year, thorns covering each green twisting branch.

The door seemed to have been completely covered by the brambles, but Grabriel reached for the handle anyway, jostling Cricket as he did.

Her lead hung to one side, giving her an up-close view of the green-covered stones around the door. There were faces covered there, she realized, the heads of wolves with very human hands raised to pull at their snouts, but whether to force their own mouths open or tear their skin off, she wasn't sure. Each of the wolves' mouths gaped open with a little stub of a candle placed inside, long since burnt down.

"Inside," Gabriel said, his voice quiet but urgent.

Cricket wasn't at all sure she wanted to go inside such a place, but in this state she didn't have much of a choice. Gabriel was already ducking into the house, taking Cricket with him.

It was cool and dark inside. Cricket could smell a hearth and the musty scent of the thatch. She was lowered onto something reasonably soft, then Gabriel moved out of her vision.

The door closed with a thump, and she had a brief glimpse of Rosaleen before she too moved out of Cricket's line of sight.

There were shapes above her head. Cricket stared up at them, trying to make them out. There was the sound of scraping, then a low light illuminated just enough for her to realize that the shapes were fat bunches of herbs hanging from the beams.

"What do we do?" Rosaleen asked. "Wait for the dead to come and find us?"

Gabriel grunted. "They wouldn't dare come here."

"I think you underestimate the strength of the wild magic that drives them," Rosaleen said. "Perhaps in other dream worlds and other forests your power is great enough to stand as a warning against those who might trespass, but here things are not as they should be."

"Hm." There was the scrape of things being moved around, the clink of jars or pots being knocked together. Cricket could hear Gabriel's heavy tread as he moved, followed by the gliding rustle of Rosaleen's skirts.

"Light the candles at the doorway," Gabriel's deep voice rumbled. "We will see how long that keeps them at bay."

"We will see." The door opened and closed again.

Gabriel leaned back over Cricket, picking her up. "I am going to sit you up."

She had a swift view of the illuminated house: a small fire burning in a hearth, a cluttered wooden table, and a high-backed wooden chair with arms carved all over, although she didn't have enough time to really take in the design. Gabriel carefully settled her in the chair, making sure that her head was propped up and her hands were lying in her lap. She could feel her body slump unnaturally, but at least she did not fall onto the floor.

Her new position gave her a tilted view of the table covered in a mixture of objects. A carved wooden bowl and clay jug in an old-fashioned style sat next to a spoon that looked identical to the ones in Gabriel's house in the waking world, and a tarnished silver snuff box sat beside what looked like the skull of a mouse.

Gabriel cast a long shadow as he moved in and out of her vision. Cricket thought it was darker than it should have been, larger and strangely twisted.

She doubted it was the firelight.

Then a large warm hand was closing gently around the back of her head, and Gabriel was holding something out under her tipped-forward face. It looked like a copper dish of some kind with a gently smoldering ball of what looked like black tar and herbs. The smoke from the ball rose up lazily, and although Cricket could not suck in a breath, it still made its way into her system, curling into her nose and mouth.

For a moment she felt a flutter of panic in her chest as her airways were filled with the gray pungent tendrils, then it hit her like a brick to the back of the head. She was a great tree struck by lightning. She could feel the heat and awful power of it straight through her very core.

Then it was as if the last thread tethering her to her body was cut because she had no sense of it at all.

Instead, she seemed to be a tiny bird, all delicate feathers and a hard, sharp little beak fluttering just above her own head.

She watched Gabriel's shadow crouch behind him, could see the deep layers of grays and black that made the hulking form. It reached out its clawed hands and licked its great fanged jaws, its tongue lolling as it watched her helpless body over Gabriel's shoulder.

For a moment she imagined what it would be like to watch it sink those long teeth into her useless corpse, split her pale flesh and let the blood run.

The front door scraped open and closed, then there was the faintest rustle of skirts like the wind through leaves as Rosaleen glided across the room to stand beside Gabriel, looking at what was left of Cricket.

Rosaleen still wore her skin and hair and dress as she had since Cricket had arrived this time in the dream realm. She was lit from inside now, the golden light spilling through her skin making it appear almost translucent with the ghosts of bones visible underneath. A gentle golden glow like the flickering of a candle gilded each bone of her body. Her hair lifted around her shoulders as if by a breeze Cricket couldn't feel.

She was the most beautiful thing Cricket had ever seen. Her little bird heart beat hard in her chest.

Rosaleen reached out one of those golden hands and touched Cricket's cheek. Cricket wished she could feel it.

A wind blew up suddenly outside, rattling the window's shutters even with the layer of brambles across them. There was a crack as the windows blew open, although neither Rosaleen nor Gabriel reacted or even seemed to notice.

Cricket braced herself against the wind and the rain that suddenly swept into the house. She cried out, calling desperately to Rosaleen and Gabriel, who still crouched beside her still, pale body, completely oblivious to the storm and her distress.

Then she was a leaf picked up by the wind and tumbled, blind and helpless, directly into the hearth.

For a wild moment, she felt the heat and thought she would surely burn, but then she was sucked upward through the chimney in a great cloud of smoke that filled her eyes and her mouth, choking her and obscuring her sight. The wind and smoke dragged her up higher and higher in a great rushing whirl until all she could see was dark tree branches and a rushing expanse of gray sky.

Cricket screamed as she pulled ever higher, spiraling up into the darkening sky, but there was no one there to hear her anymore. All she could think about was what would happen when the wind finally dropped her. It would be so far to fall, the rushing surge of death coming up to claim her with no way to stop it. She was so high that the trees below her looked like a dark green sea, its waves lapping as the branches were bent by the wind.

The wind died around her, and Cricket fell.

CHAPTER 21

The trees rose up at her with terrifying speed, and then she was crashing through them, branches and leaves whipping and tearing at her as she fell.

She hit a branch that sent pain jarring through her entire body, then she bounced, tumbling downward. She got flashes of mossy rocks, and tangled undergrowth before she hit the ground.

Cricket lay on the forest floor, her chest heaving as she looked up at the branches of the trees she'd just plunged through and the sky above that.

It took her several seconds to realize she wasn't dead. It made sense given that she did not currently have a body to die with.

She was lying in a sort of cup in the ground, old enough for moss and plant matter to have covered the floor and sides of the indentation in green. She could smell the intensely sweet and floral scent of honeysuckle mixed with the sharper notes of crushed foliage.

Cricket rolled over carefully and pushed herself up, only to bring her hand down onto something hard and sharp.

It was more shock than actual pain that caused her to swear and jerk her hand back, staring at the mass of crushed honeysuckle vines and flowers she'd fallen onto. There was something jagged sticking up among the green, like a rock but paler in color.

Cricket reached down again and, more carefully this time, brushed the greenery away from the shattered piece of bone. It was not a big enough piece for her to tell what sort of bone it was, but as she slid her hands deeper into the mass of green, her fingers brushed against more pieces of bone.

She pulled away handfuls of crushed flowers, leaves, and stems until she could see the curved shape of a skull nestled among the foliage. It was missing its jaw but besides that still mostly intact.

Cricket touched it gently, easily able to guess who it belonged to.

Around her, the tree branches creaked as air shifted through the leaves as if in a sigh.

The stillness and emptiness seemed to press down upon her until she felt sure that she was the only one in this entire forest. It set her teeth on edge and crawled across her body like the unwelcome touch of insect legs.

She very much wished she was back in the cottage with Gabriel and Rosaleen. She longed to feel Gabriel's large warm hand against her back and hear Rosaleen's laughter, bright and a little bit dangerous.

The skull was cool at her fingertips and she picked it up, holding it in her lap. She didn't know which direction the cottage was in or if she was even in the same forest. It felt different here somehow, as if she had been blown straight out of the dreaming world she knew into another place entirely.

"How do I get back to you?" she asked Rosaleen's skull. "You and Gabriel?"

The bones did not answer her.

Getting up on her knees, Cricket scanned the trees around her. Behind her was what looked like a pile of rocks partially obscured by a tangled mass of plants. Cricket stopped and stared at it, slowly realizing that it wasn't just a pile of rocks, it was a wellhead or a mouth of an unground cistern.

As Cricket stared at it there came a sound from deep inside the well's mouth, a rhythmic tapping followed by a long, low scrape.

Her pulse sped up, the dread rolling across her skin leaving gooseflesh and a cold sweat in its wake.

The scraping continued, growing louder with each passing second as if whatever moved underground was climbing up toward her. She tensed to run, to do something to stave off whatever was coming. Her hands clenched down, fingers pressing against the cold bone in her lap.

A wind picked up again, rustling the leaves of the forest and pulling at Cricket. She wondered if she was about to be lifted up again. This time she hoped she would.

The wind carried with it a faint rushing sound, the sound of water running over rocks.

Cricket's head jerked around. Was there a stream nearby? Maybe if she could see it, she could run to it and use it as a path to guide her deeper into the forest where she knew the cottage was.

There was the sound of small knocking and cracking as they fell down the well. The sound was shockingly loud even over the wind, and Cricket's whole body jerked, her gaze snapping back to the wellhead.

Whatever was down there was getting closer.

She made to stand but something caught at her feet and ankles, tripping her as she tried to rise. On instinct she flailed before realizing the honeysuckle vines had wound themselves around her boots, creeping up her legs. "No."

The scraping sound was only growing louder. Cricket reached down to claw at the pungent greenery, filling her senses with the tang of crushed leaves.

The skull had rolled off her lap and onto the thick mass of vines that covered the ground. Cricket stared down into its dark eye sockets. "Let me go. Please let me go. I need to get away from here."

Her words echoed too closely the ones she'd told Rosaleen back in the garden before she'd agreed to the poison drinking and all the rest of it.

The honeysuckle would not let her go. For every handful she ripped away from her boots and legs, there was another twisting layer of deceptively fragile stems underneath. There was green caked under her fingernails now, bright and sticky as blood.

She clenched her teeth. "All right. What do you want me to do?"

The skull made no replay, but there was a fluttering in her chest as if in answer, the fast beating wings of a bird, the painful scrape of little clawed feet.

She gasped as the pain spread through her body, bright and immediate, filling up her mind until all she could think about was the beating of wings and that hot pain. Her hands were burning now with that flickering candle flame that Rosaleen had burned with back in the cottage.

Cricket's breath came in great shuddering gasps, and a rushing filled her ears as if her head was being forced under rapidly running water. An icy coldness starting at her feet enveloped her body, extinguishing the burning and the pain as it went.

Her hands were still cold. They were numb now, and they shook as she raised them to her face to touch the wetness on her cheeks. It ran down from the corners of her eyes like tears but tasted of freshwater, not of salt. It poured from inside of her, through her eyes and her mouth and her nose, down into the skull at her feet.

The green surged up around them. Cricket could feel it now, the tender leaves unfurling. New tendrils pushed up and out, freshly watered and hungry and eager to sink roots into richer soil, stretching vines up toward the warm golden light. Cricket could feel that hunger, smell the green vegetal scent mixed with the heady sweetness of the blooms.

She turned back toward the well just as long skeletal fingers hooked over the edge. Some of the bones in those hands were human, but some bore the long claws of a hunting animal. Cricket got a glimpse of an almost human mouth, lips peeled back from blackened teeth before the green was upon the wellhead. The vines climbed the stones as they had the remains of Rosaleen's house, digging into the cracks and wrapping themselves around every inch, pushing under those grasping fingers and dislodging them from the edge of the well's mouth.

For a moment those clawed hands dug into the pungent green, but the new shoots of vines were not strong enough to hold it, and whatever had been climbing out of the well plunged back down, taking handfuls of leaves and crushed flowers with it as it fell.

The honeysuckle covered the top of the well, putting down layer upon layer of vines, like a web, binding itself tight to the stones around it until the hole was completely sealed shut.

Cricket too was covered in vines. They curled around her arms, legs, and waist. Encircled her throat and tangled into her hair right down to the scalp. They did not push into her eyes or mouth, out of which water still flowered, cold and clear as any spring.

In the quiet of the forest, the only sounds were the rustle of the leaves all around them and the splash of the water running into the skull on the ground as if were a basin.

Cricket's gazed fixed on those dark holes where eyes had once been, and she felt a great sense of tenderness rise up inside her mixed with a bone-deep weariness.

She was so tired of the world and all the things in it, terrible and frightening.

Her body sagged softly into the green, and she pulled the skull to her, nestling into the mass of honeysuckle that already cradled all the other parts of Rosaleen's skeleton.

The water did not stop flowing from her, soaking into the forest floor. Soon it would create a stream, embracing all that remained in the water and nourishing the honeysuckle that would grow along its banks.

Her eyes slid shut. As they did, fingers tangled in her hair, long and cool.

"Not yet," Rosaleen's voice said in her ear, and Cricket heard behind it the low growl of a wolf.

That small creature that had curled up and slept, awoke now all sharp teeth and sharp claws and beating wings.

She fell back into her body as if dropped from a great height, no warning or time to scream.

Her head fell to the side, knocking painfully against the back of the chair, and her body convulsed hard, her feet kicking against the floor.

Gabriel swore, his big strong hands settling on her body to keep her from falling onto the floor.

"Put something in her mouth or she'll bite her tongue," Rosaleen said.

Then there was something being forced between her teeth and the taste of old musty leather on her tongue. Cricket would have gagged if she'd been able, but she wasn't granted that luxury. Instead, she swore internally, wishing she was back sleeping peacefully among the green.

After what felt like hours, her body stopped moving, slumping limply again.

Gabriel grunted as she turned to deadweight against him and gently laid her back in the chair.

"Well, that didn't work as I had hoped," he said into the silence. "I had hoped that allowing her to dreamwalk might give her the ability to pass more fully into this world."

"Hm." Rosaleen's fingers touched Cricket's hair, pushing into the mass of it, nails gently scraping against her scalp. "Well, the paralysis might still wear off."

"We should leave her here until it does," Gabriel said.

"No. I won't be able to do this without her." Rosaleen's fingers dug more fully into Cricket's hair. "We must do this joined."

Rosaleen was so close beside her that Cricket's head was almost lying against her thigh. Cricket could feel the whisper of her skirt's fabric against her face. She remembered cradling Rosaleen's skull, becoming the green as it choked off the well.

She knew now what Rosaleen intended to do and agreed with her.

They would need to do this together.

Gabriel sucked in a breath between his teeth. "She's defenseless like this."

"That's why we have you." Rosaleen's voice was sweet.

Gabriel grunted, unamused, but his fingers closed loosely around Cricket's shoulder and she was grateful for it.

Rosaleen's hand drew away from Cricket and she strode across the room to the door and pulled it open.

Cricket could see a slice of the forest beyond the stag-bone fence of the house plot and the mist gathering.

"We should go," Rosaleen said even as Cricket caught sight of the dark figures within the mist just beyond the first row of trees.

CHAPTER 22

Gabriel let go of Cricket and strode to the door to stand beside Rosaleen. For a moment Cricket's view was blocked by both of their bodies, then Gabriel pushed past Rosaleen and stepped out into the yard.

The wind picked up, whipping leaves from the trees across the yard and causing the stag skulls to swing from the ropes they were tied to with creaking like gallows.

The figures in the mist circled the fence at the edge of the home plot.

Cricket watched them reach out, long pale fingers brushing along the bones of the fence.

"Back!" Gabriel barked, his voice a deep booming growl. "Get back."

Cricket could not see his face, but she could imagine his lips peeling back from too-long teeth in a snarl.

The shrouded women curled their fingers against the edge of the fence, gripping at it.

Suddenly there was a flare of light as if the candles sitting in the mouths of the stone wolves had begun to burn three times as brightly. Cricket saw the shadows they cast on the ground, long wolves with human limbs writhing and crawling forward.

Gabriel cast a dark shadow in the glowing candlelight too, open mouthed and slavering. It circled him, stretching out toward the gate even though Gabriel himself did not move. Cricket watched it stretch out clawed hands. Those sharp claws sank into the pale grasping fingers of the dead women on the other side of the fence, and the murmur of voices rose into a shriek.

The shadow wolf opened its huge jaws, its tongue rolling out, a long trail of drool sliding between its teeth. Those jaws closed over the head of a ghostly form whose hands were now pinned against the top of the gate.

An unholy wail filled the air, many voices lifted up in a desperate keen that made Cricket's skin prickle all over and sweat gather at the nape of her neck.

The two other shadow wolves cast by the stone carvings crept forward. Gabriel's shadow reared in one savage motion, ripping the head clean off the shadow woman's shoulders.

Cricket could imagine the crack of bone, the rending of flesh even though the motion was not accompanied by any of those noises. The only sound that filled the clearing was an eerie silence as the voices stopped.

The other ghostly figures disappeared back into the forest as all three wolves fell upon what was left of the one pinned against the gate, tearing and ravening at it.

Cricket's view of the violence was suddenly blocked by Rosaleen leaning over her.

"It's time to go." Rosaleen reached for Cricket's body, pulling her from the chair as Gabriel ducked back into the house.

"Here." His voice was calm as if he'd merely stepped out for a bit of air. "I'll carry her."

His big arms encircled Cricket again, picking her up and resting her against his chest as Rosaleen led the way outside and into the woods.

They traveled in silence back the way they had come.

Cricket knew where they were heading, and the helplessness of her position began to truly settle in like a lead weight being slowly lowered on top of her, threatening to crush her alive.

They were heading to the hole, and this time they would be going in.

She lay in Gabriel's arms completely helpless and still, unable to move, to breathe, to blink.

What was in the hole? She had no idea, but she could feel it even now, waiting and hungry, a piece of the earth peeled back to reveal something festering and rotting underneath.

It was as if some of that rot had crept inside her the first time she'd stumbled unwittingly into the field and seen the hole. A sort of slow-acting decay inside her mind, gradually eating away at the soft, sweet, delicate parts of her that made her whole, made her who she was.

Rot was natural, a normal part of life and death and decay, but it did not make it healthy or good. If a limb rotted, it would have to be removed; when fruit or grain rotted it became poison.

This poison had never been meant to see the light of day, to come to the surface where it could creep inside of human beings, eating and rotting them from the inside out until they turned on each other.

Cricket watched as the trees above her parted and all she could see was the gray, overcast sky. She could hear wind blowing through the tall grasses.

Then they stopped.

"How do we get down?" Gabriel asked.

Cricket wanted to scream, wanted to yell, wished she could run from that place as fast as she could and not look back. Her heart should have been hammering in her chest like a caged feral thing trying to claw its way to freedom. She should have been able to feel tears prick at the corners of her eyes with the overwhelming terror that gripped her.

Instead, there was nothing, just the complete and binding stillness and the stretch of sky above her.

"It's not as far as it looks," Rosaleen said. "The land likes playing tricks here. We can jump without too much trouble."

"And what about her?" Gabriel did not seem wholly convinced by this plan.

"I'll go first," Rosaleen said. "And you drop her down to me."

There was a fraught pause in which Cricket internally gave up any sort of composure and screamed silently.

"All right," Gabriel said.

There was the rustle of skirts in the quiet field and then, far too long after and too far away, a dull hard thud.

The sky above her moved, and Cricket knew she was being held over the hole. Her mind was filled with the memory of falling when the wind had taken her, the terror that had gripped her as she'd hurtled downward. This time would be far worse because she possessed an easily broken body again, one that could bleed and tear apart in the most horrible ways.

With everything in her, she willed Gabriel not to let go, not to actually drop her like a sack of so much wet meat into the gaping chasm she remembered from her previous trip here.

I will never forgive you for this, she thought, rage cutting through the horror for one crystalline moment.

He let her go, and she was falling once more.

CHAPTER 23

She fell without any grace or control, but she did not hit the bottom and have to experience all her bones shattering and her internal organs being forced out of her in a dark, wet spray.

There were a few seconds where her mind went completely blank with the force of the fear that gripped her hard around the throat, and then she slammed into Rosaleen.

The two of them went down onto the ground with a jarring pain of impact that Cricket felt from her toes to the top of her head.

Under her, Rosaleen grunted and swore colorfully before rolling Cricket's limp body off of her.

Cricket was treated to an up-close view of the dirt and a jagged slice of sky before Rosaleen reached down and picked her up as Gabriel had. Rosaleen was not as large as Gabriel, but she still held Cricket's smaller body with an ease that spoke of strength beyond mere muscle and bone.

Cricket stared up at the sky, her insides roiling with the aftershocks of her fear. She wanted to cry, to fall into a shaking, quivering heap on the ground. She couldn't, though, and perhaps that was a small mercy as she was spared the embarrassment.

A ground-shaking thud rattled through her body again.

"Now what?" Gabriel asked from beside them.

"Now we wait for it to change," Rosaleen said. "Ah, it has already."

When she heard Gabriel's indrawn breath, Cricket wished she could turn her head to see. As if sensing this, Rosaleen carefully rolled Cricket's head a little to the side.

They were no longer standing at the bottom of a hole. Instead, they were standing at the mouth of a cave or passageway that led into the ground.

It was not a large opening, a narrow, jagged crevasse of the sort Cricket could remember from her childhood. It was the sort of space usually found in forests or rocky hillsides, carved out by the passage of water and not usually very deep.

She very much suspected this one would go deeper.

"Shall we?" Rosaleen asked.

Gabriel grunted in response.

Cricket watched him squeeze his large frame through the passageway, his shoulders knocking against sharp stone edges that stood out like jagged teeth. When he was in far enough that they could no longer see him from outside, Rosaleen stepped forward too.

Once again, her helplessness gripped Cricket like a vice. She wanted to shut her eyes but could only stare unblinkingly as Rosaleen eased her into the passage.

It was dark inside, and it smelled of wet stone, dead plants, earth, and stagnant water somewhere far off still.

Her shoulder jarred painfully against a pointed outcropping of rock as Rosaleen wedged her in, Gabriel's hands reaching for her as Rosaleen let go to push herself into the small space.

The world swooped dizzyingly before Cricket's eyes as Gabriel was forced to grip her under the arms, her legs dragging against the cold, wet ground and her vision filling with the black cloth of his shirt. At least the cotton was soft against her face and she could smell him underneath it, earthy and a little bit like sweat.

"How are we going to move her?" Gabriel asked. "I'll be lucky to fit myself through a passage this narrow, much less carry her. Unless… Could you get her up onto my back for a little while at least? I may have to go sideways if it gets any narrower. Then we'll need to think of something else."

Cricket was treated to more swooping perspective changes as she was manhandled between the two of them and finally draped like a sack of flour across Gabriel's wide back.

Her face pressed against the back of his neck, and she could feel his hair against her cheek. She could really smell his scent now, leeching into her very pores as if it was trying to become her own. Tiny tickling hairs at his nape pressed against her lips.

She was very aware of his arms under the crook of her legs, her arms draped over his shoulders, and the fact that she was straddling his waist, albeit backward and completely without her control.

The farther from the opening of the crevasse they went, the more absolute the darkness became. Cricket didn't think it was because her face was pressed against Gabriel either. If she'd been able to move, she would have needed a candle or lantern to make her way through the narrow passageway, which was not something they currently had. Even so, Gabriel's pace didn't falter. *He must be able to see in the dark,* Cricket thought, an aspect of the wolf that would serve them well down here.

A luminescence pricked at the edges of her vision. It looked like pale candlelight against the dark wet stones all around them. Rosaleen's body must have been illuminated again as it had been back at the cottage, burning like a flame in the darkness.

Cricket lay limp, feeling the rough stone walls pressing in on either side of them. The walls caught at their clothes and narrowed at sudden intervals, the sharp stone gouging at their shoulders, elbows, and any other limbs left unprotected. Her knees knocked painfully against the passage walls with enough force that she was sure she'd have at least bruises if not bloody scrapes from it.

At the same time, she was aware Gabriel was taking the worst of it with his wider frame. He needed to keep his arms out at his sides to support her rather than being able to tuck them in. Still, he didn't make many signs of pain except for an occasional grunt when he jarred his shoulder too hard against an outcropping of stone.

They crept forward through the dark and the wet passage slowly sloped downward, taking them deeper and deeper into the ground.

Toward what, Cricket had no idea.

Slumped across Gabriel's back, she could not help but think about the book she'd read regarding cave exploration and all of the dangers associated with such endeavors. In the near complete darkness, her mind conjured up images of sudden drops into nothingness, fissures just large enough for a person to drop into but not big enough to crawl out of, passages that would suddenly narrow, trapping one inside, pits of water that looked shallow but were in fact unfathomably deep.

There was always the possibility of a sudden cave-in or the loss of air to breathe. A terrible mining accident had happened in the mountains where she'd grown up. Twelve men had suffocated in the pressing dark before the rescue crew could get to them.

Cricket's insides crawled and roiled at the very idea, her skin prickling all over.

Eventually, Gabriel came to a halt. Cricket strained her eyes in the darkness but could make nothing out. Slowly, she realized that she could no longer sense the walls of the passage pressing on them from either side.

The glow in her peripheral vision moved as Rosaleen came to stand beside them. The light she cast illuminated their surroundings enough for her to make out the ledge they were currently standing on, a sort of rocky plateau surrounded by darkness. The passage went on ahead of them, narrowing again as it sloped still farther down.

"I'll go first," Rosaleen said. "I think it's safer that way."

"Safer from what?" Gabriel pitched his voice into a low rumble, but it still sounded unnaturally loud bouncing off the rock around and above them.

"The dead can't be far away. The magic protects itself."

Cricket's skin crawled at that idea, remembering the mouths in the mist. They had nowhere to run now.

Gabriel took a deep breath. Cricket could feel the rise and fall of his chest, and it felt as if he was breathing for her too.

Rosaleen pressed forward into the narrow gap, and it looked as if the land itself was doing its best to consume her whole.

Internally Cricket braced herself as Gabriel followed, knowing that no matter how careful he tried to be, she was still going to get jostled against the rocky sides of the tunnel again.

The darkness of the narrow passage was lit by the warm glow of Rosaleen up ahead as they moved, the rough stone walls and ceiling slowly closing in around them the deeper they got. The rock walls felt cold where Cricket's legs and arms bumped up against them, cool and almost wet to the touch. She wondered if there was some underground body of water close to them or if this was moisture leeching down from the surface. Whatever it was it clung to her skin, slick and cold in a way she found unpleasantly like mucus, not at all like the water she enjoyed.

Under her weight Gabriel grunted as the passage became harder for him to move through.

A coolness brushed against Cricket's ankles like a breath being exhaled against her skin. It wasn't a breeze but something heavier than that. She wished she could look down, although she was afraid that if she did, she would see the pale mist that wasn't mist at all beginning to gather around their legs.

Fear began to take hold of Cricket's insides, making them fill leaden in her gut.

Gabriel stopped, his breath coming in large panting breaths underneath her. "I can't."

Rosaleen stopped as well and turned back toward them.

"It's getting too narrow." He shifted and Cricket realized just what he meant as he lowered himself into a one-legged kneel, his shoulders pressed against the rough stone walls of the passageway. "Pull her over my shoulders."

Rosaleen's long fingers closed around Cricket's arms, hoisting her over Gabriel's shoulder like a sack of potatoes. Cricket's legs hit the ground painfully and at an awkward angle, but Rosaleen did lower her top half down more carefully. She began to drag Cricket farther down the passageway as the space continued to narrow around them.

Gabriel had risen behind them and was trying to follow, turned sideways now to allow his wide shoulders to pass.

The mist where Cricket lay on the ground had thickened. It draped heavily over her skin like a wet gray shroud. She hadn't even realized she'd been straining to hear sounds besides Gabriel's labored breathing until she finally heard it. There was the soft scraping of bony fingers or maybe claws being dragged along the walls of the passage behind Gabriel, back the way they had come.

"Behind you!" she wanted to say, but of course the words wouldn't come out.

Just as true terror seized her, Gabriel half turned in the cramped space, his lips peeling back in a snarl. The darkness around him jumped and danced in the faint light of Rosaleen's illumination. Around Gabriel's bulk, Cricket caught a glimpse of a hunched skeletal figure, its clawed hands up and fangs bared in the dark gaping hole of its mouth.

Gabriel's shadow lengthened, the shape of its head stretching into a muzzle with lips drawn back from equally long fangs.

"Go," Gabriel said, his voice rumbling with urgency.

Rosaleen began to drag Cricket faster down the passageway, Gabriel shuffling after them, his head still turned to look behind.

The passage closed around an outcropping of rock, the space so narrow, Rosaleen had to pull Cricket through on her side rather than her back. Gabriel pressed his shoulder into the space, but it was far too narrow for him.

Rosaleen lay Cricket on the ground and stepped over her prone form. "Here, let me help you." She reached out her hand to Gabriel, grasping his arm just above the elbow. His big hand wrapped around her arm, and she began to pull as Gabriel pushed.

Cricket could hear the scraping coming closer down the passage, then a sort of hissing wail that she'd never heard before but was also terribly like sounds she'd heard out in the forest.

Gabriel growled, pushing harder. Then he yelled, the sound echoing off the walls around them as his hand slipped from Rosaleen's arm. Half stuck in the passage, he shoved at the thing that had gotten hold of him.

Cricket couldn't see it, but she could imagine those long-clawed fingers sinking into his arm while that open mouth tore at his shoulder. She wanted to scream. Even in this state, she could feel the scream rising up inside her to fill her entire chest to bursting.

Rosaleen grabbed Gabriel's thick arm with both of her hands, pulling him with all her might.

Gabriel yelled in pain again. There was the sound of tearing cloth, and he was at last yanked through the narrowest point.

As soon as he was through, he turned back with low noise of pure malice.

Cricket watched the bones in his hands contort and twist under the skin until they were impossibly long. As he raised them Cricket saw the glint of claws.

The spindly bony thing was forcing its way through the crack as well, its mouth still open, teeth now stained with blood. Gabriel grabbed its head, but its clawed hands came up, digging into the flesh of his forearms until blood ran onto the floor.

With one vicious movement, Gabriel tore the skull from its shoulders and tossed it back down the passage behind the creature. Cricket heard a rattling crack as it landed.

Rosaleen's hands wrapped around her arms again, dragging Cricket onward, Gabriel following fast behind them.

The passageway finally opened to another large flat ledge of sorts.

Rosaleen stopped and settled Cricket more comfortably in a lying position before turning back to Gabriel. "Let me see." She pointed at his arms, which were still running with tiny trails of blood.

He held them out for her inspection.

Her hands closed around his arms gently. She unbuttoned the cuffs of his shirt, pulling away the cloth from his skin and bathing them both in warm light.

"You could have left me there," Gabriel said, his voice lower now. "I would have blocked the passage dead or alive, allowing you and Cricket to escape."

Rosaleen was silent for a long minute, looking down at his arms and the wounds there. "That's true," she said, finally bringing her gaze up to meet his.

"But you didn't." A small smile touched his face. "Maybe I'm not as expendable as you thought."

"Maybe not." Rosaleen's mouth turned up in a smile of her own for a moment before she looked back down at his arms. She tore the ruined cloth of his shirtsleeves and bound the pieces around the wounds. "That will help for now."

"Now what?" Gabriel asked, his deep voice reverberating around them.

Rosaleen stepped forward, parting the darkness as she went and illuminating a hole in the floor not far from where they stood. "We need to go down."

Gabriel leaned over the hole, another rocky, jagged crevasse sloping even farther into the ground.

Cricket thought they'd either need to crawl or slide down this one in order to fit. She wasn't even sure Gabriel would be able to with her on his back.

"To what?" Gabriel asked. "What exactly are we looking for down here? There is only so far I can go while carrying Cricket, and only so far any of us can go with any hope of climbing back out again. In fact, we may have passed that point already."

The fear of being trapped down there permanently squeezed at Cricket's throat. She wished she could close her eyes and call up an image of still mountains and deep waters in a desperate attempt to clutch at a little bit of calm.

Rosaleen looked as if she was about to speak when there came a low scraping sound that caused her and Gabriel to freeze, both going silent as their gazes swept through the darkness around them. Cricket's eyes strained too, but it was impossible for her to make anything out behind the weak circle of light around Rosaleen.

The scraping sound came again, along with a certain shuffling, the unmistakable sound of something moving through the darkness just out of view.

Cricket listened with everything in her. The noise hadn't sounded like a person; it had not been steps or the crunch of boots, but all sound seemed distorted here, warped and thrown out of proportion.

She tried to listen for the sound of breathing, either animal or human. She heard nothing, which only made her feel worse. All she could see was the darkness over her head, both Gabriel and Rosaleen now out of her line of sight.

If whatever was out there attacked them, she wouldn't even be able to see it until it was right on top of her. That thought made her insides writhe with terror, but there was nothing she could do about it, trapped and unmoving, unable to even cry out.

All she could do was listen for the scraping, scuttling sound to come again and hope that whatever it was, it was not strong enough to get through Gabriel and Rosaleen together.

The noise came again, louder this time. It was definitely not footsteps, but it didn't sound like the tread of an animal either. It sounded like something large, much larger than the thing in the passage, dragging itself across the stone rather than walking on it. A weird, slow, heaving sort of grind.

She could hear its bones, she realized. She wasn't even sure she could put into words how she knew that, but she was sure that was what the noises were. Bones grinding together and dragging across the floor as it moved.

There was a low growl, a vicious sound and a warning. It bounced off the walls, becoming louder and louder until it filled the space around them.

There was a wordless shout from Rosaleen, and Cricket was suddenly being bodily hauled up.

Rosaleen's illumination showed stone walls and a flash of Gabriel's face twisted into a snarl, a huge and misshapen form looming up through the darkness.

Then Cricket was pitched headfirst down the hole in the floor.

CHAPTER 24

She fell sickeningly, her body half rolling, half sliding down the crack in the ground. Her limbs, which she had no control over, twisted up underneath her, smacking against the dirt of the shaft before flailing out to smash against the stones surrounding her.

There was no way for her to slow herself, break her fall, or even protect her head and face as she rolled and slid downward. She simply had to endure.

Above her, she heard Gabriel bellowing in fury, then that was gone, replaced by the frantic beat of her own heart in her ears, a rushing, buzzing pulse as she tumbled down the hole.

Cricket's body stopped falling eventually, and she lay crumpled in the darkness. One leg was twisted at a painful angle, and one arm was pinned underneath her body in a way that made pain lance through her shoulders. Her eyes stung with dirt and God only knew what else. Her head rang. Her whole body hurt, and she was sure she'd been battered and bruised all over.

She couldn't feel any serious pain, she realized after a few frantic moments. Nothing felt broken or dislocated, although she could hardly move or flex anything to find out. Her hair was half covering her face, obscuring part of her vision. Not that she could see anything in the total darkness that now engulfed her. Her eyes had begun to water until she could feel tears running down her cheeks.

For several long moments, she let the pain and terror completely consume her. She cried in the darkness, surrounded by silence not even broken by her own breath.

Eventually, the first cold edge of terror began to feel less acute. Fear was still there, certainly, its claws firmly embedded deep inside her bowels. She knew if she began to seriously contemplate what it might be like to lie here indefinitely while her body slowly starved to death or succumbed to dehydration, the terror would rise back up again. For now, she was just grateful she hadn't hit her head too badly on the way down or punctured anything or seriously broken a limb.

That, at least, was one foot on the road to surviving all of this.

She tried to quiet her own mind, pushing aside the fear as much as she could, and listened hard.

Any small clues about this new space would help, as would knowing beforehand if anyone—or anything—had come down the hole after her.

The ground under her body seemed relatively flat, covered in dirt and stones like the one above her. As far as she could tell, it did not slope down, or at least not at the same severe angle as the passage she'd fallen through. It was likely that she was lying on another plateau or in a cavern of some kind.

All around her was stillness and silence, but as she listened to it, she realized there was something there. She could hear something— not a drip or the lap of waves, but a very slight noise that made her think of water nonetheless.

She concentrated on the air moving through her nasal passage and between her slightly parted lips, trying to make out the smell and taste of it.

Was there moisture there? The tang of old, wet pennies that she associated with still water too long under the ground? Cricket thought so, although maybe it was her imagination. Still, she'd bet good money there was water somewhere within this cavern, maybe even a pool of it, although she wasn't sure how close by.

It wasn't remotely the same as a lake, but still, the presence of water calmed her a little bit. She took a breath and tried to think of what to concentrate on next.

There was the sudden rattle of stones, shockingly loud as it reverberated around this new space, bouncing off walls and ceiling. Something was coming down the passage toward her.

Cricket's full attention snapped to the sound. She couldn't tell how large it was, not with the amount of noise it was making.

Terror surged up inside of her for a moment before warm light washed over her.

"You look a mess. Are you injured?" Rosaleen knelt beside Cricket, leaning over her fallen body. Her long fingers brushed aside Cricket's hair and eased her arm out from under her, bending her leg the right way. "There now. That's better. There doesn't seem to be anything broken." She bent over Cricket again.

Where is Gabriel? Is he coming? Cricket wanted to demand. Her stomach knotted painfully at the idea that he wasn't.

She didn't, couldn't…

"You're breathing," Rosaleen said suddenly, bending even closer to Cricket until her face was all Cricket could see, her skin translucent over her skull. She was so close that Cricket could pick out individual bones and the faint outline of each of her teeth underneath her lips.

"Blink!" Rosaleen's hands gripped either side of Cricket's head hard enough for her fingers to dig into Cricket's skin. "Blink, I know you can."

Cricket honestly didn't think she could, but now that Rosaleen had pointed it out, she realized that she was breathing, her chest rising and falling for the first time since she'd entered this dreaming state, air being pulled between her lips and into her mouth.

She could taste the water now—old, still water that had not seen the light of day in a very long time.

Cricket fought with herself, struggling with all her might to bring her eyelids down across her sore and stinging eyes.

Slowly, so very slowly, her vision darkened until Rosaleen's light was gone.

For a long, exhilarating moment, Cricket just *breathed* into the darkness.

When she opened her eyes again, she saw an equal expression of triumph on Rosaleen's face.

"Now" —Rosaleen leaned closer still, so close their lips almost brushed—"blink twice if you are willing for me to enter you to combine our wills and powers together so we can end this once and for all."

Cricket remembered holding Rosaleen's skull in her hands, letting the cold mountain water from inside of her flow into it. She thought of Gabriel and whatever that thing on the plateau above them was.

Slowly, she fought her eyelids down once, then twice.

When she forced her eyes back open again, Rosaleen kissed her. It was fierce and desperate on Rosaleen's side, a crush of cool lips against Cricket's own, although the angle was a little awkward and obviously Cricket did not kiss her back.

"Finally," Rosaleen said, her tone just as fierce as her kiss. "At last, Cricket, you are too perfect."

Cricket still could not make words come out in order to respond. Not that she would have gotten the chance anyway— between one breath and the next, Rosaleen entered her.

If Cricket had thought about it before, she would have imagined some sort of light or ethereal spirit leaving Rosaleen's body to flow into hers, filling her up like a cup being gently poured full of water, much as she had filled Rosaleen before.

Instead, it felt like she'd lain too long on the forest floor and plant roots had grown up through her, piercing the wet fleshy bits of her, twisting around her bones and filling up the spaces inside of her with leaves, flowers, tender curling fern heads, and strange soft fungus spores. She didn't just smell honeysuckle but tasted its heavy sweetness on her tongue with the bitterness of leaves and tendrils of vines down her throat.

She was a seed pod being pulled apart and opened. Cricket was cocoon woven from skin and viscera that Rosaleen peeled open with sharp bone fingers and crawled inside. Rosaleen filled her up completely, this old dead thing in the shape of a woman. Her teeth behind Cricket's teeth. Her blood, old and sluggish as cooling tar, mixing with Cricket's blood.

In another life, if she had been a different person, she might have been trapped there among the green, buried deep in a dream of wild honeysuckle. Then Rosaleen—or what called herself that—would have been able to wear Cricket's skin and do as she pleased with it.

But not in this life. In this one, Cricket could feel the water rising up inside of her, dark, cold, and deep, smelling like rain off of the mountain, like rotting plants and the secret dark places among the rocks deep under the water's surface.

Cricket lay on that silty lake bottom, seaweed tangled in her hair, algae slowly eating away at the waterlogged hem of her dress, ice-cold water flowing in and out of her lungs like air.

She did not sleep.

There was a struggle as the implacable rising lake water met the creeping ivy and honeysuckle. When it finally ended, there was stillness.

Lying on the ground, deep under the earth, Cricket took several long deep breaths and finally, shakily climbed to her feet.

She glowed, casting long, strange shadows around the cavern.

It wasn't large, she now saw, but there was a pool of water that looked black in the near darkness. She'd fallen right at the edge of it. If she'd gained more speed falling down, she might have ended up in it, unable to swim or save herself.

There was a heavy scraping sound behind her, and she whirled to see Gabriel's hunched form coming out of the hole. He straightened up, and the relief Cricket felt at the sight of him was so palpable it was almost pain.

His gaze fell on her, and she saw his expression change in the low light. "Cricket?"

She took a step toward him. "I thought…" Breathing was suddenly hard, like there were metal bands around her chest, squeezing tight. "I thought you might not come." Her voice was tight, high, and strange in her own ears.

He took a step forward. "What happened?" His voice was low and urgent.

Cricket didn't really know how to answer that. "Rosaleen."

Gabriel's expression hardened. "But you're not her." It was mostly a statement, but there was a question in there too. He took another step toward her so he was well within the light she cast, his gaze searching her face.

"No," Cricket said, although that was not entirely the truth. "I can feel her, but I am here too."

"Ah." Gabriel took a step back, and the fact that he had made Cricket feel hollowed out inside. "We should keep moving." He turned away from her to peer into the darkness of the cavern they now stood in. "I'm afraid the thing up there will come for us again soon."

"What is it?"

Gabriel glanced at her before looking away again. "Dead." He strode to the edge of the pool, looking down into the water. "You wouldn't happen to know the way out?"

Cricket moved across the cavern to stand beside him. The part of her that was Rosaleen knew the shape of this cavern as if on instinct. Her bones had lain in this ground for a long time, her hair, organs, and other soft parts of her rotting into it, becoming part of it.

"We'll have to go through the water," she said, completely certain that was the only way out besides the hole they'd come through.

Gabriel sighed. "I don't like that."

Looking down at the dark water, Cricket didn't like it either.

"There's a passage about seven feet under the water," she said. "We'll need to dive down and crawl through that. The passage slopes up slightly, so it's mostly free of water once you get inside."

Finding the opening to the passage in the dark water before they ran out of air would require a high level of swimming skills and comfort in the water. Doubly so if the water was as cold as Cricket suspected it was. From up here, there was also no way to tell how large the passage was. Maybe it wouldn't be big enough for Gabriel's large frame, or worse, he might run the risk of becoming wedged under the water, unable to breach the surface on either side.

A low scraping noise jerked her out of her thoughts. It was the dragging, shuffling sound of something hard and misshapen being pulled across earth and stone. Cricket had only heard it once before, but it would be etched in her mind forever.

There was the clatter of small stones and bits of rubble being pushed down the passageway as something big forced its way down the hole toward them.

As both she and Gabriel swung to face it, Cricket was keenly aware of how small the cavern they were standing in truly was, and how little space the two of them had between the water and whatever was coming down the hole toward them.

Dead, Gabriel had said. Cricket felt the skin along her back prickle.

She remembered the shambling creatures from the forest. The magic got into everything that had lain within the ground, Rosaleen had said, dead things slowly soaking up the leeching, spreading magic until they became something else entirely.

Gabriel growled low in his throat and hunched over, his body contorting in desperate spasms.

Cricket had never seen him change before and would not have been able to fully describe the process now that she was seeing it for the first time.

It was like watching someone's body be forced open in the most vulnerable way possible, his most secret and sensitive flesh bared, quivering and wet. She watched his face contort in the light cast by her own body, watched his muscles tense and flex, his body stretching and twisting as if he was falling apart and yet coming back together whole for the first time.

The cloth of his suit gave like another layer of flesh peeling away in ribbons, buttons hitting the stone floor with a shockingly loud noise like a gun's report. Gabriel was on the ground, his back arching into a perfect tortured line as his body broke apart piece by piece.

Then he was more wolf than man, his monstrous jaws opening to allow a red tongue to loll past far too many sharp teeth like jagged spikes on a chain. His massive bulk seemed to fill the tiny cavern, his breath thunderously loud in the tiny space.

Again, there was that scraping noise as the dead thing crawled out of the hole.

It moved partly like a spider and partly like a human that had forgotten how to walk standing upright. The thing was huge, a creature made out of bone that had never seen enough sun to become bleached, brown and yellowed by the flesh that had rotted off of them. Here and there pieces of flesh still hung on the bones, along with great clumps of hair or maybe fur that still clung to parts of it, dirt caked into every crack and joint. The pieces it was made out of—carcasses of animals and what must be people—were hard to distinguish. It was just a thing now, huge and monstrous, creeping toward them from out of the darkness.

Spindly legs reached out as the creature ducked into the cavern.

The part Cricket guessed was its head was mostly obscured in dirty hanks of hair that looked far too human. As it moved some of that hair parted, revealing a terrifying set of jaws with mismatched teeth, some human, some animal.

Cricket could feel her own limbs locking at the sight of it. For a frozen moment, all she could think about was that she had no weapons, her knife left in Gabriel's house within the waking world.

Then the wolf growled, great jaws opening, muscles bunching under fur. He sprang at the creature in a burst of terrifying speed. The cavern was suddenly alive with the sound of bone cracking and splintering as great jaws clamped down around one of its limbs, wrenching and ripping.

The creature shuddered, writhing against the attack. Its jaws opened and opened, fully revealing a huge maw filled with line after line of teeth behind the hair. It made no sound aside from the clacking of bones. It reared back and swung a huge limb up and down at the wolf, who twisted away from the blow but not fast enough.

The sound of it hitting the side of the wolf was sickeningly visceral.

Cricket cried out, the light around her flaring up brighter. She was suddenly very aware of the ground around them, the smell and feel of the rock, the grit of the dirt, and the brackish water she could taste at the back of her throat.

Despite the blow, the wolf's jaws had not loosened on the limb. As the creature reared back again for another blow, the wolf twisted, his head snapping back and forth like a dog with a rabbit in its mouth.

There was more cracking and shattering bone, and the wolf tore the limb from the creature's body, tossing it aside to clatter against the cavern wall.

Now the creature made noise, a chattering sound as it clicked its many dozens of teeth together in pure rage. It lunged at the wolf, mouth open, rows of teeth bared.

The wolf lunged too, meeting it halfway in a whirl of growling, biting fury.

They tore at each other with the sound of cracking bone and the too-wet noise of rending flesh.

It was this last sound that made Cricket's knees feel like they would buckle, made her pant in great opened-mouth breaths. There was blood on the stone floor, and she knew perfectly well it wasn't the creature's.

Don't you die, she thought desperately at Gabriel.

Get in the water, Rosaleen said inside her. *We have to keep going. We're so close now.*

I can't, Cricket thought back. *You didn't leave him before. I'm not going to leave him now.*

There were big hunks of bone on the ground now. Cricket stared down at all that blood mixing with the dirt. She breathed shallowly, tasting iron on her tongue.

The air smelled like blood and decay.

Her ears rang with the wolf's snarls and the occasional angry chatter of the creature he fought.

The longer she stared at that one patch of ground, the more it began to look like it was moving, the earth rising and falling as if it was the side of some great beast taking panting breaths.

It felt like a dream, like the hallucinations she'd had when she'd been sick as a child.

Still, she drew up one hand, only half aware she was doing it, pointing at the spot.

The ground under her feet shuddered as if something was slowly awakening.

The wolf sprang away from the bone creature, still growling, the hair along his back raised. There was blood matted into his fur, but it was hard to tell how deep the wounds were or how many of them there were.

Her gaze went back to the ground. It shifted again, this time in great shuddering heaves.

Unbalanced with one less limb to stand on, the creature staggered and fell with a scraping crunch of bone against rock.

The wolf circled, sides heaving, his growling changing in tenor to one of warning.

Cricket felt a bead of sweat start at her hairline and run down the back of her neck. She was very aware that they were deep underground with many tons of dirt and rock hanging just over their heads, only the structural integrity of this tiny space to protect them from sudden, smothering death.

The wolf lunged back at the creature, his jaws cracking open far wider than should have been possible, his gold eyes rolling in his head. He made a noise that was neither human nor animal, then his jaws snapped around what passed for the creature's face.

Big mats of hair fell to the floor.

Those two great, hideous jaws locked together. A high whining noise was punched from the wolf's throat as more blood flowed down onto the stone floor of the cavern

Cricket heard a loud pop. The wolf wrenched his head back in a long arc, the creature's jawbone clamped in his mouth.

The creature collapsed, soundless except for the clattering noise of its body hitting the ground. Its limbs twitched spasmodically, but it did not rise again.

Cricket and the wolf watched it reflexively jerking. The cavern filled with the heavy, ragged sound of Cricket's own hard breathing and the wolf's panting, punctuated ever so often by the click of bone against rock.

The wolf dropped the jawbone some ways away from the creature and turned his massive head toward Cricket.

She watched those jaws open again, the long red tongue lolling out.

There was blood on his muzzle, blood on his sides and shoulders. She stepped forward, her fingers brushing against his fur for the first time. It felt like a dog's fur, like the thick pelt of a wolf.

Cricket parted the hair with difficulty to see one of the wounds on his side. It was just as deep and ragged as she'd been afraid of. Here she had nothing to bandage him with, no cloth or salves, not even clean water to wash away the blood.

For several long moments, she just stood there, looking at the blood seeping from the gash in his flesh, listening to his breath.

She leaned forward and pressed her face against his neck, his thick fur against her face, the smell of animal all around her. "I'm sorry. You are going to have to stay here. I need to go on, but you can't come with me. Not injured."

The tips of her fingers gently brushed the fur of his snout, shorter and finer than on his body, just grazing the damp corner of his mouth.

"I'll come back," she told him softly, although she wasn't at all sure it was a promise she'd be able to keep.

She stepped away from him, unbuttoning her shirt and letting it fall to the ground before undoing the buttons at the waist of her skirt as well.

Normally she'd be horrified at the very idea of disrobing in front of him, but that part of her seemed faraway down there in the dark with the scent and taste of dirt and blood still filling her senses.

That left her only in her underclothes and boots. She debated taking the boots off as well, but the idea of trying to climb sharp rocks barefoot kept them on her feet.

Cricket crossed the space to the edge of the pool and sat on it, her feet just above the water. Her mind conjured all sorts of things that could be under the surface, from the possible to the fantastical.

She tried to steady herself for the cold plunge into the unknown.

Behind her, the wolf barked, a sharp sound that reverberated off the walls of the cavern.

Cricket glanced over her shoulder at him. "I'm sorry."

She pushed herself off the edge and dropped into the pitch-black water beneath her.

CHAPTER 25

The water was cold, far colder than any water she'd ever experienced, even water straight off the mountains in winter.

Cricket could feel her limbs becoming heavy with the shock of it almost immediately. She kicked hard, trying to fight through the coldness of the water and the weight of her underclothes and boots as they became saturated.

She kept the top half of her body above the water as she edged around the side of the pool toward where she knew the hole was. Her hands clung to the slippery rocks as they dug into her fingers and palms.

Just water. You know water.

She could sense the wolf watching her from the edge of the pool, but she didn't look at him, keeping her gaze fixed on the next rock she'd have to grab. Her knees and shins knocked and scraped against the rocks under the water. When she was still a few feet away from the wall where the hole was located, she ran out of rocks to grip and realized she was going to have to swim the rest of the way.

Cricket took a breath and sank deeper into the water, still trying to keep her head above it. It was so cold she could feel her heart slowing. She kicked off the rocks, cutting through the water toward the wall with strong controlled strokes.

When her wet hands slapped against the wall, she stopped. She could sense the hole below her, several feet down.

It needed to be now or never. She took a very deep breath and dove.

The light she cast was dimmer under the water, muted and shadowy, not illuminating very much at all save for murky water and stone.

That was unfortunate. She'd been hoping the light would make this easier.

With how cold the water was and how fast her limbs were going numb and useless, she didn't know how many dives she'd be able to do if she missed it on this first one.

The water glowed a dark, sickly green around her as she dove into its icy depths. She could smell and taste it, the coldness of it and its strange mineral qualities so unlike the fresh water she was used to.

Rocks loomed up like splintered teeth below her, dark crevasses between them. They seemed to be waiting for her in the depths, watching her descent. She was careful as she kicked, knowing it would be too easy to get a foot caught in one of those tight little spaces. Then the pool would be able to hold her under until she ran out of air to breathe and filled with water instead.

The stone wall was smoother in places where water had run over the course of centuries, but in some ways, that was just as treacherous. There was nothing for her to grab to steady herself or pull herself deeper.

Her hands slid uselessly against the smooth surface, and she was forced to swim further, eyes straining open even as the water burned them.

It felt like she spent centuries in those desperately cold depths, although Cricket knew it must have only been moments before she saw the opening—a dark, hungry, gaping space.

She didn't have time to second guess swimming into it or to think of all the ways she could go wrong. As strong a swimmer as she was, her chest was already starting to ache and burn.

She swam for it desperately and edged her body into the space, her fingers slipping and sliding against slick stone walls. The darkness was profound in the hole, her light barely cutting through it.

Above her there would be air. There had to be or she'd die.

She kicked as hard as she could, heedless of the way her foot smacked against unforgiving stone, her knees scraping agonizingly. The dark water seemed to part as she propelled herself through it, up and up. Her chest was screaming at her, a mass of red hot pain, oxygen-deprived muscles, and tortured lungs. Desperately, her body was telling her to suck in air, but she kept her mouth closed through sheer force of will until her head finally broke the surface.

Cricket gasped, her chest heaving so hard that her throat almost closed back up on her again.

The air was stale with a strange tang she'd never experienced before, but it was still breathable.

It was only after her breath had somewhat steadied that she realized the passage she was in went almost vertically up smooth stone walls so steep, she seriously doubted she could climb them.

On the other hand, the water was too cold for her to stay in much longer, so she braced her hands against the nearest surface and began searching for finger holds.

It was slow going, but her semi-numb fingers finally found a crack. She dug into it, careless of the way the stone bit into her palms, and began hauling herself forward.

Her feet slipped against the stones without anything to push on, and she searched for a foothold. For a too-long moment, she thought there would be none to find and she'd drop back into the water again, but her foot hit something that was enough for her to propel herself up on tired legs.

Cricket got another shaky handhold and then another, keeping her body pressed against the curve of the passage in order to use what little angle there was to her advantage. She felt like some kind of spider scaling the inside of a jar. She tried not to think about that or falling back into the water. Instead, she directed all her focus onto finding the next hand and foothold.

Eventually, the angle became less steep, and it began to feel more like making her way through a tunnel rather than scaling a cliff face. Cricket crawled in the dark, every part of her body aching with every movement. Her nose and eyes still ran from the water she'd had to swim through, and her hands felt bloody and raw.

She rubbed an arm across her face, clearing her airways enough to suck in a genuinely deep, shaking breath.

The smell, *that* smell, vegetal and sweet with ash and rot and the metallic tang of old blood curled around her, hanging pungent in the air as if seeping out of the rocks themselves.

Cricket grimly pushed herself up and started moving forward again.

She had to be close now.

She didn't want to think about trying to go back the way she'd come. Even if they got to wherever Rosaleen was leading and managed to accomplish what they'd come here to do—and survived— she'd have to come back here, scale the tunnel going the other way somehow, swim through that cold, dark water again, and find her way back up to the surface.

It all felt impossible with a body on the verge of giving up, but the idea of simply not doing it, of allowing herself to die down here in the dark, made her even angrier.

If she was going to let herself slip into death, it was damn well going to be on her own terms at the time and place of her choosing: in the place she loved best, not here in this hole.

Something pricked at her, something that should not have been there but was.

She stopped, her ears filled with the sound of her own panting breaths bouncing off the stone walls of the tunnel around her. All she could smell was stone and dirt and the strange minerality of the water she'd swam through. All she could taste was the water. The faint light she was still producing showed her the narrow stone passageway disappearing into the darkness ahead.

Still, she made herself pause and concentrate.

Somewhere beyond her own breath and the beating of her heart, she heard them again. That murmuring sound rising and falling like the movement of water against her senses.

A sudden hot rage took hold of Cricket as if by the throat, and she started forcing her tired body to move forward with purpose now.

The part of her that was Rosaleen told her it wasn't far now, and the part that was very much still Cricket was just about ready to tear whatever was ahead of her apart with her bare hands.

She dearly wished she had her knife with her for this.

The tunnel narrowed suddenly, and Cricket gritted her teeth as she was forced to go flat on her stomach, pulling herself through the tiny space.

The smell was so strong, filling up her head and mouth, creeping its way down her throat.

The floor underneath her hands was beginning to turn soft and almost slick as if covered by something that had grown and died there.

Danger, her body told her. Cricket couldn't disagree.

She squeezed herself through a particularly narrow outcropping of rock, her fingers scraping through the dirt, and then there was nothing under her hands.

She nearly pitched forward, falling face first into the darkness but froze instead, scooting back as best as she could as her gaze swept the space in front of her.

There was an opening with a drop, she thought as she edged forward so her head and shoulders passed the tunnel's mouth. In the dim light she still cast, she could see that there was a drop down to the cavern floor, but it was only a few feet at most. Still, the space she'd had to crawl through on her belly was so small, there would be no nice way of climbing out.

Cricket was forced to slither forth face first, more like a creature than a person. Her underclothes clung to her body, still soaking wet from her swim, and her hair hung in great sodden clumps, falling into her face.

She dropped onto the cavern floor like a pale spider shaken from the mouth of a jar. The ever-present scent of wild magic growing up from so deep in the earth pressed in on her from all sides like a weight. It slid into her ears and mouth and all of her other orifices until she felt stuffed and bloated with it, struggling to move or think.

As she moved, she was able to make out the shapes on the floor, rock or something else rising up in folds and crevices, pockmarked with holes of all sizes. Her mind conjured up images of a cliff face carved out by the waves of some great ocean. That wasn't quite right; it was more like a massive dead log fallen onto the forest floor, worn, rotted, and grown upon until it was hollowed out and twisted by hundreds of millions of growing and crawling things. All of it was covered by the white mist of the magic, dense and interlocking like cultivating mycelium covering the decaying surface of the cavern and climbing up the wall, stretching, overlapping in thick mossy mats until everything seemed furred with the stuff.

Cricket was just one more of those crawling things—the insect she was named after, creaking across the bark and growths on her hands and knees.

She was too far from where she'd come to turn back with any speed when the sound changed again.

As Cricket listened, frozen on all fours, it began to sound more like a breathy sort of moaning, then the shuddering breath of something huge deep below her.

She closed her eyes briefly, trying to will away the panicked part of her mind that said she could feel tiny movements in the stone under her fingers as if the ground itself was rising and falling with each of those labored breaths. She was suddenly sure that if she looked down through the fist-sized hole only an inch away from her fingers, she would find some massive fleshy body of a giant, inhuman, miles-wide fungal fruit squatting in the darkness, sending its pathways up toward the surface and the light.

They -all human beings - were merely ants to it, tiny and fragile vesicles to carry its parasitic spores. Sacks of nutrients for those spores to eat and discard as it spread, colonizing and digesting as it went.

She wondered suddenly if the ants that were paralyzed and consumed by the parasitic *ophiocordyceps unilateralis* thought of it as some wild and hungry magic too.

How exactly are we supposed to contain it? She thought at Rosaleen's consciousness tucked deep inside of her. *Aren't you supposed to have a plan?*

Call down the forest, Rosaleen sighed inside her head.

What? Cricket had no idea what that was supposed to mean.

Do it!

An image began to form in Cricket's mind, not just of the stretch of forest she'd walked through so many times since she'd come to Gabriel's house, but other trees, thick and green and lush, their colors like a stretch of emerald stones against a dark gray sky. The forests of her childhood rolling across sloping mountainsides straight up to the shores of the lake.

Cricket closed her eyes and took a deep breath, fancying she could taste cold mountain air filling her mouth, curling down her throat.

She could picture every leaf, every tiny, mossy frond and fir bow. The air around her trembled with the soft shushing of branches against branches, the rustling of small creatures moving through the underbrush, the soft crunch of leaves and small twigs underfoot.

She could feel the sunlight, the way it spilled in patches against her hands and her face, the great stillness and presence of all those trees and their slow, exorable ascent toward the sun and stretch downward deep under the ground.

Under her hands the earth shook, very slightly at first but gathering in strength, a deep rumbling inhale and exhale, a pulsing that passed through her hands and up her arms until her entire body throbbed with it.

There was a faint pattering sound, almost like rain.

Cricket opened her eyes and blinked down at her hand, confused to find it covered in a very fine layer of grit.

More dirt hit her hand, and she realized she could feel it against her hair and her back too. A steady rain of dirt was being shaken loose from the ceiling above her.

Her gaze swept up without her permission to the ceiling high above her. There was something happening up there in the shadows.

The ceiling above her head exploded.

There was a great groaning, cracking noise like the side of a ship in a storm, and bits of rock and dirt came hailing down on top of her, falling into the holes and bouncing off the floor.

Cricket yelled, the sound of her voice ricocheting around the room. She brought her arms up to protect her head.

The air around her was so full of dust and dirt, it was hard to even know what was happening until she realized the shadows bouncing off the walls were writhing as if great limbs were trying to thrust themselves straight through the ceiling down on top of her.

Cricket cried out again in fear, her gaze searching the darkness of whatever it was that was breaking the ceiling apart at that every moment. The dust stung her eyes and made them water even worse. She blinked away tears, her eyes straining. She could barely make out the growing mass above her, pale limbs twisting and entwining, pulling apart dirt and rocks as they sank down through the roof of the cavern toward where Cricket crouched.

It took far too long for her mind to claw its way past the sheer terror of the situation to realize what she was looking at were roots. Great huge roots from more plants and trees than Cricket could even imagine, burrowing far faster and deeper than any tree ever had before, seeking their way down under the ground to entrap and ensnare.

So this was Rosaleen's plan. Even as she thought it, she realized she could barely feel Rosaleen in her mind at all. What was there was pale and faint like a photograph left too long in the sun.

Under her hands, the pulsing had grown stronger. Above her, Cricket realized grimly, the roots' descent had slowed. She watched a huge spider's web of them crawl down the cavern wall above her head until the roots stopped moving altogether.

Far below her she could hear the moaning again, a great wind that did not exist passing through passages she could barely imagine. Maybe it was something else completely.

There came a scraping sound from above.

More dirt and small stones rained down from the ceiling. Cricket looked up in hopes that the roots had begun to move again, but the great twisted mass that now engulfed the entirety of the cavern roof did not move. Instead, there were things moving inside of it.

A clattering sound joined the scraping, a kind of rustle.

Her gaze tracked the movement as best as she could through the dust and gloom as whatever it was crawled through the roots toward one of the walls.

Cricket took a deep breath. The dust stung her throat and lungs, making her double over, coughing uncontrollably.

For several moments the sound of her own retching coughs drowned out everything else in the cave. When her coughing died away, Cricket could hear more clicking, shuffling, rustling noises, noises that seemed to come from everywhere now. When her gaze went up again, it was as if the mass was alive with movement.

Although she very much doubted life had anything to do with this.

There was a clattering noise from one of the cavern walls. When Cricket's head snapped around to look, she saw it was another monstrous creature like the one Gabriel had fought creeping down the wall like a huge obscene spider.

Rosaleen should have realized this was possible, Cricket thought grimly. They already knew the wild magic located in the cavern could reanimate in a manner of speaking. The roots from the trees Cricket and Rosaleen had called down must have brought all sorts of things from more shallow parts of the earth down deeper with them.

Including bones.

Cricket hoped most of them were animal bones because the idea of the remains of people being torn from their resting places and so used churned her stomach.

She climbed to her feet, not knowing what she was going to do but pretty sure she wanted to be standing for it.

She had no weapons and no ability to fight a construct the wolf had struggled to defeat.

A calm started to eat through her fear as she watched more and more of the things claw their way out from the roots above her head like some grotesque mockery of birth. They began their slow descent toward her, crawling and creeping. Their bones clicking and scraping together as they moved was the only sound in the great cavern aside from her own ragged breath.

When they reached the ground, she would die. The absolute certainty of that wrapped its cold fingers around her.

They would smash her brains out on the rocky floor or tear her to pieces where she stood. She hoped it would be the first; that was at least a faster way to die.

Nausea rose in her throat, and Cricket fought it back. She didn't much feel like spending her last moments in life puking up her guts, even if it was a completely understandable reaction to the current situation.

She couldn't stop it, though. The reflex took ahold of her strongly, and all she could do was double over before she was retching and gagging against it. Her mouth filled with the iron taste of blood and she spat dark red globules onto the ground. She could feel the muscles in her abdomen spasming against it, and her throat felt raw. She reached up more blood red masses, mixed with what looks like hair and maybe a finger. Cricket fell to her knees but at this point she couldn't stop. Her body spasming over and over again.

Cricket gasped for breath, blinking against the tears running down her face, obscuring her vision.

Cool fingers wrapped around her wrist, sudden enough to startle a shriek out of her. Rosaleen was next to her now, where she had not been before.

"Run," Rosaleen said in her ear.

They ran, Cricket stumbling and tripping as Rosaleen dragged her back toward the hole they'd originally come out of.

Cricket could hear the bone creatures scrabbling along the stone walls behind them and wondered if they'd reached the floor yet. Their bones clicked together to make a dull chattering sound as they moved together in a swarm.

They reached the wall with the hole in it, and Cricket gripped the edge of the mouth, ignoring the way the rough stones bit into her already battered hands. She hauled herself up into the hole, propelled by sheer fear. She fell belly first into the tunnel and began crawling as soon as she had her hands under her. She could sense Rosaleen crawling behind her, and Cricket prayed with everything inside her that the passage was too narrow for the creatures to follow them.

For minutes they crawled through the darkness, the only noise the sound of Cricket's breathing.

Rosaleen said, "We need to go back."

Cricket clenched her jaw. "And do what? It didn't work. We failed. And if we go back…" *I'll die.*

She remembered the jaws on the bone creature Gabriel had fought, all those rows upon rows of teeth. She could still see the jagged bite they'd taken out of him, how deep it had been and how vicious. It was too easy to imagine the creatures behind her descending on her, their mouths opening wide, their teeth tearing at her until there was nothing left but blood and bone and viscera dripping through the holes in the cavern floor.

Maybe Rosaleen didn't care. She was already dead, after all; the creatures probably couldn't hurt her. Cricket was probably expendable to her. When Cricket's body was laid out in pieces across that dark cavern so far down no one would ever find them, Rosaleen would simply go back up and start over, invading someone else's dreams.

Rosaleen's deathly cold fingers closed around Cricket's ankle. Cricket kicked out at her hard, hoping to connect. Rosaleen dragged her back with her inhuman strength, knocking Cricket to her stomach in the narrow passageway.

Cricket clawed at the dirt floor and walls, and finally at Rosaleen as she was dragged. Soon they were grappling together in a small space. Cricket punched and kicked and bit, fighting with all her will against Rosaleen. Their bodies pressed together in an echo of intimacy. Cricket yanked at a handful of Rosaleen's hair, then reared back enough to headbutt Rosaleen as hard as she could in the face.

Pain exploded like bright stars within her own head, and the passage seemed to swing dizzyingly around them.

Cricket could taste blood in her mouth even before Rosaleen grabbed her and smashed her back against the ground with force.

More pain and light exploded behind her eyes.

"Listen to me," Rosaleen said. They were so close together they could have kissed under different circumstances. "You need to take my power."

Cricket tried to suck breath through her nose, which both failed and hurt enough that she suspected it was broken. "We tried that," she spat. "It didn't work."

"No." Rosaleen sounded grim. "We haven't. We've tried joining together—*that* didn't work. What I am suggesting now is that you take my power. It will become yours, and I will cease to be."

"No." Cricket tried to squirm against Rosaleen's grip. "I want to go back to Gabriel." *I want to go home.*

"And lead those creatures to him?" Rosaleen asked ruthlessly. "It knows you exist now. It knows you are a threat. Do you think even in the waking world you'll be safe?"

"You're lying," Cricket said through clenched teeth, but there was a new sort of fear inside her. All her senses strained for the sound of scraping bone legs against the walls of the passage.

Rosaleen let go of Cricket with one hand, undoing the buttons at her collar. Under other circumstances, Cricket's heart might have raced watching Rosaleen as she undid her dress and pushed it open to reveal her soft skin, the swell of her breasts. They were pressed so tightly together, Cricket could feel the back of Rosaleen's hand brush against her chest, but at the moment the only desire the touch elicited in her was the strong desire to punch Rosaleen.

"I wanted this to be different," Rosaleen said, her voice almost gentle now, the calmness wrapping around the hard lines and sharp edges of Cricket's anger and fear. "I thought selfishly that we could exist together, two spirits in one body. That I could be at peace to exist in the warmth of you. Two plants growing together in the soil of our own choosing. But I don't think that can be. Take the magic inside yourself, make it yours, and let the memory of who I used to be finally die."

Rosaleen sunk her fingers into her own chest. It was like what she'd done to Cricket in the garden, physical and ghastly to watch. Rosaleen's hand sunk into her body like it was sinking into soft bread dough. Cricket could feel the blood begin to flow between them, staining her underclothes. She could make out the white jut of bones poking out through Rosaleen's skin.

Rosaleen didn't scream or cry out, didn't make any sound at all. Her expression was a calm mask of concentration, and out of everything, that was the sharpest reminder that Rosaleen was truly not alive.

When she drew her hand out, it looked like she was clutching a great mass of bloody flesh. After a moment Cricket realized she was holding her own heart.

"Eat it." Rosaleen held it up in the dim light she still cast, far too close to Cricket's face.

Cricket's throat felt too dry for words. She licked her lips and finally croaked out, "You have got to be joking."

Rosaleen leaned down, bringing her face very close to Cricket's. The hand that still held the heart was close enough to the side of Cricket's head that it was probably dripping blood into her hair.

"Do it." All of the soft calmness that had existed in her voice moments before was gone, and every word was as hard as a hammer blow against glowing steel. Her eyes were no longer a woman's eyes but the lightless holes of a skull old and pitted by the elements and the ceaselessness of time. "Do it now, or I will break your legs and your arms and leave you here for the creatures to root out like a choice little morsel to devour at their leisure."

"Is this really how you want to die?" Cricket hissed back at her.

Rosaleen laughed. "Oh Cricket. I died a long, long time ago. It no longer scares me."

Cricket was weakening and she knew it, trapped here underneath Rosaleen with nowhere else to go and no other options. "Take the curse off me like you promised."

Triumph lit Rosaleen's eyes. "As you wish." She slid her free hand between them, caressing the thin layer of sodden cloth that clung to Cricket's freezing skin.

It was not any less painful than it had been the first time Rosaleen had dug her fingers into Cricket's chest.

Cricket screamed, even though she knew the creatures just outside the tunnel would hear. She couldn't stop herself. The pain was overwhelming, a beating, living thing that threatened to pick her up and dash her against the rocks with the force of it.

Rosaleen's fingers grasped the hateful, poisoned weed that had invaded the inside of her roots deep and twisted. She pulled and Cricket screamed again, her entire body thrashing, heels kicking helplessly against the stone floor of the tunnel as Rosaleen drew it out of her with sheer strength alone.

Then it was out. Cricket gasped, eyes streaming with tears, head aching and pounding.

She had barely a moment to catch her breath before she felt something move against her skin. A tiny, tickling sort of touch as if worms were crawling against her hands, making her jerk in reflex to get them off.

There was nothing there but her own pale skin, her fingers and knuckles bruised and bloody and her nails caked with dirt.

It came again, that sensation of crawling against her skin, her hands, her arms, and now her face.

The magic. The thought flitted through her mind like an already smoldering moth. She no longer had the curse to protect her, and now the magic was reaching out, trying to crawl under her skin, through her eyes, nose, and mouth to take root inside her where it would grow, eating her away piece by piece until there was nothing left but a husk. The stench of rot seemed to be everywhere now, sweet and sick. It was so thick she could taste it, feel the putrefying slime of it coating her skin as those tiny worms burrowed and squirmed their way toward her eyes and mouth.

She slapped her hand against her own face as if she could somehow pull away the tendrils of magic that she couldn't see or grip but could feel, with gut-churning clarity, creeping along her skin.

Rosaleen brought her heart back to Cricket's mouth so Cricket could taste the iron of blood and feel the warm, soft flesh against her lips.

"Now eat, quickly," Rosaleen said. "Before you become like the rest of them. Fill yourself up and give it nowhere to go."

As if she moved in a dream, Cricket's lips parted.

The first bite was fueled by the pure rage that swelled Cricket's chest to near bursting, rage at being trapped and used yet again. She bit and tore at the flesh in front of her mouth, looking directly at Rosaleen as she did. She thought of Walter, his mother and sisters, his whole fucking family as her mouth filled up with blood. She thought of their whole social circle with all of the rich men who'd lingered over her hand a bit too long and the women who'd judged her with little knowing smirks on their faces. She imagined devouring each of their hearts in turn, rending and tearing at them as she felt the blood run warm across her lips and down her chin.

Grief gripped at her throat. Her mind filled with memories of the bodies on the farm, of the woman in the woods, how long they must have suffered, how they died. Her gaze swam, tears blurring Rosaleen's face into streaks of nothing. She thought of Gabriel bleeding in the caverns above her, thought of her mother drinking herself to an early death, and finally of her father on the last day she'd seen him, his body tipping over the railing of the balcony of their home, falling into the dark lake below.

She was crying now, fully sobbing, her mouth full of blood.

Long fingers touched her face gently, stroked away her tears with such tenderness. "I wish I could see what shape my magic will take when it becomes truly and completely yours, but I know it will be magnificent."

Rosaleen lowered herself to lie against Cricket as she cried, her head pillowed on Cricket's narrow bony chest.

All around them she could smell honeysuckle, sweet and familiar. Rosaleen sang softly, the song she'd sung when she'd held Cricket's hand in the sitting room of Gabriel's house, low and wordless as the honeysuckle twined around them, thick and green like a cloak covering them both.

Cricket could feel it tangling in her fingers and in her hair. She could feel Rosaleen's body slowly fade to nothing but bones cradled against her as she choked down mouthful after mouthful of the heart Rosaleen's skeletal fingers still held against her lips.

When the last of it was in her mouth, she felt Rosaleen's body grow lighter and more brittle. The honeysuckle that cloaked them began to wither. The delicate flowers wilted, their petals falling against Cricket's face like silken rain. The leaves curled in on themselves, the vines drying and retreating.

Cricket swallowed, and there was nothing left but dust and the lingering smell of sweet flowers.

Complete darkness enveloped her with no more light to pierce it.

There was nothing left but her own thoughts, the sound of her own breathing, and the taste of blood on her tongue.

Within that stillness, she began to hear the faintest sound of scratching.

The sound of something scrabbling against rock.

Panic dug deep into her. She reached for Rosaleen and found nothing. She tried to anchor herself to thoughts of the forest, but they slipped away, as powerless as any of the other thoughts frantically buzzing inside her head.

There was nothing there, nothing but Cricket's aching body and bloody underclothes.

Slowly she began to roll over, trying to get up and start crawling again.

That was when she heard the other noise—a low, rumbling sound coming from the tunnel in front of her.

She froze, her eyes straining although there was nothing she could see.

In darkness that complete, there was no warning. The water hit her in a great wave, knocking her flat again and filling up her mouth, throat, and lungs before she had time to draw in a breath to hold or scream.

The water enveloped her completely, cold and tasting like the mountains.

CHAPTER 26

The lake water roared down the tunnel in one great rushing force, slamming out into the cavern. It smashed the bone creatures across the room, throwing them like splintered driftwood. It poured down through the holes in the floor, filling up all those secret passageways beneath, stopping the voices until all that remained was water and silence. It kept rising, filling the cavern up, lapping and pressing against the stone walls, creeping ever higher.

The water pushed up into the mass of roots that had broken through the roof of the cave, seeping up through the tiny holes into softer, more hospitable ground.

Some of the creatures were pushed up with the rising water, carried along like corks dropped into a pitcher. They rose as the water rose until they were pressed back into the root mass again, tangled up, broke into their respective parts, and left to sleep once more.

The ones that did not rise were pushed down through the holes in the floor by the weight of the water, each piece of bone washed into the deep places of the earth until they too were quiet and still.

In the depths of the water-filled cavern Cricket's body drifted both submerged and the source of the water. For indeed, all the water that had filled up the great space had passed through her, touching all of the secret, dark spaces inside her until she, like the cavern, was filled.

It gently flowed through her now, lapping in and out of her mouth and lungs, trickling from behind her eyes. She hung, submerged, pale and small in a cloud of dark hair, slowly lifted by the water.

There was a current in the water, faint but there.

It was a current that remembered rivers that ran through rocky places and streams that cut through the soft ground of forests. It remembered the air and the sun, still pools deep in the mountains where no humans ever went. It remembered the sea.

The current caused the water to move ever so gently around the inside of the cavern. After some time, it moved the body too, up and down and around the space, tugging it like a trailing piece of lake weed.

The current tried to pull the body down, but there were no holes in the floor big enough for it to fit through. Eventually, the current carried the body out of the cavern and away from those deep, watchful spaces that now lay silent beneath it.

The body's eyes stared into the water as it carried her but did not see it, her face and hands now finally washed free of the blood that had stained them.

She and the water rushed on, eagerly devouring each new underground space as it spilled into them until all were filled with the drumming of dark, deep water like the endless beating of a heart.

CHAPTER 27

There were hands on Cricket's face, but her eyes felt too heavy to open, leaden and bruised. Her limbs felt heavy too, her body too big or maybe too far away, it was hard to tell. For a long time, she struggled against the overwhelming weight of everything pushing down on top of her.

Eventually, she did open her eyes.

For a moment all she could see was dark green branches against a gray sky. She was also very wet, she realized, soaked through and freezing cold, lying in nothing but her underwear on the banks of a streambed. She knew it had to be a streambed because she could hear the great rush of water very close by.

She blinked again, and her vision was suddenly blocked by Gabriel's frowning face.

He looked tired, haggard really, and somehow gray as if whatever had leeched the color from their surroundings was slowly leeching the color from his body as well. "Thank God. I thought you were dead."

Very slowly, Cricket forced her tongue from her mouth and licked her lips, which were dry to the point of cracking. Her tongue felt too large, swollen and misshapen. She was not sure she'd be able to form words with it.

She was also not completely sure she hadn't been dead or wasn't dead right now.

Her gaze traveled across the arch of trees overhead, slowly searching the forest around them.

No mist stirred the undergrowth, and no grayness leeched the color from the moss or trees. The wild magic was quiet now, bound under many lakes' worth of water, no longer able to seep up to the world above, either in this realm or the waking one.

Cricket brought one trembling hand up and clenched it over her chest. She could feel her heart beating more strained and ragged than it should have been, but she could feel something else there as well. A shadow like the ghost of a dead heart, still and unbeating, encompassing her own.

Gabriel's big hand reached down and wrapped around her wrist, shockingly warm and alive against her ice-cold skin.

Her entire body felt too heavy and too battered to move, and her throat was swollen near shut.

Gabriel looked down at her and seemed to realize what it was she couldn't say. His arms closed around her, picking her up and carrying her through the forest.

Under her hand her heartbeat slowed, the dead heart closing slowly around it. Cricket let her eyes close again.

She drifted into a gray sort of darkness until Gabriel's stride slowed to a stop.

With great effort she blinked her eyes open to see that they'd passed through the gate of bones and were approaching the vine-covered stone cottage once more with the two human-wolves flanking the door.

Her eyes slid closed again, and she listened to the creak of the door opening and the sound of Gabriel's tread against the floorboards.

She was lowered into the bed, and she lay in a quiet, hazy half-sleep almost as soon as she touched it. She floated there for a long time, vaguely aware of the bed under her and Gabriel moving around the space but not fully conscious.

When she was next able to peel her eyes open, her body still felt leaden, but her head was clearer now.

Cricket coughed, her throat scraping painfully. She sat up.

Gabriel was no longer there, but the fire was lit in the hearth.

Cricket swung her legs over the edge of the bed and tested her ability to stand. Her muscles felt stiff, her limbs aching slightly but holding her.

She hobbled to the hearth and let the heat sink into her down to her bones.

The heat helped soothe some of the ache until she felt well enough to turn back to the interior of the cottage. The room wasn't that big, made even smaller by the clutter of drying herbs, jars, and the trinkets strewn across the long table.

Gabriel was definitely not in the house, so Cricket crossed to the door and pulled it open.

The sky was dimming above the trees now, the last of the sun painting it in red and gold. Twilight was gathering through the trees, the first time she'd seen night fall here.

The candles were lit in the mouths of the wolves guarding the door, casting long shadows across the house plot, but Cricket could not see Gabriel anywhere.

She hesitated, unsure if she should leave the relative safety of the house or stray beyond the bone fence. She was keenly aware of her lack of clothing and the fact that her feet were now bare, but she stepped out anyway. Crossing the house plot, she stepped through the gate and into the forest beyond.

For a long moment she stood, listening to the sound of the trees.

There was a difference to the way the forest sounded now, the way it felt. It was more settled and more alive, although her body and mind were not unaware that there was still danger here in this world made of magic and unknown things.

She circled the house, slowly picking her way through the trees adorned with the bleached skulls of stags. Gabriel was not behind the house either. Cricket found nothing there but more forest and a long, low stone sunk into the ground and half choked by weeds.

She bent over it and saw that the image of a wolf had been carved into it with something sharp but crude.

Her gaze rose to the forest. It was becoming increasingly dark in the failing light. Gabriel couldn't be that far away.

She squared her shoulders before stepping back under the trees. She had faced much worse than some dark woods.

The scent of wet earth, rotting wood, and moss was strong here, stronger than in other parts of the forest, and the space between the trees felt darker than even the failing light would account for. Cricket made her way forward, slow and careful so as not to tread upon any sharp rocks or thorns.

Luckily, she did not have to go far before she saw Gabriel's large, dark form standing still among the trees.

She coughed lightly just to make sure he knew she was there.

"You're awake." He half turned toward her in the failing light.

"I am. And moving a little more normally, at least."

"Thank God." He held out a hand to her and she took it.

He had been standing in front of a stone form, a statue much like the ones at the doorway of the house. It was a human figure crouched on hands and knees, its head that of a wolf, its hands raised as if to tear at itself.

"Is it hard sometimes? Being the wolf?"

Gabriel's fingers squeezed around hers a little bit. "Sometimes."

They were silent for a moment, hand in hand, their gazes fixed on the statue before them.

"It's a great deal of power," Gabriel finally said into the silence. "A great deal of potential for violence and destruction. I need to always be aware of that and be mindful that there is a wildness and a hunger that is greater in me than in many others. I cannot…consume everything in my path, and I wouldn't want to, but that hunger is still there, still part of me. At the same time I would not be who I am without it; it is so much a part of me that I feel as if I would cease to exist if I was not also the wolf."

Cricket thought of the part of her with teeth and claws. It was a feral creature that lived inside of her and had kept her safe and fighting for years, but she also knew how easily it could be turned upon an innocent party that was simply in her way.

She'd hurt Gabriel after all, with her single-minded need to protect herself, even from those who were not her enemies.

For so long she'd been surrounded by danger, always running, always on guard. Everything looked like a threat even when it wasn't.

What if Gabriel had not been immune to her poisons? What if she had overestimated the dose or actually managed to stab him?

Cricket looked down at her small feet on the mossy forest floor, then back up at Gabriel.

"I'm sorry." Her voice was low but still audible in the quiet. "I am sorry for poisoning you, for trying to stab you, for not trusting you…for all of it."

Gabriel made a soft noise somewhere between a grunt and a sigh. He shifted his weight slightly so his side pressed up against Cricket's. He let go of her hand to slide his arm around her shoulders, pulling her close. "It's all right."

Cricket wet her lips. She leaned against him for once, just letting herself be touched and touch in return. "Maybe…maybe I could learn some…restraint."

Gabriel chuckled low and soft and squeezed her a little tighter. "We'll work on it. Learning to tread a little bit more gently around each other."

A little bit more gently. Cricket reached up to cover his hand with hers and promised herself that she would try.

CHAPTER 28

By the time they made their way back to Gabriel's stone cottage, the sun had set and the forest was dark around them. After the true blackness of the caves, the starlight beginning to filter through the branches above them was a relief. Still, Cricket could barely see where they were going.

"How long can we stay here?" Cricket asked, keeping a firm grip on Gabriel's hand in the gathering night. "We have to wake up at some point."

Or maybe they wouldn't. Maybe the poison had truly worked too well.

Her fingers tightened around Gabriel's. She was not at all sure how she felt about that.

There was no one waiting for them in the waking world. Still, Cricket had hoped that now she was finally free of the curse, she could go back to her parents' house, enjoy that life of solitude she'd promised Gabriel and herself.

Gabriel didn't answer, and Cricket felt her heart sink a little bit.

Up ahead of them was the house, now surrounded in the faint glow of candles. As they drew closer, Cricket could see each of the stag heads had a candle within it, the light trickling from their eyes and mouths to cast long, horned shadows on the ground below. They seemed to dance and spin across the ground so dizzyingly that for a moment Cricket had to close her eyes.

When she opened them again it was as if everything had changed. The cottage and house plot was still the same and the forest still stretched out around them on all sides, but Cricket knew with a bone-deep certainty that Gabriel's garden, the forest behind it, and the field with the hole that had been a strange, twisted copy of the waking world was gone.

The world that they were in was different now, wholly unknown to her and unexplored.

Her heart lurched in her chest. "I need to check something." Her voice was high and urgent.

"Now?" Gabriel frowned down at her.

"Yes, now."

He stared at her for a moment, then shrugged. "Let me get a lamp."

His hand slipped away from hers as he crossed to the cottage and went inside, reemerging a few moments later carrying a lit lantern in one hand.

"All right, lead the way."

Cricket didn't really know where to go, but when she took several long breaths, willing herself to stillness, she felt the tug, a twisting ache inside of her, and started walking.

They made their way through the dark woods. The trees were still the same towering pines, the ground still moss covered but this was not the same forest she'd traveled through before. Like a tree growing around and over the stump of a severed branch.

The ache inside her pulled her on, drawing her through these unfamiliar trees with not a creek or stream insight.

Gabriel did not question where they were going, just held onto her arm in order to steady and guide her through the dark, holding the lantern high in the other hand. His shadow stretched long across the ground, and she was glad for it in this new dreaming space.

The trees were thinning, and Cricket could make out a glimmer of moonlight reflecting off something.

She stopped so suddenly that Gabriel stumbled and grabbed at her shoulder for a moment to right himself.

"Sorry." Cricket's gaze was still fixed to the edge of the forest and what lay behind it.

She took several steps forward.

The ground sloping down a little ways before it met the edge of the water beyond.

It was a small lake, the water black in the darkness, sparkling where it reflected the moon and stars.

Cricket stepped out from under the overhanging branches, tipping her face up to feel the wind against her skin, carrying with it the familiar scent of lake water mixed with pine trees.

For several minutes she allowed herself to just stand and inhale deeply.

"Is this what we came here for?" Gabriel asked from behind her. "Rather late for a swim, isn't it? Besides, I'd have thought you'd have had your fill of water. At least for a little while."

Cricket let her eyes blink open, squinting through the dark along the lake bank.

She saw what she was looking for a little ways away, a sharp outcropping of rock that jutted out over the water, carpeted by pine needles and leaves. "What here." She headed for the rocks.

It was not easy going in the dark with her bare feet. Small stones dug into the soles of her feet, and the dried pine needles pricked at her. She set her jaw and climbed as fast as she dared up onto the rocky lip.

"What on earth are you doing?" Gabriel called from behind her. "Cricket? Cricket!"

She straightened up, flung her arms wide for balance, took two quick paces to the edge, and jumped, diving into the dark water below.

The cold hit her, but it was nothing compared to the cave water deep underground. The taste and scent of vegetal brine filled her mouth and nose, lake plants growing and dying.

She cut through the dark water, heading for the silty bottom.

There was a tangle of very different plants there, the sort that did not grow in water, a cocoon of drowned vines and rotted leaves.

Cricket pulled at them, tearing away great handfuls that disintegrated into slimy muck in her hands.

She caught a glimpse of bleached bone within the mass.

The dead honeysuckle came away, drifting off into the current in pieces. Cricket reached out for the body that had been trapped in the center of the green.

Cricket caught her and held her close.

They floated in the dark water together. Cricket wrapped one arm tight around her dress-clad waist and cupped the back of the skull tenderly with her other hand. She kissed where the lips should have been, letting her eyes slide closed as she did.

The water stirred around them, its internal current causing Cricket's hair to float and halo them both.

Deep inside her chest there was a fluttering like the beating of wings, and arms wrapped around her in return. Lips brushed the back of her neck, kissed up her throat, and sighed against the angle of her jaw.

Then they were gone.

The body slipped from her grasp, carried away like the honeysuckle.

Her head broke the surface. Cricket blinked away the sting of water from her eyes to find her arms empty, even though she was sure she had never let go.

For a moment she treaded water, feeling panic touch cold fingers against her spine. Her mind quieted slowly, her breath settling. She longed to smell a hint of sweet flowers on the night air but there was none. Just the familiar, mineral and vegetal smell of the water.

Cricket turned back toward the dark figure of Gabriel standing on the shore.

She swam hard, cutting through the water with ease until it became shallow enough for her to stand on the silty bottom and walk against the pull of the water to where he stood.

As she grew closer, she saw that the shore was not as bare as it had been before she'd entered the water. Where there had been rocky earth with a thin layer of fallen needles and some straggling plants was now a blanket of green.

She stepped onto the pebbly shore and crossed over to where Gabriel stood, still holding the lantern.

"She's gone?" Gabriel asked, reaching out for her, hand hovering about the curve of Cricket's shoulder but not quite touching.

"Yes." Cricket straightened back up. Even though she was soaked to the bone, her hair plastered down her back and the night air was starting to feel cold against her bare arms and legs, she still felt lighter than she had in years.

They made their way back under the high arch of the trees, and Gabriel's hand slipped into hers, big, warm, and familiar.

Cricket let herself be guided back through the dark.

All the candles were still glowing when they made it back to the house plot, casting the yard in flickering light. Gabriel pulled the door to the cottage open and tugged her inside.

Only when the warmth from the fireplace hit her did Cricket realize how cold and wet she was. She pulled the chair closer to the fire and perched her sodden self on it while Gabriel bustled around the space, getting a blanket to drape over her shoulders and putting the kettle onto the hook over the hearth.

Slowly the fire warmed her limbs, seeping into her. She felt her eyes begin to drift shut.

The water in the kettle boiled. Gabriel removed it and poured them two cups before pressing one into Cricket's hands.

She'd expected tea, but when she sipped it, she tasted the smoky bite of whisky against her tongue.

"Drink," Gabriel said. "And then we can go to bed."

The inside of the cottage was only one room, and there was only one bed in it for them to sleep on.

Cricket's insides squirmed, her pulse speeding up and her throat closing. It took her a moment to realize that it was more anticipation than nerves.

She lifted the cup of hot toddy to her lips and drank.

Outside the wind rustled the branches of the trees above the cottage, sounding like far off rain mixing with the crackle of the fire.

Gabriel set his own cup aside, stood, and stretched before reaching out one hand to Cricket.

She curled her fingers around his and let him tug her gently over to the bed in the corner of the room.

It was a large bed, sturdily built if not elegant. She knew it was soft from the last few times she'd lain on it. She hesitated beside it, unsure what to do and very conscious that she was dressed only in her sodden underthings under the blanket wrapped around her shoulders.

Gabriel sat on the edge of the bed, the frame creaking a little under his bulk. He reached for Cricket's hands, taking them loosely in his own. "We can just sleep." His voice was so soft and gentle, so understanding.

Her back stiffened, her head coming up. She shrugged the blanket off her shoulders, letting it pool around her feet. She took a quick step forward before she lost her nerve.

They'd kissed once before, all hot and hungry. It was slower now when her lips pressed against his, feather light. For a moment he didn't move, then his hands came up to cup her head. He kissed her back like thunder rolling through her with the promise of lightning waiting to strike.

Her toes curled against the rough floorboards at the power and desire behind that promise.

The kiss became hungrier now, her mouth devouring his until he growled low in his chest, his hands closing around her waist and lifting her onto the bed.

She gasped as her back hit the mattress, then again as long cool fingers sank into her hair, pressing deliciously against her scalp and the nape of her neck.

Gabriel stripped off his clothes, baring soft skin in the flittering firelight and dark hair across the heavy swell of his chest and stomach and his muscular thighs.

She undid the buttons of her sodden underclothes, unwilling to bear the cold clamminess against her skin any longer. There was a moment when she was far too aware of her boniness and tininess without her usual layers of clothing.

"Gorgeous creature," Gabriel rumbled above her, and his big body covered hers.

"You as well." Her fingers tangled in his dark curls, her voice low, the words just for the three of them. "Come and eat me up."

He bared his fangs in a grin as he pulled her thighs around his waist and bent his mouth to the curve of her shoulder.

Everything after that was hunger and sweetness and feast.

CHAPTER 29

"We can't stay here forever," Gabriel said, his hand heavy against Cricket's stomach.

Pale sunlight was beginning to slide through the cracks around the window shutters. Cricket's senses were full of the scent of the bed linens mixing with dried herbs, smoke from the fire, and her and Gabriel's bodies combined. She was warm under the blankets they'd piled on the bed, truly relaxed and boneless for the first time in what felt like forever.

"Why can't we?" she asked.

Gabriel shifted beside her under the covers. "Our bodies are still in the waking world unprotected."

Cricket breathed in, feeling the rise and fall of her chest and stomach, the warmth of his skin against hers. Part of her wanted to stay here forever and let what happened to her body happen. She'd never been tied too strongly to it anyway.

But she did not know what would become of their dreaming selves if they were to die in the waking world from starvation or something else.

She sighed. "I suppose you're right. Do you have a way to get back?"

"I believe so." Gabriel's hand slipped away from its resting place on her stomach, and Cricket missed it immediately. He pushed himself up and climbed out of the bed, sorting through his clothes from the night before and pulling them back on.

Cricket rose after a moment too, pulling on her still damp and very dirty underthings since she didn't have anything else to put on.

Gabriel began rummaging around on his worktable while Cricket picked up the poker, coaxing the fire back to life.

He turned back to her with a cup in his hand. "Drink it in one go like you did with the tonic to get here."

Cricket took it, bracing herself. She met Gabriel's gaze.

He gave her a small encouraging smile, raising his own glass in a sort of salute.

She took a breath and nodded, lifting the cup to her lips.

It was bitter and acrid. All the muscles in her throat and abdomen locked up as soon as the first bit of it hit her stomach, then they began spasming, frantic to force it back out of her.

She gagged, the cup slipping from her fingers. Her whole body hit the bedroom floor, shuddering with great heaving spasms as she vomited until she felt like her insides would come up too.

Her hair had fallen into her face and was now disgustingly stuck to it.

It took her far too long to realize she was in Gabriel's bedroom again, crouched over the well-worn boards of the floor, having just projectile vomited everything inside her up onto his rug.

Her entire body shuddered with another racking bout of sickness, and she made a piteous whimpering noise in response.

Strong arms closed around her, and Gabriel held her up against his chest, petting her disgusting hair away from her face until there was nothing left inside her to throw up.

"I was right. We should have stayed in the dreaming world," Cricket croaked out.

Gabriel sighed. "You better go clean yourself up. Do you need help getting to the bathroom, or can you make it on your own?"

Cricket didn't know, but she put her hands under herself and pushed up onto shaking legs. For all she felt like a bag of refuse left too long in the sun, she did manage to stagger down the hall and into the bathroom under her own power.

There she hovered over the toilet to make sure nothing else was going to come up, then she washed herself off as best she could, cleaned her teeth, and drank several large glasses of water.

Her skin was almost translucent like she hadn't seen the sun in months. Staring at herself in the mirror, there were dark circles under her eyes and some gray in her hair that most certainly hadn't been there before. There were also disturbingly mottled bruises on her wrists, neck, and she was sure the rest of her body as well.

She looked like someone who had just recently come off many months spent in a sickbed or maybe someone newly risen from the grave.

Cricket spat a mouthful of water into the sink and turned away from the mirror.

Gabriel wasn't anywhere to be found when she left the bathroom. The bedroom had been cleaned, though, and when she made her slow, painful way down the stairs, she found that the front door had been unbarricaded and unlocked.

She pushed it open, slowly blinking against the sunlight that felt far too intense even though she rationally knew it wasn't even that bright out. It was late in the day and evening was advancing on them, casting long, if perfectly mundane, shadows in its wake.

Gabriel was some ways down the road, standing by the gate to his closest neighbor's house.

She made her way slowly down his front path and out onto the road to where he stood. The hedgerow, which had been perfectly orderly all the other times she'd passed it, was now thickly overgrown. The front gate was no more; the stone posts on either side had fallen, and the wood of the gate had rotted away to nothing.

Beyond the gate was a thick tangle of brambles and new growth trees, but if she looked hard, she could make out the ruins of a stone house, fallen now and mostly obscured by the landscape.

She looked at Gabriel.

He took her arm, and together they made their way down the road to the next house, which was also nothing but ruins now, long abandoned, the house plot almost completely swallowed up by the forest. So was the next one they passed and the one after that.

They made their way back to where the path into the forest had always been. It was overgrown now, completely obscured by long grasses. They picked their way through anyway, back across the forest to the abandoned farm. When they got there, it was just an empty field filled with long grasses, flowers, and the buzz of insects.

Cricket stared out across it. She was able to make out shapes in the grass where a well might once have been and the stone foundation of a wooden house and barn long rotted away.

Her fingers tightened around Gabriel's hand.

They stared at each other, then turned as one back to the forest.

The path they took now was far too familiar.

Cricket felt fear twist cold in the pit of her stomach as they grew closer to the field where the hole had been.

When they stepped out from under the shelter of the trees, however, she drew in a sharp, shocked breath.

There was no hole, but neither was there an empty field like the one they'd just left.

Instead, tidy rows of graves stretched out before them, stones weather beaten and beginning to green with lichen poking up among the long grasses.

Gabriel stepped forward while Cricket remained rooted to the spot. He knelt next to the closest stone, parting the grass around it and brushing his hand across the inscription.

"These graves are old," he said, his voice low as Cricket finally made herself step forward to stand beside him. "By almost a hundred years."

She swallowed hard.

He moved to the next gravestone, his fingers tracing the name. "This was my neighbor. And this one too."

Cricket stared out across the field—now a graveyard. The breeze rustled the long grass and pulled at the edge of her skirts.

It was a whole town's worth of graves.

A town that had died a long time ago and might finally be at rest.

She turned away from the graveyard, letting her hand rest against Gabriel's shoulder.

Gabriel closed his eyes and sighed. "I think," Gabriel said very quietly, almost to himself, "that it's time for us to leave now."

Cricket nodded. "Time to find someplace where we can rest."

The weariness that had taken over her was a testament to how very true that was.

The curse that had bound her for so long was gone now. Walter was gone, and she'd done all she could do for the people here. It was time to go home, back to that great moldering house in the mountains. She wanted to lay in one of the big wicker chairs on the veranda overlooking the lake and allow herself to be quiet for a while. There Gabriel could have his books and no doubt there would be plenty of work for the two of them to do once they got their energy back. The house had been very long neglected at this point and Cricket shuddered to think of what her greenhouse must look like. There would be much to put right again.

Gabriel pushed himself wearily to his feet and took her arm again, turning them back toward his house.

It took Cricket no time at all to pack once they were back inside.

Gabriel needed longer, so she went out into the back garden while he packed his bags.

She sat on the stone bench surrounded by bushes and allowed herself to just feel the garden around her, listening to the wind in the trees and the soft rustle of the long grasses. It felt emptier somehow than it had since she had arrived there, free of wild magic and Rosaleen's wandering ghost.

Later that evening they made their way down the road to the train station, suitcases in hand with plans to hire movers for the rest of Gabriel's things once they got up north.

The train station was overgrown now too, the building just a little stone hut compared to the way it had been when Cricket had arrived. They waited in the gathering dusk until they heard a train whistle coming down the tracks toward them. For a moment Cricket thought it might rush by them, but then it slowed and came to a stop.

A conductor swung the carriage door open for them. "You folks are lucky we saw you," he said as Cricket handed over her bags to him. "We don't often stop here, particularly this late in the evening." He squinted down at them with interest. "No one lives out here anymore. Where are you two going?"

"North," Gabriel said, following Cricket up the steps and into the train. "We'll need tickets if you have them." He handed over the money while Cricket seated herself, smoothing out her skirts.

Gabriel settled beside her as the train began to move, taking them away from the ruined town in the forest.

The window beside Cricket's seat was half open, allowing the cool evening air to pull at some small strands of her hair that had fallen around her face when she'd hastily pinned it up before they'd left.

For just a moment she thought she smelled the scent of honeysuckle carried on the wind. Then it was gone, and she let herself picture high mountain slopes and cold, deep lake water.

She let it fill her up starting with her heart.

AFTERWARD

All books are a communal act of creation, and this book is no different. I am deeply indebted to many people. First and foremost, S.T. Gibson, who championed this book for years and encouraged me to lean into all that is strange, dark, and messy about the story.

Thanks are also due to Marie Sager, who is responsible for the day-to-day support in the writing and publishing process. Thank you, Marie, for wrangling small dogs alone in my absence and understanding what it means when my door is closed.

I also want to thank my editing team, May Peterson and Jessica Cale, who have worked with me on several books now and never fail to lift up my best intentions while doing their best to correct my sloppiness.

It was a pleasure to work with the amazing and talented artist and illustrator, Hippolyte Girardin, on the interior illustration for this book. I would also like to thank my agent, Eva Scalzo, for her continued support in all my writing endeavors.

ABOUT THE AUTHOR

EE Ottoman is a romance and speculative fiction author specializing in trans and queer fiction with a historical setting. He is also a historian who has written extensively on the life of 19th century trans physician Dr. James Barry. EE also works as a writing coach and research assistant. Helping other authors with project and career planning, goal setting, writing without plotting, accountability buddy services, brainstorming, and help with historical research.

EE Ottoman currently lives outside of Philadelphia with his wife and an entire house full of dogs and cats. He is passionate about history, stories, and the queer spaces between the two. In his free time, Ottoman is an avid vegetarian cook, practicing fiber craftsperson, and novice mushroom cultivator.

You can follow him on Instragram @acosmistmachine

Find out more at www.eeottoman.com